Character design: Yummy Book Covers

Cover design: Covers By Sophie

BRAT Christmas

MELODY TYDEN

CONTENTS

Chapter One

~Maxine~

The first time Josh's phone buzzes with a text from a new number, I don't think much of it.

A cool October breeze blows through the window next to me. Leaves in shades of yellow and orange sway in the tree outside, and Josh's phone lies face-up on the kitchen counter, next to the carrots I just finished slicing.

Glancing over, I catch the name as it pops up on the screen.

"Who's Sam?"

At the other end of our cramped galley kitchen, Josh rummages in the fridge. "Someone new I'm training at work. Do you want the teriyaki or chilli and garlic sauce?"

"Teriyaki. And grab the bean sprouts while you're in there."

He tosses them over without looking, narrowly avoiding the handle of the wok on the stove next to me. An inch to the left and sizzling hot oil would have gone flying, but I press my lips together to stop from pointing that out. Getting him to help me cook each night when we both get home from work took long enough; I don't want to give him an excuse to stop.

The sharp scents of ginger and garlic waft through the air as I tip everything into the hot pan. "Is Sam going to be on your team?"

Josh swipes his hair out of his eyes as he continues to stare into the fridge. *Time to make an appointment for a haircut*, I add to my mental checklist. If I don't do it, he'll put it off for weeks.

"Yeah, looks that way. I might get one more developer before the end of the month too. Brad thinks this new app has real potential."

"That's great."

Usually, I have trouble shutting Josh up about the apps he's developing. I know the ins and outs of each project he works on, but tonight, he's the one who changes the subject, frowning down at the bottle of teriyaki sauce.

"Actually, I think I'd rather go for the chilli and garlic."

Then why ask me what I wanted? I can't help wondering, but again, I bite my tongue.

"Okay. Fine by me."

The next week, we're making a chicken caesar salad when I ask how the app is going.

"Sam noticed a flaw in the initial design that means we have to start over," he tells me.

I grimace in sympathy. "Shit. Sorry."

To my surprise, he smiles. "No, it's a good thing. Better now than when we're two months in. I can't believe we all missed it. Some people just have a knack for seeing the big picture, I guess."

Personally, I think that's a skill I also possess, but it's been a while since he pointed out any of my good qualities.

I paste a smile on my face to push down the thought. "So, I had some ideas about a couples costume for Ellie and Brad's Halloween party."

His eyes almost immediately glaze over. "Sure. You can pick. I don't care."

Great. Another year of shopping for costumes alone.

Another two weeks pass before I notice Sam's name on his phone again. This time, it's while we're eating, and Josh snatches the phone up from the coffee table when it buzzes and lets out a soft chuckle when he reads the message.

"What?" I ask when he doesn't offer an explanation.

"Just something funny that happened at work today," he mumbles as he taps out a quick reply.

After hitting send, he places the phone back down, face-down this time. A few more seconds go by before I prompt him for more. "What happened?"

He glances from the TV to me and back again. "It's kind of an inside joke."

Something dull and uncomfortable lodges in the bottom of my stomach but I force myself to ignore it. "Sam's working out well on the team?"

His eyes don't leave the screen this time. "Yeah."

"Well, that's good. Do you want to invite him to watch the game this weekend?"

As life-long Bears fans, Josh and I host a group of friends at our place most weekends during the football season. Moving in together right out of college, we were the first to get 'settled', and even though our apartment is no longer the nicest or biggest, the tradition of hosting stuck.

However, Josh shakes his head. "Actually, I meant to tell you: Paul's having a small group over. Guys from work only. We found a potential investor for the app and need to do some brainstorming, so we'll do it while we watch the game. You can have your girls over here without me in the way."

He makes it sound like he's doing me a favour but I'm left with the distinct feeling of being boxed out.

It's never anything big, but as another two weeks go by, he seems less and less eager to talk. I tell myself I'm being paranoid and chalk it up to the way he always immerses himself in a new project. Besides, I'm busy at work too. We had our first snowfall, and people always seem to forget how to drive the first time it snows each year. Auto accident claims skyrocket.

Two weeks later, I get a text as I'm leaving work the night before Thanksgiving. Neither of us has any extra vacation time, so we'll be staying in the city over the holiday weekend rather than seeing our families.

At least we have each other, or so I think until I read the text.

> Gotta work late tonight. Go ahead and eat without me.

Late nights aren't unusual in the development phase of a new app, so I text my friend Ellie, who also happens to be Josh's boss' girlfriend, as I wait on the L platform for my train home.

> Hey! Just heard the guys are working late tonight. Want to come over and watch some trash TV?

Rather than texting me back, she calls me ten minutes later. I cover one ear, straining to hear her over the rumbling of the train. "Hello?"

"Hey, Max. I just talked to Brad."

Her unusually heavy tone immediately sets off alarm bells, though I don't yet know what they mean. "Okay?"

"We actually have dinner plans tonight, and he hadn't said anything about being late, so I called and asked. He says he's on his way home and everyone else has already left the office too."

What the hell?

I wrack my brain for a reasonable explanation for the mixed wires. "Maybe they changed their minds? Josh is probably heading home too."

"Well, I wondered, so I asked Brad why Josh might think they were working late. He got really quiet and told me it was none of our business."

The train lurches to a stop at the next station, and my stomach flips with it. "What does that mean?"

"I don't know, but it suggests there's some kind of 'business' going on. I'm not trying to start trouble, but I know you'd tell me if the shoe was on the other foot."

I would, and I'm glad she told me, even if I'm hoping for an innocent reason behind Josh's obvious lie. "Got it. Thanks. I'll talk to you later."

By the time I get home, my stomach is still unsettled and my appetite has disappeared. Josh isn't there, and there are no new texts from him either. My imagination has already conjured up every worst-case scenario, but the most obvious one is the one I can't stop thinking about.

There's one clichéd reason a guy would lie about 'working late', and while a couple of months ago, I would have thought the idea of Josh cheating on me was crazy, it doesn't feel so impossible anymore.

In the apartment, Josh is everywhere I look, each object telling a story of our past and the future we've planned, a future that's feeling more precarious with each passing minute. Each movement of the clock's second hand sounds like a ticking bomb, waiting to explode.

At twelve minutes past ten, the door finally opens. Josh bustles in and starts unwrapping his scarf before he sees me sitting on the couch. His eyes flit to the dark TV, then to the quiet computer at the desk, searching for a sign of what I'm doing. "Hey. I thought you'd be in bed."

Normally, I would be tucked in with a book by now while he scrolled on his phone. Not tonight, though. I haven't read a word, unable to think past the whirlwind of doubts in my mind.

"How was work?"

He sighs as he kicks his boots off. "Hard, but good. The extra time paid off. We made some progress."

There's no alternate explanation, then. He's sticking with the original story.

"Did the whole team stay?"

"My team, yeah."

The lie slips off his tongue so easily, I feel like I'm going crazy.

Answers are what I need, and I can only think of one way to get them. "Can I see your phone?"

Only when I thought about it after my conversation with Ellie did I realize that Josh has been keeping his phone on him a lot more than usual lately. I haven't seen it lying out on the table or counter for quite a while.

His brow furrows at the sudden change in topic as he shrugs his coat off. "Why?"

"I want to see it."

I keep the words carefully neutral but he's not an idiot. He knows something's up, and his posture quickly turns defensive, shoulders curling in. "What's wrong with yours?"

"Josh." I say his name slowly and clearly, letting him know I'm not in the mood for games. "We have an agreement, remember? If either one of us asks for the other's logins, histories, whatever, we turn it over. No questions asked."

Every muscle in his face tightens. "That was *your* rule."

"That you agreed to."

"Because I didn't have a choice," he mutters, turning away from me to head to the bedroom. "It's late. I'm going to bed."

If I had any doubt that he was hiding something, he just blew it to pieces. "Are you fucking serious?"

When he doesn't stop, I spring to my feet and follow him down the hall. He slams the closet door open, making me jump, but I don't back down.

"Don't treat me like an idiot, Josh. Give me the phone. Now."

I hold out my hand for it like a teacher demanding a note she caught students passing. Why am I *always* the authority figure in our relationship?

He scowls back at me but to my relief, he reaches into his pocket and tosses the phone to me, not even bothering to walk it over. I manage to catch it awkwardly, but when I try to unlock it, the code doesn't work.

My eyes lift to find him staring at me, nostrils flaring. "Why did you change the code?"

"Why do you think?"

A long, horrible silence swells between us as we simply stare at each other, each one daring the other to say the words out loud.

Neither of us do, but we don't have to. He's fucking cheating on me and we both know it.

For the first time in what must be years, I don't bother to moderate my words. "Get out."

His face reddens. "This is my apartment too, you can't just..."

"Get the fuck out!"

My voice comes out so loud and sharp that he flinches. For just a second, I could swear something close to regret flashes across his face, but it's gone in an instant. With a scoff of feigned bravado, he turns back to the closet, grabs a duffle bag and starts stuffing his clothes into it.

My arms wrap around my stomach as I watch him in silence, the tips of my fingers feeling cold and numb.

This can't be real, but no matter how many times I try to pinch myself, I don't wake up.

When the bag is full, Josh zips it shut and turns back to the door. He has to walk past me to get to it, and he pauses for a brief moment when he reaches me. I don't breathe, waiting to see what he'll say.

The air hangs thick and heavy between us, all the easy familiarity of our four years together gone.

Four fucking years.

In the end, he says nothing, hoisting the bag up and over his shoulder as he heads out the bedroom door. I don't move as I hear the rustle of his coat and the clomping of his boots. I don't move when the apartment door opens and closes again.

I don't move until silence falls and the numbness fades. Then, all at once, the weight of my loss crashes down on me. Frustration, anger, betrayal, sadness; I don't know which is stronger, or which hurts more. I just know it *hurts.*

This wasn't supposed to happen to me. I followed the rules, did everything right.

What the hell am I supposed to do now?

Chapter Two

~Maxine~

I need another drink.

Three days have gone by since I kicked Josh out. Two days since my friends assured me he'd come crawling back, whether I wanted him to or not. Despite having Thanksgiving plans, they all managed to jump on a group video chat where they loudly proclaimed that he'd never deserved me and they didn't like him all that much anyway.

Yesterday, Janine tracked down a picture of Josh and his new girl-friend, and the man himself texted me to say he'd come by on Saturday to pick up his things.

And now it's Saturday, and I'm sitting in a dimly-lit bar down the street with my four best friends, the scent of stale beer and fried food thick in the air, simply so that I'm not at home when my piece-of-shit ex-boyfriend comes by.

It shouldn't take him long. I already packed his stuff during my solo Thanksgiving, tossing everything into garbage bags and leaving them piled in the living room. His signed Jimbo Covert jersey? In the bag. The suit he wore as a groomsman in my sister's wedding? Bag. His college sweater, the one I used to wear around his dorm with nothing else on? That's in there too.

Years of memories, wrapped up in plastic and disposed of, as if they never mattered at all.

Like *we* never mattered.

"Time for shots!" Ellie announces, appearing at the table with a tray of tiny glasses sloshing with an unsettlingly thick green liquid. Her red curls bounce with every step, her energy in stark contrast to the depression weighing me down.

Tamara wrinkles her nose, which nudges her glasses down. She pushes them back up as she peers at the drinks. "What are those?"

"Some Christmas-themed special," Ellie replies, depositing two of the weird drinks in front of each of us. With Thanksgiving over, holiday themes are popping up everywhere, but I've never felt less festive in my life. "If we drink enough, maybe some well-hung elves will appear."

Willow snorts into her perfectly-manicured hand. "That doesn't even make sense."

"That's because you're all too sober. *Especially* you." Ellie eyes me pointedly before plopping an extra shot in front of me.

Janine picks up a glass, tilting it so the gloopy liquid nearly spills. It glistens strangely under the bar lights. Is that... glitter?

"To Max and her newfound freedom," she declares, sweeping her dark hair over her shoulder. "And all the lucky single guys she's about to hook up with."

I force a smile and raise my glass, even as my insides churn. After so many years with one man, being with a stranger feels completely unrealistic, not to mention a little bit terrifying.

Glasses clink, and I throw back the shot. Icy mint slams into my tongue, so strong it burns my throat on the way down. A second later, the alcohol kicks in, spreading a sharp heat through my chest.

I wouldn't say it feels *good,* but it's better than self-pity.

I down the second shot without hesitation.

"When's the last time you fucked someone other than Josh?" Willow asks when the burn fades.

"She's *not* a cheater, so obviously before they met," Tamara points out.

Willow rolls her eyes. "Obviously. But *when?* Give us a name. A date. *Details.*"

For a brief moment, I consider lying. I could invent some ridiculously satisfying one-night stand that would make Josh sound disappointing in comparison. It might fool Willow, and maybe even Ellie. Unfortunately, Tamara and Janine both knew me back then so they'd sniff out my bullshit instantly.

"I slept with a grand total of three guys in college before Josh," I admit, swirling a few stray drops at the bottom of my shot glass, "and I don't remember anything spectacular about any of them."

"Typical overgrown boys," Janine agrees. "But trust me: those same boys are men now, and men get better with age. Time to broaden your horizons."

She and Willow share a knowing look before Willow gasps, a lightbulb flicking on in her brain. "We should go dancing tonight! Show you what you've been missing."

Janine's eyes gleam in return. "Yes! We'll do a little makeover and..."

"No." The word falls from my lips, flat and final. "Not tonight."

I'm definitely not ready for that. Chances are much higher I'd end up sobbing in the club bathroom instead of taking a guy home, and quite frankly, neither option appeals to me right now.

Tamara nods quickly to back me up, her glasses once again slipping down her nose. "It's reckless, especially when we don't know where Josh and Sam might..."

She stops short, grimacing like someone kicked her under the table.

Thanks to Ellie's interrogation of Brad, I now know that 'Sam' is short for *Samantha*. The new coworker Josh let me believe was a man. Thanks to Janine, we've all seen her social media, especially the picture she posted with Josh, captioned 'so glad we met'.

Josh always said there weren't enough women in app development. I never knew that was because he wanted to *date* them.

We couldn't be more different. She's blonde, blue-eyed and perpetually sun-kissed in her photos, while my brown curls, brown eyes, and pale winter skin make me resemble a mole rat in a wig next to her.

"We're doing just fine right here," Ellie declares, downing her next shot. "I'll get another round."

Three hours later, my buzz is strong enough to convince me I can walk the two blocks home alone. I wave off my friends as they pile into a cab, giggling like teenagers. Josh texted an hour ago to say he was done and left his key on the kitchen table. No mention of next month's rent that's due on Tuesday. He never handled any of the financial stuff, just transferring whatever I told him he owed into my account where I could take care of everything.

"You're better at managing all that stuff," he used to say.

I'm a lazy man-child who can't look after myself, I should have heard.

The late-November air is sharp against my cheeks as I walk down the quiet residential street, breath curling in pale puffs over my head. The streetlights hum above me, casting pools of yellow across the sidewalk. Despite the chill, the alcohol in my veins ensures that the cold doesn't bite.

I'm almost enjoying the walk until I see it: a sleek, baby-blue car parked in front of my building, its polished surface gleaming under the streetlight.

My steps slow until they come to a full stop and I yank my phone from my coat pocket, scrolling through Janine's texts until I find the link she sent for Sam's social media. Beneath her picture with Josh is another of her standing next to this exact car.

My stomach twists, and just to be sure, I zoom in on the license plate.

I'm not going crazy; it's a match.

What. The. *Fuck.*

Why is *her* car here?

My buzz instantly shifts from warm and light to something heavier and darker. The emotions I've been drowning all day come rushing back.

Anger.

Hurt.

Betrayal.

This *bitch* stole my boyfriend and has the nerve to park outside my building, like she owns that too? They were supposed to be gone an hour ago.

Before my brain catches up, my hand is already in my pocket, fingers curling around my apartment key.

One sharp edge.

One smooth, perfect paint job.

A match made in heaven.

Pressing the key against the car's side, I drag it from headlight to taillight. The metal screeches in a satisfying squeal.

At the rear bumper, I pause to admire my handiwork. The scratch is there, but it's not *deep* enough. Not as deep as four wasted years.

So I do it again.

And again.

Three long, jagged lines now decorate the car's side, a physical manifestation of the way I feel, ripped open and raw. Sure, it's petty, but I *always* play things safe. Just once, it feels good to let my impulses take over.

Shaking off the rush of adrenaline, I exhale and turn towards my building...

... only to slam straight into a wall.

Blinking, I stumble back. Why the hell is there a *wall* in the middle of the sidewalk?

No. Wait.

Not a wall. *It has arms.*

My gaze drags upward, tracing over broad shoulders, a thick winter coat and the curve of a tense jaw line, until it meets piercing blue eyes.

A dark blue wool hat sits low on his forehead, but it does nothing to soften the hard glare he levels at me.

His voice is deep and even colder than the night air.

"What the fuck are you doing to my car?"

Chapter Three

~Reid~

This is the last fucking thing I need.

As if this day hasn't already had its share of frustrations between being short-staffed at work and my ex-wife throwing another tantrum about Christmas. Now, I get to deal with some punk vandal keying the shit out of Sam's car.

The bundled-up figure doesn't even try to be discreet, dragging the key in slow, deliberate strokes across the paint before stepping back to admire the shiny scratches beneath the streetlights.

What the actual fuck?

I close the distance in a few long strides, fully prepared to deal with some snot-nosed kid. However, when they turn around and barrel straight into me, I'm surprised to see the vandal is actually a woman.

She looks about Sam's age, with smooth skin, cheeks flushed pink from the cold, and big brown eyes, framed by thick lashes, that blink up at me in an unfocused daze. When I demand an explanation for why she's fucking with my car, she stares at me like she's struggling to process my words.

"Your car?"

"Yes, my car."

Sam might be the one who drives it but I paid for the damn thing and keep it insured. For the purposes of this conversation, that makes it mine.

The woman glances back at the vandalized car, her confusion shifting into something that looks an awful lot like panic. "Oh, no."

At first, I think that's some half-assed attempt at an apology, but then her hand flies to her mouth. Turning away, she stumbles towards the nearest tree and proceeds to empty the contents of her stomach all over the roots.

For fuck's sake.

Heaving a sigh, I step forward and place my hand lightly on the back of her coat. "Are you okay?"

"No," she sniffs. "I'm... I'm sorry about your car."

"I mean: are you going to be sick again?"

Hand still hovering near her mouth, she straightens and scans the street, as if testing her nausea level. When her arm finally lowers, she exhales a shaky breath. "I think I'm okay. Sorry. I've been drinking."

Of course she has.

"You shouldn't be out here alone if you're drunk."

"Thanks, Dad," she mutters.

The sarcastic tone should annoy me, but there's something about her complete lack of filter in this moment combined with the vulnerability I just glimpsed, that affects me in a completely different way. An old instinct flares beneath my skin, an urge to push back against that snarky attitude with a firm hand, in a way we'd both enjoy.

Where the hell did that come from?

Shoving the thought down, I fix her with a glare instead. "You owe me a few thousand dollars to fix the damage you just did. If I were you, I'd try not to piss me off any further."

Her face drains of colour, and for a second, I think she might be sick again. "I don't have that kind of money."

"Maybe you shouldn't go around destroying other people's property, then."

Defiance flares in her big brown eyes, and for a moment, I think she'll give into it and put up a fight. Instead, she seems to make a conscious effort to suppress her natural instinct, just like I did a moment ago. Her lips press together, keeping whatever thought she had to herself.

"Where do you live?" I ask when it's clear she's going to hold her tongue.

"Why?"

"Because I'm going to get you home safely, and then we're going to talk about how you're going to repay me."

Something shifts in her expression, a flicker of something I can't quite name, and it takes me a second to realize why.

Fuck.

I meant repaying me with money, but when the words replay in my head, I hear what else it might have sounded like. And the fact that it's making her blush rather than run? That tells me she's trouble for someone like me.

My earlier instinct was obviously right, a little voice somewhere deep inside that recognized its counterpart in her. That voice has been quiet for so long, I honestly thought it might be dead.

When she doesn't answer right away, I lay out my position more clearly. "I'm not leaving you alone out here in your current condition, so you can either tell me where you live or call someone else to come and take you home. That'll give us plenty of time to talk about the money you owe me while we wait for them to arrive."

After weighing those options for a moment longer, the woman raises a weary hand towards the apartment building next to Sam's car. "I live right here."

That makes things easier, at least. "Alright. Come on."

She doesn't resist when I slip an arm around her waist to steady her. Her body is lithe beneath my grip, but not delicate. It suggests a hidden strength that matches that spark of fire I saw in her eyes earlier.

Fumbling with her keys at the front door, it takes three tries before she manages to get the door open. The building is a little run-down but clean, functional rather than fancy. Of course she lives on the fucking third floor, and after we make it up the stairs, she gets the apartment door open with less trouble.

Inside her apartment, she doesn't even glance at me before sighing heavily and toeing off her boots. Her gaze flicks to an empty spot in the living room, lingering there as something unreadable simmers in her eyes.

Before I can prompt her to keep moving, she abruptly snaps her head away. "I'm going to brush my teeth."

"Good plan."

She disappears down the hall while I wander into the kitchen and pour her a glass of water, leaning against the counter while I wait. The small cooking space offers a clear view back into the living room, the whole space giving off a warm and welcoming vibe that suggests its owner is usually a little more put together than she's coming off this evening.

When the woman returns, she's shed her heavy coat and her lips glisten with freshly-applied gloss. She looks softer than she did down on the street, and a little less guarded.

More appealing than a drunk woman who just keyed a stranger's car has any right to be.

I hand her the water and she drinks deeply before setting the glass on the counter with a quiet clink. When she turns back to me, I fix her with a hard stare.

"Why the fuck would you let me in here?"

She blinks, the doe-eyed innocent look returning in full force. "You said..."

"I know what I said, but you have no idea who I am. You don't know if anything I told you is true. What if I saw you key that car and made some shit up about it being mine to get into your apartment? What if I just put something in that drink?"

Finally, some sense of self-preservation kicks in. Her posture stiffens and her fingers flex against the counter as she considers grabbing something, anything, to use as a weapon.

Before she can move towards the knives in the block on the counter and hurt herself, I hold out a hand. "Lucky for you, I was telling the truth, but you need to be more careful. You can't trust men."

Her expression darkens and her gaze returns to that same empty spot in the living room. "You don't have to tell me that."

"Apparently, I do."

Fire creeps back into her brown eyes as they dart back to me, and I hold her stare for a long, silent moment.

A moment just a *little* too long to be entirely innocent.

Now that we're in the warm light of her apartment, it's impossible not to notice things I shouldn't, like the way her shoulder-length curls frame her face, or the subtle highlight of makeup on her cheekbones. Or most of all, the way her plump, glossy lips part, as though she's about to push back and test my limits.

With an inward groan, I force my thoughts back to business, to the car downstairs and the fact that she needs to pay to repair the damage she caused.

When I speak again, my voice comes out rougher than before thanks to the effort it's taking to stay on track. "Let's start with why the hell you were out there keying my car in the first place."

Chapter Four

~**Maxine**~

I must be drunker than I realized. That's the only reasonable explanation for why I can't string together a coherent thought around this man.

The way he scolds me for letting him into my apartment when he's the one who insisted on it in the first place rattles every feminist bone in my body, making me want to tell him exactly where to go. But then there's the way he checked on me when I threw up, or offered me a glass of water to help me feel better, looking after me like it's second nature, and instead of irritation, his solid presence stirs something far more confusing.

I don't want him to think I'm stupid.

I shouldn't care *what* he thinks.

It doesn't help matters when he reaches up and pulls the woollen hat off his head, revealing dark hair speckled with gray at the temples. The scruff along his sharp jawline is the same: mostly dark with the occasional gray. It gives him a distinguished air that adds to the sharpness behind his blue eyes, a look that suggests he's already figured out the world and doesn't have the patience for any bullshit.

He's old enough to be my father.

He's one of the most attractive men I've ever seen.

Two things can definitely be true at once.

When his stare hardens, I remember I still haven't answered his question about why I keyed the car, so I let the words tumble out before I can overthink them.

"I thought it belonged to someone else. I don't usually go around destroying stranger's property."

What are the odds that another car with that exact shade of baby-blue paint would show up outside my building today of all days? The universe must be playing a joke on me, though I don't think it's very funny and apparently, the car's owner doesn't either.

An unimpressed eyebrow arches over his left eye. "Why were you keying *that* person's car, then?"

He's going to think it's immature. I can already picture his condescending glare, but what's the point in lying? Nothing I say is going to impress him, so I stick with the truth. "She stole my boyfriend. He cheated on me with her."

I brace for the mocking, the disapproval, the look that says I'm just as pathetic as I feel, but it doesn't come. Instead, his expression softens, something unreadable flickering across his face.

"I'm sorry. Nobody deserves that."

The sincerity catches me completely off guard. "Thanks," is all I manage to mutter.

"However."

Of course there's a 'however'. The hard edge returns to his tone and I have to fight the urge to roll my eyes.

"You're an adult. Being drunk is no excuse. You need better discipline than that."

Discipline.

The word lingers between us, his tongue darting between his teeth on the final syllable. A shiver creeps down my spine and I have no idea how to interpret it.

What the hell was in those shots?

Before I can stop myself, I blurt out, "So, now you're going to punish me?"

Something flares in his eyes, the same something I noticed earlier when I sarcastically called him 'dad'. I have a feeling I've hit on something he doesn't want me to see, and now that I have, I want to poke at it.

The idea of getting under his skin is... *exciting.*

Seriously, what was in those drinks?

His stare stays locked on mine, the air between us charged. He doesn't answer right away, as if he's forcing himself to think before he speaks, and when he finally does, his voice is tight.

"Now, you're going to take responsibility for your actions by paying for the repairs."

Just like that, the tension shatters and reality slams back into me.

Thousands of dollars.

That's what he said downstairs, and my stomach twists as I do the math. With the gaping hole Josh's absence is going to tear in my finances, I can't afford this. The momentary satisfaction of keying what I *thought* was Sam's car suddenly seems like the worst trade-off imaginable.

Still, I'm not the kind of person to walk away from my responsibilities. I *did* damage the car, and I got caught, so I'll have to make it right.

"Would you be willing to work out a payment plan?" I ask hesitantly. "I can't give it to you all at once, but I could do a few hundred a month."

Things will be tight for a while but I can make it work if he agrees. If he doesn't, I'm not sure what I'm going to do, so I hold my breath while he considers that offer.

When he gives me a small nod, a little of the tension leaches from my shoulders.

"You just earned yourself some brownie points for not trying to tell me to go through my insurance. I can make you an offer."

"Okay," I agree warily, not ready to fully relax until I hear his terms.

"I'm willing to let you work off the debt. You don't have to pay me anything."

My body immediately stiffens as outrage coils in my stomach. The alcohol fuels my indignation, and I spit out the words without a second thought. "If you think I'm going to prostitute myself over a few scratches on a car, you're not only a pig, you're delusional."

His eyebrows raise again, both of them this time. "Is that so?"

"I wouldn't touch you if my life depended on it."

That's a lie, and worse than that, I think he knows it. His lips twitch, almost as if he's *enjoying* my outburst. "Are you finished?"

"No, I also want to say that..."

When I jab a finger towards him, his smile breaks free and it completely transforms his face. He has an *incredible* smile, and my stomach twists again, this time with plain, old-fashioned lust.

Maybe 'working off' my debt to him wouldn't be *so* bad.

Except... did he actually say that's what he meant?

He takes a step closer, still grinning. "You want to say what?"

I have no idea what I was about to say, so I force myself to take a metaphorical step back.

"What kind of work?"

His chuckle vibrates deep in my bones. "Maybe that's the question you should have asked in the first place."

Cheeks burning, I glare at him. I don't know who I'm angrier with: myself for jumping to conclusions or him for finding it so amusing. Why the hell did my brain jump straight to sex?

His explanation turns out to be much more innocent than I'd imagined. "I need some admin help with my business. We're short-staffed with people out sick and the holidays coming up. We have extended office hours so you can come in around your schedule at your regular job, and I'll offer you a fair wage until your debt is worked off. I assume you know your way around a computer?"

I nod out of habit, still processing everything he just said. "I actually manage an admin team."

"Perfect. Give me your phone."

He holds out his hand, and for a moment, I'm back in the living room with Josh, asking him to show me what's on his phone. The memory hits me so hard, I have to blink it away as I reach into the pocket of my jeans. I unlock the phone and hand it to him, no questions asked.

I've already asked enough stupid questions for one night.

As I watch, he navigates to my contacts, enters his own information, and sends himself a text. Once his phone dings, he hands mine back to me and pulls his device from the pocket of his coat.

"What's your name?" he asks, staring down at his screen. It looks tiny in his large hands, and I can't help noticing there's no ring on his finger.

"Maxine. Everyone calls me Max. What's yours?"

He types my *full* name into his contacts and slides the phone back into his pocket, lifting his gaze to meet mine again. "You can call me Reid, Maxine."

There is *no* reason for my stomach to dip the way it does when he says my name.

"I'm going to go now and you're going to drink another glass of water and get your ass into bed." His stern tone makes it clear he expects me to follow his instructions. "Tomorrow, I'll send you proof that the car is mine, an estimate for the damage repair, and the address of my business. Any questions?"

I start to shake my head before one pops into my brain, uninvited. "Why does a man like you drive a car like that?"

His expressive left eyebrow lifts again, this time in curiosity. "A man like me?"

What *do* I mean by that? I'm not sure I know, so I end up just shaking my head. "Never mind. You've wasted enough of your time here already. I'm sorry again about your car."

"I'm sorry about your asshole boyfriend."

Hearing this man who could probably crush Josh with one hand call him an asshole is the first thing to make me really smile all day. "Yeah. Me too."

We move back towards the door, and he inspects the deadbolt on his way out. "Make sure to lock this behind me."

This time, I don't bother to stop my eye roll. "Does your business specialize in giving people obvious advice?"

His lips twitch but sadly, his magnificent smile stays hidden as he repeats his order. "Lock it."

"Yes, sir." I give him a mock salute and that damn eyebrow lifts again. How the hell does he make a simple facial movement look so sexy?

Before he can say anything else, I close the door behind him and turn the lock loudly enough that I'm sure he'll hear.

I really need to stop drinking.

Chapter Five

~**Reid**~

Lazy Sunday mornings are my one true indulgence. Early on in my career, I realized how easy it would be to lose myself in the work needed to build a business from the ground up. I could put in long hours every day and still not be satisfied. So, I drew a line: Sundays were off-limits, a day for my family and life outside of work.

'Lazy' is a relative term, though. At ten o'clock, I've already worked out in my home gym for an hour, showered, took Sam's car into my regular body shop, and sent Maxine the information I promised her last night. She hasn't answered yet, and if I had to guess, she's probably having a lazy morning of her own, feeling a hell of a lot worse than I do.

Part of the reason I woke up so early might have something to do with my fleeting dream about *disciplining* the young woman from last night in the way she accused me of wanting to, not to mention the way I woke up with my dick harder than it's been in years, but I'm not going to dwell on that. My rational, conscious brain knows better than to go down that road with Maxine. Not only is she young enough to be my daughter, she's *connected* to my daughter, whether she knows it or not.

It's a fucking terrible idea, no matter how long it's been since a woman lingered in my mind the way she has.

Now, I'm sitting in the living room of my Craftsman-style home in Beverly, far from downtown Chicago, nursing a cup of coffee and reading a book. *Trying* to read a book, more accurately, because every time I attempt to focus on the philosophical questions in *The Brothers*

Karamazov, my thoughts end up wandering back to that small downtown apartment and the brunette who lives there.

Unfortunately, they also keep coming back to the reason she gave me for keying Sam's car. Although I hope Maxine got some of the details wrong, deep down I'm afraid she didn't.

The front door lock whirrs open as someone enters their access code, and since my son and daughter are the only ones besides me with their own codes, I'm not surprised to see Sam waltz in. A younger version of her mother, she's beautiful as ever. Her cheeks are tinted pink from the chilly November morning air but her pout detracts from her angelic appearance.

"Where's my car?" she asks in greeting as soon as her eyes land on me. Her tone hints at both hurt and accusation, as if I let her down by not having it running and waiting for her after she asked me to pick it up last night.

Usually, I would agree, but this morning, I ignore the question. "Come and sit down. I want to talk to you."

"Dad, I'm going to be late," she protests.

"I don't care. Sit down, Samantha."

At the sound of her full name, she drops the pout, a look of confusion taking its place. "What's wrong?"

"That's what I want to know. Sit your ass down."

Keeping wary eyes on me, she kicks off her boots and tugs off her coat before stepping into the living room. Her feet sink into the plush area rug that takes up most of the floor space. Shades of brown complement the bronze leather sofa set, everything masculine, comfortable, and unpretentious.

Needless to say, I completely redecorated once Sam's mother moved out.

My daughter perches on the edge of the sofa across from my armchair. "What's going on?" she tries again.

I snap the book in my lap shut, giving her my full attention. "Remind me why I needed to go pick up your car last night?"

She squints over at me, her heavy lashes almost covering her eyes completely. "I decided to go out, so I took a taxi home rather than drive. That's what you always said I should do."

That's true enough. I have the same deal with both my kids: if they need a ride or they need their car taken care of so that they're not getting behind the wheel after a drink, they can call me and I'll handle it. Jamie hasn't taken me up on it in years, and at 22, Sam's probably getting old enough that she can figure things out for herself too.

I don't mind that she called, though. That's not what I'm talking about. "Why did you have your car downtown in the first place?"

"I was helping a friend move. I told you that. It took less time than we expected, so we went out afterwards."

She did tell me, and I didn't press for details at the time. Now, I want to know more. "What friend?"

She shrugs. "One of the guys I'm working with. You don't know him."

"Just a guy that you work with? Nothing more?"

Her fingers twitch in her lap, a surefire sign that whatever's about to come out of her mouth next is a lie. It's a holdover from when she was a little kid and used to cross her fingers behind her back when she stretched the truth, thinking that gave her an out. It's kind of cute that she hasn't completely eliminated the instinct yet, but I'd prefer she didn't lie to me in the first place.

"Yeah, just a friend. You'll meet him at the pitch meeting this week."

Up until those words came out of her mouth, I was actually looking forward to the pitch meeting. When Sam hinted that her new company needed an investor for her first project with them, I thought it could be a great way to support her at arm's length, giving her some of the independence she's been craving while still having her back. I agreed to let them try and sell me on it.

Now, the presence of Maxine's ex-boyfriend at that meeting has me questioning that decision, among other things.

"Why was he moving out of his apartment?" I ask next. I know my daughter, and although she's very smart in many ways, thinking on her feet has never been her strong suit. If she's lying, I just have to keep pressing her until she trips up.

"He, um..." She pauses, and I can almost see the wheels turning as she tries to come up with a reasonable explanation. "It just made sense for him to move. I think he got a better deal somewhere else."

Weak, Sam. "How long had he been in that apartment?"

"I don't know. A couple of years?"

"And he found a better deal when rent prices have gone up more than 4% in the last year and it's almost always a smaller increase to extend an existing lease than to move to a new one?"

She crosses her arms, her shoulders drawing up to shield her. "I don't know, okay? People move all the time. Why does it matter?"

"Because you're lying to me, and based on what happened to your car last night, I want to know why you were in that neighbourhood."

Instantly, her arms drop and her lips part in horror. "What happened to my car?"

"Answer my question first and I'll tell you. The truth this time."

With an aggravated sigh of defeat, she gives in. "Alright, he's not just a friend. I didn't want to tell you yet because I don't want you to get the wrong idea."

"About what?"

"About why you should invest in the app. I'm not asking just because we're dating and it's his project. It really is a good investment. I was going to tell you about us dating afterwards."

"So, he's a guy you work with and you're dating." When she nods, I go back to my original question. "And why was he moving?"

"Because... he moved in with me?"

She phrases it as a question since she knows damn well I won't like it.

My grip tightens around the book in my lap, the pages crinkling under my fingers. "I've never even met this guy and you're living with him? What do *you* know about him? Have you done a criminal history check? Met his family?"

Her hands fly out as if she could calm me down the same way a lion tamer appeases an angry cat. "He's not dangerous, I promise. He's a really nice guy. And yes, it's fast, I know that, but he had nowhere else to go."

And we're back where we started. "*Why* didn't he have anywhere else to go? Why did he have to move?"

Her eyes dart around the room, looking for help in any of the framed family pictures on the mantelpiece or the pieces of art decorating the walls. Apparently, there's no inspiration to be found, since she gives me the real answer.

Almost.

"His roommate kicked him out."

"His *roommate*."

I repeat the word, emphasizing it to show I don't buy it, and Sam grimaces. At least she doesn't lie as brazenly and cavalierly as her mother. I suppose I should be grateful for that.

"His ex-girlfriend," she finally admits. "They were living together."

I lean forward, propping my elbows on my knees. "And were they exes when you two started seeing each other?"

Her eyes drop, unable to hold my gaze. "Not... exactly."

"Samantha."

The single word is so full of disappointment that she seems to shrink beneath its weight as she starts babbling. "I didn't know about her until two weeks ago, and Josh says they were going to break up soon anyway. It wasn't because of me. You don't even know him."

From the pain I saw rippling in Maxine's eyes last night, I have a strong feeling she would give me a different version of events. If Sam is also telling the truth, and based on the lack of her usual tells, she seems to believe her words are true, perhaps this Josh asshole was lying to them both.

"From what you've just told me, I know enough."

Sam leans forward, her lips pulled down in a pout. "Dad, please give him a chance. A person can make bad choices without *being* a bad person. It's not always black and white. You're always so critical just because Mom..."

She trails off, realizing a little too late that she's crossed over a line we usually steer clear of.

Yes, my wife cheated and blew up everything I thought we'd built on solid ground. No, I haven't been close with anyone since then.

But it doesn't change the fact that Josh sounds like a piece of shit, and Sam wanting to make excuses for him turns my stomach.

"Someone keyed your car on the street last night," I tell her bluntly, changing the subject and leaving Maxine out of the narrative. "It's getting fixed, so you can use my Chevy in the meantime. Keys are in the truck in the garage."

She doesn't move. "Please don't be mad at me."

Mad isn't the right word. More than anything, I feel like I'm not sure I fully know the young woman sitting across from me, and that's worse than anger. It's fucking heartbreaking.

I should say something reassuring, something that tells her she'll always be my little girl, and no matter how much she messes up, as long as she wants to make it right, we'll figure it out together.

But right now, I just can't.

"I've got work to do," I say instead, pushing to my feet. "I'll see you at the pitch meeting."

Before she can say anything else, I stride out of the room, leaving her to see herself out.

Chapter Six

~Maxine~

I wake up to the Sahara Desert in my mouth and a jackhammer drilling into my skull. Those damned green shots really did a number on me.

Groaning into the empty space around me, I grab my phone off my nightstand to check the time.

11:34. *Shit.*

I have errands to run today since yesterday was a write-off, and several messages are waiting for me. I check in with my friends first before I reach the one from 'Reid', sent at 9:47 this morning.

My stomach knots as our interaction from last night comes rushing back to me. In spite of my drunkenness, I don't seem to have lost any part of my memory, though whether it would be better if I *could* forget some of it is up for debate.

What the hell was I thinking when I... well, did any of it, really? The whole evening was so unlike me, from keying the car in the first place to the back and forth between us, but somewhat surprisingly, I don't regret it as much as I probably should. If anything, I'd say the nervous feeling bubbling in my stomach is closer to... anticipation?

I tap the message open before I can get too carried away.

> Here are my papers for the car and the estimate from the garage. They already started work.

Damn. He doesn't waste any time.

Holding my breath, I open the invoice, and blow out a relieved sigh when I see the total of $1800. That's not as bad as I feared since the scratches covered the body panels and doors. I assume that baby-blue colour isn't all that easy to find either. It could have been worse.

In fact, as I squint down at the fine print, I see a 'premium customer' discount applied that significantly reduces the price. It *would* have been worse without Reid's discount.

Not quite sure how to feel about that, I return to the rest of his message.

> You can find the address and background on my company, Bear Construction, on our website. There's someone in the office until 9 pm every weeknight and all day on Saturday. Let me know what day you can start and I'll connect you to the office manager.

> Chin up, Maxine. Today will be better.

Pressure unexpectedly builds behind my eyes at those final words. The last few days have been pretty awful, but somehow, those two short sentences make me feel a little better, even if they come from a man I don't know at all.

Blinking back the urge to cry, I click on the link he included to the company website. I don't know what I expected, but the sleek, professional site that greets me comes as a surprise. *Chicago's top luxury construction firm*, the headline banner reads. *25 years of making the impossible possible.*

That's quite a claim, but as I scroll through some of the pictures of their projects, I have to admit I'm impressed. Close-up detail photos show a level of craftsmanship beyond anything I could ever dream of affording, and one picture in particular catches my eye: a carving of a bear on an ornate wooden staircase that's both subtle and stunning at the same time.

"Wow," I whisper before returning to my exploration of the site. There's an 'about us' section, and as soon as I click on it, a picture of Reid pops up.

Holy fuck.

In my drunken haze in my kitchen last night, I thought he was one of the best-looking men I'd ever seen, but seeing him in a suit, the deep blue of his tie bringing out the striking indigo of his eyes, my mouth somehow goes even drier.

I read his bio out loud to make sure I don't miss anything. "Reid Larson trained as a carpenter at Southwestern Illinois College before founding Bear Construction. The firm quickly built a name for itself by providing quality woodwork along with excellence in general construction. With strong relationships across the trades, Bear Construction provides a one-stop-shop for all your luxury construction needs."

For a 'personal' bio, it doesn't contain much personal information at all, and I scroll down, hoping to find more. There are more photos, including Reid on a construction site in a hard hat and jeans, and one of him wearing safety goggles and working on an intricate piece of wood carving.

Honestly, I can't tell which look suits him best. The man is *seriously* hot, and the skill those hands must have...

Nope. Not going there.

Especially not when I'm going to be working for him and he already thinks I'm a complete disaster.

More pictures follow, showing him with other construction workers, at a ribbon-cutting ceremony, and with a group of young people, but there's no further text at all. My disappointment is so strong, I have to laugh at myself. What did I expect? A dating profile?

Returning to his message, I'm about to respond when I realize I haven't opened the document showing that he actually owns the car. I can't imagine he'd go to all this trouble just to get an admin assistant if it *isn't* his car, but I should probably look at it anyway.

Reid's voice rings in my head with his words from last night: *You can't trust men.*

As if I didn't just learn that first-hand for myself.

When I open the file, everything looks legit. There's his name and address, in a pretty swanky part of the city, along with the car details.

I scroll down, just to make sure I haven't missed anything, and that's when I see the text at the bottom of the page, superimposed over the image itself.

> If you see this, tell me what you had for breakfast and I'll give you one hour off the time you owe me.

My laugh is equal parts surprise, amusement, and annoyance. He really doesn't trust that I'd check the documents properly, and that irritates me, even though I very nearly didn't.

Part of me is tempted to pretend I didn't see it, just to see what he'd do.

I toy with the idea, waffling back and forth before deciding that I really shouldn't push my luck right now.

Next time is fair game though.

> I missed breakfast but bacon and eggs for lunch sounds like heaven right now.

Almost instantly, three dots appear, and his answer steals my breath yet again.

> Good girl.

Two simple words shouldn't have the power to send the sharp jolt through me that they do. My stomach flips, and I'm not even sure why.

What the fuck? I don't want to be called that.

Do I?

My phone pings again before I can even think about how to respond.

> Do you know what day you want to start?

Ignoring the first message for the sake of my sanity, I answer his question.

> I could be there at six on Tuesday.

> Sounds good. I'll have Rebecca get in touch before then.

Rebecca must be the office manager he mentioned before, and I do my best to ignore the pang of disappointment that accompanies the realization that she'll be the one meeting with me, not Reid himself.

Okay. Thanks. Go Bears.

I add the last part without even thinking until I see the words looking back at me in black and white after I hit send. It's game day, and I always end my texts to Josh or any of my friends with a little encouragement for our team. It's a ritual born of superstition that turned into habit, but to a complete stranger, it makes me look crazy.

I'm about to apologize when one more text comes through on his end.

Go Bears. Have a good day, Maxine.

That whole exchange ended up being much warmer than I expected. Maybe I'm not as much of a disaster in his eyes as I thought?

I put the phone down, ready to take a minute to psych myself up for what I need to do today, but to my surprise, I'm actually feeling much better than I was before. Agreeing to this whole indentured-servitude thing might not have been my finest hour, but at least it's keeping my mind off Josh, and at least for today, that's a win.

With a new spring in my step, I throw back the covers and swing my legs out of bed, ready to take on the day.

Chapter Seven

~**Reid**~

At 5:45 on Tuesday, Rebecca's head appears around my office door. "What are you still doing here?"

"Last time I checked, I own the building," I grumble at her, flipping another page of the printed report on my desk that I've been reviewing. "I'm allowed to be here."

My office manager lets out a delicate snort. "Just tell me to mind my own business if you don't want me to know, Reid. Sarcasm doesn't suit you."

Not many of my employees would speak back to me that way, but Rebecca isn't just any employee. She joined the company when we were first starting out, walking my young and inexperienced ass through the teething years as I made a name for myself. In her late '50s now, her once-black hair a steely shade of gray, she still keeps this place running more than anyone else, me included. I have no idea what I'm going to do when she retires, which is why I pay her an obscene amount to make sure she sticks around as long as possible.

Still, it doesn't mean I have to tell her *everything*. She definitely doesn't need to know that I'm lingering in the office on purpose because Maxine keeps popping into my head, uninvited, and I want a chance to exchange a few words with her when she comes in for her first shift.

I could tell Rebecca that checking in on a new hire is standard practice, but we both know I don't usually make a point of introducing myself to temps, and I sure as hell don't rearrange my day to do so.

"Do you want me to add you to the dinner order?" she asks next.

With our office open longer than the usual nine-to-five, we provide dinner for anyone working past six. I've always believed that when you look after people, they'll do their best for you. That philosophy never lets me down.

Well, *almost* never.

"No, I won't be much longer."

With a brisk nod, she walks away, and of course, almost as soon as she does, my stomach rumbles.

"Actually, get me a beef sandwich," I call out through the open door. "Hot and wet."

No sooner do the words leave my mouth than a figure appears in the doorway. However, the curvy silhouette doesn't belong to my office manager.

No, the woman standing there is significantly younger and wearing an expression hovering between confusion and amusement. "Excuse me?"

For a split second, I don't recognize her. The drunk, messy woman from Saturday, all sharp edges and emotion, has been replaced by someone tidy and professional, with a sleek navy blouse, fitted black skirt, and hair tamed into loose curls.

The eyes give her away, though: big, brown, and sparkling with mischief.

"Maxine." Her name almost gets stuck in my throat and I clear it hard before continuing. *What the hell?* I don't get nervous around women. She took me by surprise, that's all. "Where's Rebecca?"

"That's what I'm trying to figure out. The woman at the front desk told me she came this way."

Heather at the front desk is the daughter of one of my foremen who begged me to give her a chance in the office, and I agreed because we need the extra help right now. Sending a new employee wandering through the office on her own is unfortunately par for the course for how things are going.

Maxine's gaze flicks curiously around my office before coming back to rest on me. "What was that about wanting something hot and wet?"

Fuck.

This woman has some nerve. After our previous interactions, she should be staying out of my way rather than teasing me, and I should be irritated with her impertinence. I *should* shut it down.

Instead, something tightens low in my gut at the challenge.

"So, your mind is always in the gutter, not just when you've been drinking. Good to know."

The reminder of how she accused me of trying to extort sex from her hits the mark, and her cheeks quickly redden.

Still, she doesn't back down. "If you'd stop saying such suggestive things, maybe I wouldn't get the wrong idea."

This is what I've been missing: someone I can have fun teasing who'll give it right back to me.

Before I can respond, however, Rebecca reappears. "Ms Lisney?"

Maxine turns, a professional smile replacing the more playful one she wore for me. "Yes. Hello."

"Hi." Rebecca gives her a once-over, assessing the new arrival with her usual cool efficiency. Based on Heather's performance, she was less than thrilled when I told her we were taking on another temporary employee. Maxine will have her work cut out for her to win Rebecca over. "You'll be over here with me. Sorry for bothering you, Reid."

The apology isn't necessary, so I wave it off. "It's fine. While you're here: I will have supper after all. Beef sandwich."

"Hot and wet," Maxine adds, understanding settling in her eyes and her lips twitching as she shoots one more glance in my direction.

The two of them walk away and it takes me a minute or two to realize I'm smiling as I finish reading through the report.

Weird.

Half an hour later, I get the message that the food has arrived, and I head to the kitchen to pick mine up. A dozen people already fill the room, chatting as they divvy up the meals, but conversation dwindles when I walk in. Maxine, standing near the counter with her back to me, talking to two of the men from accounts, turns to see what caused the sudden lull. When our eyes meet, instead of looking away like everyone else does, she smiles.

"Yours is over there," she says, pointing to a small bag sitting on the other end of the counter. "Just how you wanted it."

A dozen pairs of curious eyes dart between me and the new girl and I can practically hear the internal questions behind them, wondering who the hell she is to speak to me so familiarly. It's not that I'm unapproachable. At least, I don't think so, but there's always been a divide between me and the office staff.

On site, I'm one of the guys, but here, I'm just the boss.

I grunt out an acknowledgement, picking up the bag and leaving everyone in peace while I head to Rebecca's desk. She's eating her salad in front of her computer, as I knew she would be.

"Are things working out with Maxine?"

She glances up at me, gaze sharp as always. "It's been half an hour, Reid."

"And you can size someone up in two minutes," I counter. "So what do you think? Is she going to help?"

As much as this arrangement is about Maxine working off the repair costs, it's also about taking some pressure off Rebecca and the rest of the team. If Maxine won't be pulling her weight, I might have to reconsider.

Thankfully, Rebecca's first impression is a good one. "She's already read up on the business, has relevant experience and is asking good questions. I don't think she'll be a burden."

Unlike Heather, she means. "Alright, good. Keep me updated."

As I turn to head back to my office, I almost run straight into Maxine, who's come up behind me. I'm not sure if she overheard our conversation, but based on the knowing look she gives me, she can at least guess what I'm doing there. "Checking up on me already?"

"Naturally," is my gruff answer. "Making sure we're not wasting anyone's time here."

One eyebrow raises in challenge. "And?"

Gone is the unsure, emotional woman I encountered on Saturday, replaced by the one I only caught glimpses of that night.

Confident. Fiery. Impulsive.

Begging to be shown a firm hand.

Fuck. I really shouldn't have added that last one.

"Jury's still out," I tell her, giving Rebecca a nod before I leave them both. "Don't let me down."

Her chin lifts in defiance, but I catch another emotion lurking in those big brown eyes. She *wants* to prove herself to me. *Craves* it, even.

Which is exactly why I need to walk the fuck away.

Chapter Eight

~**Maxine**~

My plan is kind of backfiring.

I showed up at Bear Construction for my first shift, determined to prove to Reid Larson, and to myself, that I am *not* a sociopathic menace to society, but actually an intelligent, confident woman who has her life under control.

What do I do instead? *Flirt* with the damn man.

It's not entirely my fault, though. I thought I was prepared. I studied the pictures of him on the website until I was sure I could handle those blue eyes looking at me in real life if we happened to run into each other. I did my best to put the nightly dreams I've been having about him firmly in the 'fantasy' category of my mind. I even gave myself a pep talk in the mirror, reminding myself that I *just* got dumped and am in no position to even think about another man, let alone one I'm going to be working for.

And then I walk by his office door, hear his gruff, sexy voice talking about 'hot and wet' things, and all my best-laid plans fly out the window.

That doesn't even take into account his office wall, the one that's practically a shrine to my beloved Chicago Bears. I didn't get a close look at any of it, but I could swear at least one of the photos is of Reid *on the field* with some of the team.

Not only is he successful and gorgeous, he's also a Bears fan?

This isn't fair. Someone is messing with me.

At least I don't have too much time to dwell on it since Rebecca flies through our training session, leaving me scribbling notes and asking multiple questions to try to make sure I don't miss anything.

In my day job, I work for a car insurance company, managing the team that processes all of the administration for car accident claims. Everything is always urgent: customers impatient to get their repairs completed and body shops impatient to get paid. We deal in volume, getting through as much as we can as quickly as we can.

Bear Construction is different. They're about quality rather than quantity, as Rebecca reminds me multiple times. Their clients are exacting and if they don't get what they expect, they'll take their business, and their considerable wealth, elsewhere.

Part of the reason the office stays open each night is just in case any of those clients need to touch base outside the usual 9-to-5. The other reason is that Reid offers his employees flexible work hours if they have kids or other commitments. That's on top of the generous rate of pay, even for a temp like me, meaning I'll have my debt to him paid off in about 70 hours of work. I can probably pull that off by the end of January or early February.

All in all, it seems like a great place to work, but one that insists on competence, and by the time she finally gives me my first task for the night, I'm low-key terrified of screwing up. I don't want to let either Rebecca or Reid down.

"These are invitations Mr Larson has received for holiday parties," she explains, dropping a surprisingly large stack of envelopes on my desk. "For each one, figure out who's hosting the party and look them up on our client database as I showed you. If they're not in the database, RSVP 'no' with our apologies. If they're clients, add them to a list with the client name and date of the party. I'll review the invitations with Mr Larson later this week to make up a schedule. I'll leave it to you to figure out how to organize the list."

That feels like a test, but it's one I'm up to. Reaching for the invitations, I flip through the stack of heavy envelopes. They even *feel* expensive. "This is going to keep him busy all month."

"Mr Larson will only take the most important ones himself," she explains. "Others, he'll delegate to Jamie or one of the other managers."

"Jamie?" I don't remember seeing that name on the website.

"Mr Larson's son."

Something twists low in my stomach at the word *son*, and it takes me a second to identify the feeling as… jealousy?

What kind of woman would appeal to Reid Larson enough that he has a child with her? What would it be like to be so intimate with him? Not just in a sexual way, although that has plenty of appeal on its own, but to have a family together?

I've never even really given much thought to having kids of my own, but having *his* kids feels like this woman won the lottery in a way I can't even begin to explain.

Maybe I *am* a sociopath after all.

"I didn't know he had children," I manage to say despite the strange tightness in my throat.

Rebecca makes a noise that I can't interpret. "Two of them. Only Jamie works here though."

"And his… uh… wife… attends these parties with him?"

The older woman's gaze narrows, making me fear that she can guess the reason for my question or the completely unreasonable fantasies that have flitted around the edges of my dreams. I probably shouldn't have asked, but I need to know. He doesn't wear a ring, but that doesn't necessarily mean he's unattached. Finding out he's married would shut down my inappropriate thoughts immediately.

Sociopath or not, I am *not* a cheater.

"It's best to never mention the former Mrs Larson," she snips. "I'll worry about his plus-ones."

In other words: *mind your own business, Max.*

Message received, but my breath comes a little easier after hearing the word 'former' applied to the mother of Reid's children.

I start on my task, getting so wrapped up in it that I barely even notice when Reid leaves the office around 7:30. Rebecca follows him half an hour later, telling me to put aside any invitations I'm not sure about and we can review them tomorrow. The office is still open for another hour and I might as well get as many hours in as possible now that I'm here.

The invitations range from simple postcards to stunning works of art. In what sometimes feels like a different life, I studied graphic design in college, and it's fascinating to see all the layout and font choices made on each invitation, and to consider why they work or don't.

The one from the Stamer Hotels chain, displaying a pop-up scene of the Chicago skyline with the Stamer hotel front and centre, takes my breath away. Snow sparkles on the rooftop and tiny lights twinkle in its windows.

Their holiday party will be in the hotel ballroom with a black-tie dress code. Although I've heard how beautiful the hotel is, I've never had a reason to go inside it. I can barely imagine how elegant the party will be.

Did Reid work on that hotel, I wonder?

Sure enough, when I pull up 'Stamer' in the client database, the business pops right up with a note that all contact with them is to be handled by Reid himself.

Nobody can say he isn't hands-on when it comes to his business.

He seems like a pretty hands-on kind of guy in general.

The kind of guy I wouldn't mind having his hands on *me*.

Stop it, Max.

Clearing my throat, I force myself to refocus and manage to finish going through the stack of invitations at quarter to nine, giving me enough time to pretty up the spreadsheet I made and email it to Rebecca. The invitations themselves, I leave in three neat piles: the ones I've responded to, the ones on the spreadsheet, and a couple that I had questions about. When I shut down the computer and grab my coat at nine o'clock, I'm proud of the work I got done and actually looking forward to coming back the next evening, despite how long the day has been.

However, when I walk through the doors of Bear Construction just before six o'clock the following day, something immediately feels off. Rebecca isn't at her desk and the stacks of invitations I left out are gone, replaced by a note.

See me in my office.

The note isn't signed but it doesn't need to be. That bold, masculine print can only belong to one person.

My eyes flit to the other side of the open-plan office where Reid's door is open, the window blinds drawn. Trying my best to ignore the way my heart pounds, I leave my coat at my desk and stride over to the open doorway as confidently as I can.

Sitting at his desk, he's staring down at printed papers, his sharp, chiselled features unreadable. I take the opportunity to steal one last breath before I knock.

His piercing blue eyes find me as his head raises, and my body reacts before my mind can catch up. Heat pulses through my body and something seems to tug me towards him, as if gravity itself has rewired to centre around this man.

He's so fucking hot.

However, I push my lust down when I realize there's not even a hint of a smile in those eyes.

"You wanted to see me?"

Somehow, my voice comes out steady, but I honestly have no idea how. My legs have started to tremble.

"Come in. Shut the door."

A warning bell rings in the back of my brain, an alarm telling me that being alone with this man is a terrible idea in so many ways.

I do what he says anyway.

With the door closed behind me, I wait until he gestures at the chair across the desk from him. "Sit."

Again, I obey, watching him warily the whole time. His cologne, something woodsy that feels exactly right for a carpenter, drifts over to me, making it even harder to concentrate. "Is there a problem?"

From a drawer in his desk, he pulls out a large stack of envelopes that I immediately recognize, and tosses them onto the desktop between us. "Is there a reason you left these sitting out overnight?"

I sense it's a trick question, but I answer honestly. "I wasn't finished with them yet."

His sharp gaze never leaves me. "And Rebecca didn't give you a key to your desk drawers?"

That question makes it a little clearer what the problem might be. "She did, but I didn't realize I needed to lock everything away."

"Did you ask anyone?"

Just like on the night we met, his tone gets under my skin. I hear what he's saying and I understand he has a point, but he doesn't have to be such an ass about it.

"No, I didn't. I'm sorry, but now I know, and I'll make sure I use the drawers going forward. Is there anything else?"

His eyes flash with that same... *something*... I caught a glimpse of that night in my apartment. A sign that I'm succeeding in riling him up just as much as he's doing to me.

"Do you have somewhere to be? Am I inconveniencing you, Maxine?"

Don't say it, my brain begs. *Don't say it.*

I say it.

"Actually, you are. This could have been a text or an email. Or do you only get off on pointing out other people's mistakes in person?"

Storm clouds seem to gather in those mesmerizing eyes. If I listen closely, I could swear I hear thunder in the distance. "I *get off* on people doing their job properly."

The emphasis he puts on those words turns my insides liquid, conjuring up all sorts of images I've been trying so hard to avoid for the past few days.

"Our clients take their privacy very seriously," he continues.

"I understand."

"And I expect my employees to do the same."

"I said I understand," I snap back at him. "I didn't know the rule, and now I do. Though I'm a little surprised you don't hire better security if you're that worried about people snatching things off desks."

His eyebrow raises in a mix of irritation and intrigue. "So this is my fault?"

"No, but I don't know what else you want from me. I apologized and I promised not to do it again. What's left? Are you going to spank me for it?"

I have *no* idea where those words come from. I've never spoken to anyone like this, and I can't even blame alcohol this time. I haven't had a drop in days.

Something about this man brings out a rebellious side I barely even knew I had, one that urges me to push back when it would be far safer to retreat. And maybe that's not the worst thing in the world. After all, I played it safe with Josh, and look where that got me.

But it's obviously not the smartest thing either, at least not in this situation.

Sucking in a breath, I brace myself for an explosion. Will he fire me on the spot? Honestly, I couldn't even argue if he does. Who the hell speaks to their boss this way?

But Reid doesn't explode. His nostrils flare and his hands grip the armrests of his chair tightly as he takes one controlled breath, and then another. Electricity crackles between us.

And in those seconds of silence, our eyes locked together in a battle of wills, I'm hit with one complete and utter certainty.

Spanking me is exactly what he wants to do.

Chapter Nine

~**Reid**~

I force myself to inhale, every muscle in my body so tight that the air has to squeeze into my lungs.

She did *not* just say that. I must have imagined it, just as I've imagined dozens of similar scenarios far too many times in the last couple of days.

Except she fucking *did* say it.

My lips part, knowing I need to say *something* in response, but the words dry up before they can even reach my tongue.

Nope, not yet. Keep breathing.

Another forced inhale and another attempt to calm the pounding of my heart and the throbbing of my dick.

I didn't call her into my office to spank her. That would be insane.

No, I simply wanted to correct the mistake she'd made, a mistake I happened to notice when I arrived at the office that morning and grabbed the invitations off her desk before Rebecca could spot them. It was an innocent enough slip, but a mistake all the same, and I didn't want Rebecca to have any reason to think badly of Maxine when she was just starting out.

I had no plans beyond that, but the defiance in her big, brown eyes and the way she pushes back against me knocked on a door I've kept closed for far too long.

I've met women who talk a big game, but when the moment comes, they back down. Maxine isn't doing that. She's staring me down and daring me to take what I want.

And fuck, do I want it.

I couldn't entirely hide it from her that night in her apartment, and I have a feeling she glimpses it now too as I struggle for control. This is the moment where I either shut this down for good or...

Or the moment I truly let her see me.

With each passing beat of silence between us, Maxine's expression shifts. Rebellion blends into confusion before landing on something new. Not disgust, or even fear, which would both be perfectly reasonable responses to the situation.

What I see in her eyes is *curiosity*, mixed with a flicker of excitement.

It's that excitement that finally makes me speak, my voice coming out rough and deep.

"Is that what you want, Maxine? Are you a... *tactile* learner? Would it help you to remember not to make the same mistake again?"

We're walking a razor's edge that's getting more dangerous with each sentence passing between us. One misstep, one word taken the wrong way, and we fall.

The reasons I should send her out of my office right now repeat on a loop in my head. She's working for me. She's half my age. She used to date Sam's new boyfriend.

It's so fucking inappropriate.

But her ass would feel so good beneath my hand.

I don't know what she can see in my eyes, if she can get even a glimpse of the internal war I'm fighting, but her resolve seems to harden right in front of me, uncertainty morphing into determination.

"I guess that depends on how memorable you make it."

My restraint snaps like a frayed leash, and desire floods my veins. It's thick and all-consuming, expanding with every breath. This exchange of power and the rush it brings has been pushed down for too long, for *years* since my divorce, and I don't want to ignore it anymore.

"If we're doing this, it isn't because I'm your boss. It isn't because you owe me money. It's because you want to, and as soon as you don't want to anymore, it stops. Do you understand me?"

Her eyes widen as realization settles in that I'm deadly serious. After only a short pause, however, she nods.

"Words, Maxine. Give me your words."

Fire flares in those beautiful brown eyes, and still, she doesn't back down. "I understand."

Those are the sweetest two words I can imagine right now. My dick swells even further but I resist the urge to reach down and adjust myself. This isn't about me. *Not yet.*

"On your feet."

That fucking doe-eyed, innocent blink of hers will be the death of me.

"Don't make me repeat myself." My voice is pure gravel. "Stand up."

This time, she obeys, rising slowly. Every shift in her posture, each small movement, mesmerizes me. Unfortunately, she's not wearing a skirt today... or maybe that's a good thing. It would have been too tempting to lift it up and take things even further.

We should start slow.

Funny how I'm already thinking of this as just the beginning.

"Bend over and put your elbows on the desk. Keep your eyes on me the whole time."

Her fingers flex at her sides while her lips tighten. The defiance is back, clashing against her curiosity.

This time, I don't repeat myself. I just arch a brow, daring her to disobey me.

A beat passes as she breathes in and out, a clash of wills taking place without a word until, with an intoxicating mix of resentment and surrender, she lowers. Bending at the waist until her elbows rest on the desk, her eyes never leave mine.

She looks absolutely perfect this way.

A dozen ideas flood my mind of ways I could touch her and things I could teach her, but I lock my hands into fists, forcing myself to stay in control.

One thing at a time.

Every movement slow and deliberate, I get to my feet. Maxine's expressive eyes follow me as I step around the desk until she can't see me anymore, but she doesn't turn her head when I leave her line of sight. She doesn't break position.

Such a good girl.

From the side, she somehow looks even better. Her boots have a small heel, highlighting the curve of her calves and the lift of her ass as she bends over. Her body is braced and waiting, but I don't see any fear.

Am I afraid? Probably not as much as I should be. Each inhale feels thick, as though I'm breathing in something stronger than air. My palms itch, already aching for the contact they haven't made yet.

Once I touch her, I can't take it back. Once it happens, it can't be undone. Maybe I should walk away while I still can.

I don't fucking want to.

Lifting my hand, I let it hover just above her skin, savouring the way her body tenses in anticipation.

One heartbeat, and another.

I wait just long enough to make her wonder if I'll actually follow through, long enough for her weight to shift, confirming she wants it, before my palm sails in a perfect arc and lands with a loud *smack* against her round, beautiful ass.

Chapter Ten

~**Maxine**~

Smack.

The sound registers in my brain before the actual impact does, and my breath whooshes out of my lungs in a sharp exhale. *He actually fucking did it.* Part of me thought this might be some kind of test or power trip, but as the sting begins to radiate out from where his palm connected with my ass, reality sinks in.

This is not a drill, and definitely not a dream. If a pinch can wake you from a dream, that smack would have had me shooting out of bed. But I'm still here, in his office, bent over his desk, my ass throbbing from where he spanked me.

Stranger than that, it's not the only thing throbbing.

Wetness pools between my legs, my clit begs for friction, and a steady beat of desire pulses deep inside me. The sensation is overwhelming, an electric current running through my nerves and short-circuiting logic and hesitation.

I've never been this turned on in my life.

Just as the sharpness of the pain begins to override my shock, Reid's hand returns, rubbing slow, firm circles over the spot he just struck. Heat spreads through me in waves, my breath shuddering as his touch soothes and ignites at the same time.

"Is that enough? Or do you need another reminder?"

I force myself to breathe and try to string together a coherent thought. Even in my inexperience with this kind of thing, I know punishment isn't the end goal. At least, not entirely. It turns *him* on too. If I looked behind me right now, I have no doubt I'd see his arousal pressing against the seam of his expensive dress pants.

That's about the only thing I *do* know. The rest is entirely new.

Josh was the very definition of vanilla. I asked him once to spank me during sex, just to see how it felt, and his attempt was so awkward and devoid of any urgency or need, that I never asked again.

I convinced myself it wasn't that important. Maybe I wouldn't even enjoy it.

Reid just cleared that up for me, at least.

I fucking *love* it, and I don't want it to end just yet.

So, I poke the bear. "You might need to do it once more. I'm not sure I'll remember that."

"Son of a…" he mutters under his breath, and I bite my lip to hide my smile. Safe in the knowledge that he can't see my face, I can revel in his unravelling. Seeing him lose control is the single hottest thing I've ever witnessed, but hearing it comes a close second.

On a fundamental level, we both know what we're doing. Pushing him excites me, and he enjoys being pushed. From the moment we met, we recognized it in each other, even if I didn't fully understand it until now.

I'm still distracted by that thought when his hand lands again.

The impact jolts my body forward, my elbows slipping against the smooth surface of his desk. A sharp sting flares through me, layered over the lingering heat from before, and my breath stutters on impact.

Instantly, his hands find my hips, steadying me before I can face-plant into the wood.

"Better?"

The smug satisfaction in the question makes me want to push him *even more.*

I should stop. I should think about what this means and the consequences, but I can't resist pushing just a little farther, to see just how far I can take it. "Better make it one more."

A pause follows, a long one, and a different kind of anticipation coils in my stomach. This time, I'm fully braced for it, but the waiting is somehow worse than the actual contact. He's letting me sit in the expectation, *marinate* in it, and my jaw clenches in frustration.

Smack.

Even though I was prepared this time, my lips part on a grunt when the impact actually comes. Tears sting my eyes from the force of it, and I bite down hard on my lower lip to keep from whimpering.

In pain? In pleasure? I can't be sure.

Reid's hand is on me again in an instant, rubbing gentle, deliberate circles over the burn he just left behind. The pain lingers, but so does something deeper. If he offered to fuck me over this desk right now, I would beg him to do it, and I've never begged a man for anything.

I don't know who I am right now.

The thought flits through my mind, a thought that should terrify me but doesn't. If anything, it feels...

Freeing.

He *doesn't* offer to fuck me, though.

Instead, he steps back around the desk, lowering himself into his chair as if he has all the time in the world. His intense gaze locks onto mine, watching me with a satisfaction that makes my stomach tighten. "You can sit down now."

It takes my body a second to obey. My muscles are stiff from the tension, my ass still aching from his hand, and when I lower myself into the chair, the pressure makes the sting worse. A wince slips through my defenses.

Reid doesn't miss it.

His eyes track every twitch of my face, cataloguing each one. "It's going to hurt all night, and probably tomorrow too. Every time you feel it, you'll remember what you did wrong. I'm sure you won't make the same mistake again."

I can say with absolute certainty that I will never forget anything about this interaction.

But as the adrenaline starts to fade, uncertainty creeps in to take its place. What the hell did I just do? Did it mean the same thing to him as it did to me?

I can't help voicing the thought out loud: "Is this how you train all your employees?"

A muscle ticks in his cheek. "Don't ever think that. I've never done this in my office before. I fucking shouldn't have done it now."

"Then why did you?"

His stare seems to see straight into my soul, understanding the insecurity driving my questions. "I think you know why. I think you feel it too."

I *do* feel it, but it seems impossible that he feels the same. He's extraordinary and I'm… just me.

It doesn't make sense and I don't want to assume anything. I need to hear him say it, so I throw his own order back at him. "Words, Reid. Give me your words."

Blowing out a breath, he shakes his head as if he can't decide whether to laugh or bend me back over his desk. Maybe he wants to do both.

"You've got spirit and a hell of a lot of nerve, and I find that incredibly attractive. It drives me crazy, but in a good way."

Fuck.

No one has ever been this blunt with me. No one has ever *owned* their desire so completely.

"And you're not in a relationship with anyone else?" I have to ask, just to be sure.

That same muscle works in his cheek. "Of course not. I told you before: no one deserves that kind of disrespect."

I remember his words from the night we met, and it pleases me more than it probably should that he remembers it too.

"Have you ever done anything like this before?" he asks, gesturing at his desk in reference to what just happened between us there.

"No. Never."

"A natural," he mutters, mostly to himself, before his eyes lock onto mine again. "Did you enjoy it?"

I'm sure he already knows the answer, but I appreciate that he asks instead of assuming. "Yes."

He nods without a hint of surprise. "This is awful timing, with you working here and just getting out of a relationship and..."

He trails off there but I have a few guesses about what might have come next. Something about our difference in age, maybe, or something about his ex-wife. Heeding Rebecca's advice, I don't bring her up.

Besides, there's something I want to know even more. "If none of that mattered, what would you do?"

His eyelids lower, just a touch, and my stomach flips. My body has never reacted to anyone the way it responds to him.

"I would train you properly."

The intensity between us should scare me. It *does* scare me, if I'm being honest, but not enough to make me walk away. "Train me to do what?"

"To understand what you want when you act like a brat and to help you get it."

One word stands out to me above all the others in that sentence, blunting the lust simmering inside me. "Hang on. I'm not a brat."

"Yes, you fucking are."

My mouth pops open to argue but he silences me with that damned raised eyebrow.

"It isn't an insult, Maxine. It's simply what you are, and the fact that you take it in a negative way tells me you don't understand yourself."

He's so fucking presumptuous. "And you know me better than I know myself? After spending less than an hour with me?"

We're back to arguing again, but this time, Reid doesn't take the bait. He simply leans back in his chair and points to the door.

"Rebecca will be waiting for you. We can talk about this again when you're ready, or we can pretend it never happened. It's up to you."

The dismissal stings almost more than the spanking did, and my face heats as I push up to my feet, snatch the invitations off his desk, and stalk towards the door, trying to ignore the way my ass aches with every step.

"Drink some water and sleep on your stomach tonight," he orders behind me.

The last thing he sees as I walk out of his office is my middle finger over my shoulder.

Chapter Eleven

~**Reid**~

A full 24 hours after my encounter with Maxine in my office, my palm still tingles with the ghost of our contact. Not as much from the spanking itself, but from what came after: the way I soothed the sting, my fingers tracing the curve of her ass. A pulse of heat stirs low in my gut as the memory plays out.

Some doms are sadists, getting their primary satisfaction from the pain they inflict. That works for them, but it's never been my style. Pain is a tool, a necessary one, but my sweet spot is what comes after, the moment when discipline shifts into pleasure and the line between punishment and reward dissolves into something deeper. One doesn't work without the other. Without the pain, no lesson is learned, but without the pleasure, the *right* lesson doesn't sink in.

Both need to exist; one, then the other, always ending in pleasure we both enjoy.

That's the balance I need, and Maxine needs it too, whether she realizes it yet or not. Perhaps she needs it more than anyone I've met before. Her reaction in my office made that crystal clear, but I won't push her into asking for more. She has to want it for herself and come to me knowing exactly what I'm offering. Until she does, I plan to stay out of her way, far from temptation.

That's made easier on Thursday night by the fact that I can't work late even if I wanted to. I promised Sam I'd go to the pitch for her app, so at seven o'clock, I find myself outside a three-story building twenty minutes west of downtown. The ground floor houses a café, and up a narrow flight of stairs, I reach Great Lakes Development Studios.

The door flings open before I can even press the buzzer.

"Mr. Larson." A tall, skinny man with thick-rimmed glasses beams at me from inside, his hand outstretched. "Brad Flanagan. So glad to meet you."

Since he hasn't given me a reason to dislike him yet, I shake it. "Is Sam here?"

"Yes, sir. She, Josh, and the rest of the team are in the boardroom. They've got a great presentation planned."

"Wonderful." Somehow, I make that sound sincere as I follow him inside.

To be fair, the office isn't bad. When Sam first told me she got a job with an app development company, I pictured a bunch of college kids coding in someone's basement, fuelled by energy drinks, but the background check I ran on Brad and the company came back clean. They have a few working products, they're solvent, and their bills get paid. If Sam wants to work for them, I have to trust her judgment.

It's not as though I haven't tried to get her to work for me but she insists she needs to find her own path. I should be proud of that. I *am* proud, but pride and concern don't cancel each other out. They just sit side-by-side, forced into a reluctant truce.

We reach the 'boardroom,' which is just a regular meeting room, and through the window, I see Sam seated at the front with four others, all men. It doesn't take a genius to figure out which one is Josh. She leans towards him, laughing at something he said, but as soon as I walk in, she immediately straightens, her expression shifting from warmth to controlled professionalism.

The rest of them do the same, like I'm a drill sergeant coming for inspection.

"Let me introduce you to the team," Brad says, gesturing around the table. "This is Devon, Mark and Abdul. You know Sam, obviously. And this is Josh, the team lead for this app."

Josh stands up, ready to come over and shake my hand, but I lower myself into the chair at the head of the table before he gets a chance, flexing my arms as I lean forward to make myself look as big and intimidating as possible.

He falters mid-step, uncertainty flickering across his face before he forces a smile and pivots back to his seat. *Smart choice, kid.*

"Let's jump right in, then," he says, a nervous laugh serving as punctuation at the end of his sentence. A glance down at Sam for encouragement earns him a nod before she shoots me a pleading look.

Be nice, Dad, that look says.

She asked me to be here, and I'm here. Being nice was never part of the deal.

Josh launches into his pitch, a PowerPoint lighting up the wall behind him, but I barely hear a word. Instead, I study *him*, trying to figure out what both Maxine and Sam see in him.

He's a good-looking kid, I suppose. Clean-cut. His hands move when he talks, long fingers gesturing in a way that screams nervous energy. They've never seen a hard day's manual work, I'd wager, and I know he wouldn't last five minutes on one of my job sites.

Most of all, he's completely unthreatening.

Objectively, I can see why that might appeal to Sam. Despite her prom-queen beauty, she's always felt more at home among the bookworms and theatre kids of the world. While other kids were out at parties, she'd be home on her computer, lost in her own world, and as a dad who knew exactly what teenage boys saw when they looked at her, that suited me just fine.

Though she might be spoiled, in no small part thanks to me, she's not a snob. Most people would consider her out of Josh's league, but she doesn't see herself that way.

So, the two of them, I can almost understand.

But Maxine?

That just doesn't track. He wouldn't push her, wouldn't challenge her. Wouldn't give her the structure or the boundaries she needs. What the hell did she get out of their relationship that had her so distraught when it ended?

As I try to figure it out, the room falls silent, and I realize all eyes are on me.

Shit.

They must have asked me a question, and I tuned it out completely.

"Sorry, can you repeat that?"

Josh forces another awkward laugh. "I was just wondering if you could see yourself using the app in your day-to-day life."

Considering I have no clue what the damn thing does, that's a hard question to answer. I turn to Sam instead. "What do you think?"

"Well, I don't think you'd use the dating side of it." She laughs as though the idea of me dating is completely absurd. "But you're always getting tickets for stuff through work. You could use it to find someone to go with you."

Wait. What the hell *does* this app do?

As Josh continues, I catch up. It's a platform for people with an extra ticket to any kind of event to find someone to go with them. They can sell it or offer it for free, specify whether it's a date or just a friendly outing.

"And how do *you* make money?" I ask. "Are you charging people to list things?"

Josh shakes his head. "Our profit will come from advertising. The app itself is free for users."

They're all watching me, eager for another question, so I dig one up. "Aren't there already apps doing this?"

One of the other men chimes in. His name is Kevin, I think? Or Devon, maybe? I've already forgotten. "Other apps offer similar features, but nothing does exactly what we do. Because the original ticket holder is still going, no money changes hands through the app, so we avoid commerce fees. We're just a meeting place for people connecting over a shared event."

I lean back, considering the pitfalls. "And what if people start listing 'tickets' for illegal stuff? Drugs, sex, weapons, that kind of thing?"

Brad jumps in. "We have a strict system to catch violations of our terms. We'll monitor activity closely. Great questions, Mr. Larson."

They talk through their financial projections, and though I'm not their target audience, I can see the potential. The investment money they're asking for isn't outrageous, and a week ago, I'd have been happy to sign up simply to support Sam. Making things easier for the people I care about is the most satisfying thing I can imagine.

Having Josh involved changes the dynamic, though. Yesterday, I told Maxine no one deserves the disrespect of being cheated on, and that's exactly what his actions demonstrate to me: a lack of respect and responsibility, and I'll be damned if I'm going to reward that behaviour by bankrolling a project that, despite Sam's involvement, is ultimately his.

It's a dilemma that's not going to be resolved sitting in this room or in front of a crowd.

"I'll look through this over the weekend," I say, flipping through the papers they handed me. "If everything checks out, I'll arrange a meeting directly with the team lead."

Josh swallows the golf ball-sized lump that seems to be stuck in his throat. "That sounds great, Mr. Larson. I'll look forward to it. Thank you for your time."

Brad leads me back to the main door, but we don't get far enough away before one of the men exclaims, "You didn't tell us he was *that* terrifying, Sam."

Brad winces but doesn't acknowledge the comment, perhaps hoping I didn't hear it. "Josh can answer any questions you have about the app, but please feel free to get in touch with me if you need any information on the business itself."

He strikes me as a decent guy overall and I respect anyone who starts their own company from scratch, so I shake his hand once more. "I promise I'll give it some serious thought."

He has no idea just *how* serious.

Chapter Twelve

~Maxine~

The search results on my screen have me completely under their spell. Even though I need to start getting ready for my Friday night out with my friends, I'm unable to look away.

I brooded over Reid calling me a brat all day on Thursday, wincing every time I shifted on the hard, uncomfortable chair in my cubicle at the insurance company. Where did he get off being so judgemental? I had a whole speech prepared for Thursday evening when I got to Bear Construction, fully psyched up to give him a piece of my mind, only to find that Reid wasn't in the office that evening.

"He rarely works late," Rebecca said when I mentioned his absence as casually as I could. "It's unusual that you've seen him here twice this week already."

Deflated, with all that energy built up for nothing, I completed my tasks and headed home, feeling not only unsatisfied but disappointed too. Had I been *looking forward* to seeing him? That was ridiculous.

But I didn't know what else to call the melancholy that lingered over me during my work day on Friday. I definitely wouldn't see him that night either, since I already had plans with the girls and wouldn't be working at Bear Construction. Who knew when I would see him again?

Sure, I had his phone number and I could call him up to give him a piece of my mind, but that would be... well, kind of a bratty thing to do. I didn't want to give him more ammunition.

So, when I drag myself off the L and hurry back to my apartment in the frigid late afternoon, I'm half-tempted to cancel my night out. I'm just not in the mood.

But on a whim, I sit down in front of the computer and type "what is a brat" into the search engine.

The first result is exactly what I anticipated: "a child, typically one that's badly behaved."

Gee, I wonder why I took that as an insult.

The next result makes me hesitate, though. "Someone who is confidently rebellious, unapologetically bold, and playfully defiant."

That doesn't sound *so* bad, but I also don't feel like it's exactly what he meant either. Reid doesn't strike me as the kind of man to be up-to-date on pop culture references.

After scrolling through a few pages of results without getting any further, I amend my initial search by one word: "what is a *sexual* brat?"

Words immediately leap off the screen at me, and when I read through enough of them, it's almost as though a light switches on in a corner of my mind, illuminating an area that had previously been dark.

The more I look at it, the more sense it makes.

According to the wisdom of the internet, a brat is a specific type of submissive partner. Rather than following orders without question the way a 'typical' submissive would, they like to tease, defy or disobey their partner, pushing their buttons to provoke a reaction.

I can see myself in that description, I have to admit, especially during my interactions with a certain frustratingly-attractive older man.

Which makes Reid my opposite: a dominant partner who enjoys the challenge that a brat provides.

I'd train you properly.

His words from the other night repeat in my head, sending a shiver down my spine. He didn't say anything about sex, and the websites make it clear that sex doesn't *have* to be part of a dom/brat relationship, but it usually is. And my body responds to that idea, just as it did when I was bent over his desk. A throbbing deep in my core has me glancing towards my bedside table and the toys I keep there.

Before I can reach for one, though, my phone rings, making me jump as if I've been doing something wrong. I snatch it up from the bed where I tossed it earlier, glancing at the screen before answering.

"Hey, Janine. What's up?"

"Just checking you're not bailing on tonight." Her tone is already accusing even though I haven't said a word about not showing up.

And I don't tell her that I'd been considering it, because after the discovery I just made, I need to talk to somebody. "I'm coming, don't worry."

"Good." She sounds surprised and a little relieved, clearly having anticipated a fight. "And wear something red. We're going to go dancing after some drinks, and the club is giving a discount to anyone in the Christmas spirit. Tamara's getting us all Santa hats."

"The bare minimum effort," I laugh. "I like it. Alright, I have to start getting ready. See you soon."

An hour and a half later, I find the rest of our group already squeezed around a table at one of our regular bars downtown. We usually drink first in a quieter spot so we can catch up, then hit the club. With Christmas on the way, this is the one and only Friday this month that everyone's free, so we'll have to make it count.

"Here she is!" Janine welcomes me with a sideways hug, placing a shot in front of me before I even get my coat off. "You sounded so much better on the phone than I expected."

Brutal honesty: alcohol's best and worst side effect. "How should I have sounded?"

"Well, last weekend, you looked like your dog died," Tamara informs me bluntly. "Today, you look human again."

"You guys do wonders for my self-confidence," I tell them dryly before raising my glass. "To getting over break-ups."

They all cheer as they lift their own shots, and Willow slams her empty glass onto the table after downing the drink.

"That's what I'm talking about! Tell us your secret, Max. What put that spring in your step?"

Janine gasps, grabbing Willow's arm. "Oh my God. She got laid."

"What? No, I..."

"Who is it?" Ellie asks, leaning forward across the table. "Someone we know or a stranger?"

"A one-night stand!" Willow declares. "It must be."

"I didn't..."

Ellie turns to Janine. "I told you she's been really secretive about where she's been all week."

"It must have been more than once," Janine agrees.

"I hope you were careful," Tamara chides me. "Heartbreak is no excuse to be reckless."

"I hope he's so much hotter than Josh," Willow adds. "Was he bigger too?"

"There is no..."

No one lets me speak as they continue to speculate amongst themselves about the mystery man who's responsible for the turnaround in my mood. I lean back, raising my hand to get the waitress's attention and order another round of shots for the table.

Only when they arrive and I lift mine in another toast do the rest of them *finally* let me talk. "I did *not* get laid, but I did meet someone. Kind of. Nothing has happened yet, and I don't know if it even will, but I can honestly say, Josh has barely crossed my mind all week."

Squeals of delight meet my proclamation, along with a whole host of new questions.

"Who is he?"

"Where did you meet him?"

"Why don't you think anything will happen?"

I slam back my shot, letting the alcohol's warmth fuel my resolution to be honest and vulnerable with my closest friends.

"I took a second job and he's my new boss. He's ridiculously hot but he's also older and, as I mentioned, my boss, which makes things tricky. But he did spank me in his office the other day and I kind of loved it."

For once, every single one of my friends is speechless.

"You're going to need to start at the beginning," Tamara finally says, and the others all nod in agreement.

"Skip *nothing*," Willow instructs.

We switch to drinking cocktails as I fill them in, telling them how I accidentally keyed Reid's car, how he proposed I work for him to pay off the damage, the intense vibe between us, and everything leading up to the bruise on my ass. They make the perfect audience, gasping in dismay at the right spots and sighing at my descriptions of Reid's attractiveness. His name and business, I keep to myself, not because I don't trust them but because it's new and fragile and I want to shelter it just a little bit longer.

Janine pouts about not being able to see a photo of Reid for herself but Ellie supports my decision. "I can't believe you let him spank you, though," she exclaims, shaking her head. "It's so..."

"Hot?" Willow suggests.

"I was going to say kinky. I just didn't know that was your thing, Max."

"Neither did I, but maybe there's more out there that I would enjoy that I just haven't tried yet. And now, there's nothing to stop me from finding out."

Tamara nods. "It's a perfect time for exploration. Josh dumping you might actually be the best thing that could have happened to you."

Someone tries to kick her under the table but ends up getting me instead. "Ow."

"Oops." Janine laughs, her eyes twinkling with mischief. "I thought you liked that kind of thing now, though."

"This is what I get for being honest, isn't it?"

"Yes," they all chorus in unison.

The conversation shifts to other things, and we're all riding a good buzz by the time we get to the club. Men come over to dance with us, their faces blurred by the alcohol and the flashing lights. None of them stands out to me. They're all too bland. Too soft. Too young.

They're not Reid.

It's only when I think of him, imagining him brooding in the corner as he watches me dance, planning out how he's going to punish me for letting these other men think they have a chance, that my body begins to heat.

By the time the taxi drops me off and I stumble back into my apartment, I've made up my mind.

I'm going to ask Reid to train me. He said we could talk about it again when I was ready, and I'm ready now. Just the idea of it has me throbbing again, and I pull out one of the vibrators from my drawer, riding it to a quick and dirty orgasm to take the edge off before I drift into sleep, where Reid will be waiting.

Chapter Thirteen

~Reid~

I have no reason to linger at the office on Friday night, so when six o'clock passes with no sign of Maxine, I assume she's not working tonight and pack up before Rebecca becomes suspicious.

"I've seen more of you this week than I normally do in a month, Reid," Rebecca says when I stop by her desk on my way out. "Is everything alright?"

"I'm fine," I assure her a little too quickly. "Just making sure *you're* okay. I know we're still a little short-staffed. Do you need more help?"

I'm not sure she fully believes my excuse, but she humours me anyway. "I think we're in good shape, actually. Max is going to be a big help. I've got her scheduled to do the year-end letters tomorrow. It'll take her all day, but it'll free up time for the rest of us."

"And you'll be able to go on your holiday without stressing?"

Rebecca and her husband have a trip planned to visit their son in Germany for Christmas. They leave next weekend, which is another big part of why we needed the extra help. I don't want her worrying about work when she's not here. If she believes things are under control, she'll be able to relax and come back fully rested in the new year.

"I think so." She sounds almost surprised when she says it. "Unless something goes dreadfully wrong next week."

She knocks on her wooden desk to avoid inviting trouble in.

"And you're not coming in tomorrow?" I throw the question out casually, as if I don't care about the answer.

"No, I'm braving the stores downtown to finish my shopping." She shudders in an expression of dread that I'm sure is mirrored on my own face. That sounds like hell. "You're spending tomorrow at the Morgan Park site?"

"That's the plan."

One of my teams is doing a restoration of a historic home in the neighbourhood, and I'll be doing some of the more skilled woodwork on site. Though I have a team of craftsmen, there are some jobs I still prefer to do myself.

Which means there's no reason for me to be walking through the front doors of Bear Construction at nine thirty on Saturday morning, but I find myself there anyway, concocting some bullshit story about wanting to check the reference files one more time before I head to the house.

As soon as I walk in, though, I see Maxine's curly brown hair pulled back into a messy bun that bobs as she looks back and forth between her computer screen and something on her desk, typing away. My heart rate kicks up a notch, and I can't lie to myself any longer.

I came here to see her. Even if we don't talk, even if this glimpse is all I get, it'll make me feel more alive than anything else has over the past two days.

Not since I first met my ex-wife has someone consumed my thoughts the way Maxine has. Not that Maxine reminds me of my ex in any way; they have nothing in common other than the way they both managed to get under my skin almost immediately, and kept pushing when most people would back off. That's my type, apparently, and even after the way my marriage ended, it's still what I crave.

"Good morning," I say as I walk past her on the way to my office, not even stopping to make eye contact. Rebecca isn't here but there are still other employees around and I don't need to give anyone any fuel for gossip.

"Oh. Uh, good morning," Maxine stammers from behind me, and I fight back a smile. Good to know I have the ability to throw her off too. I'd hate to be the only one affected by this energy between us.

She doesn't stay uncertain for long, though. Not even two minutes later, while I'm still getting settled in at my desk, she appears in my doorway, knuckles rapping softly on the door.

"I'm going to get myself a coffee from the kitchen. Do you want anything?"

These are the first words she's said to me since storming out of my office on Wednesday, flipping me off as she went, and it's clearly meant as a peace offering.

I accept it in that spirit. "Sure. Coffee sounds great."

"Hot and wet, right?"

A laugh blows past my lips before I can stop it. "That's usually how it comes, yeah. I'll take it black too."

"Got it." She tosses me a full smile, clearly delighted with having made me laugh, and that now-familiar tug of need hits low in my gut.

It only gets worse when she turns and leaves. Saturdays are casual days in the office, and tight jeans hug the curve of her ass as she walks away, appearing in tantalizing glimpses as her loose red sweater sways side-to-side. My fingers ache to feel it again.

Wanting to give the appearance that I have a reason for being here, I pull out the pictures of the house pre-restoration and begin flipping through them. I'm still in the middle of it when Maxine reappears, two steaming mugs in her hands. She doesn't wait for an invitation before striding in and placing one of them down in front of me.

"Thanks." I don't look up, waiting to see what she'll do next without any direction from me.

Maxine leans a little further over the desk, her attention fixed on the photos. "What are those from?"

"It's a house we're restoring. See this staircase here?" I flip one of the pictures around so she can see it better. "It's falling apart, so we're replacing it with an exact replica. Hand-carved."

"Wow." As she leans down even more, her sweater gaps at the neck, offering a glimpse of soft skin and lace. Is she doing that on purpose? I can't decide if it would be better or worse if she doesn't realize it.

"And you do this carving yourself? I saw on the website that you're a carpenter."

My eyebrows are raised by the time she looks back up at me. "Reading up on me, were you?"

"Doing my research," she shoots back. "Isn't that what you told me to do?"

She's referencing our last interaction here in this office, and I lean back, my eyes still on her. "It is. When did you get so good at following instructions?"

Her big brown eyes hold my gaze without a waver. "It's something I might like to work on."

I take a long sip of my coffee to cover up the way my mouth goes dry at the possibility she's saying what I hope she's saying. "Meaning?"

A laugh somewhere out in the main office makes us both glance towards the door. Anyone could walk in at any time, making this conversation risky.

It doesn't stop either of us.

When Maxine turns back to me, her jaw is set. "Meaning I want you to train me. Like you said."

No beating around the bush at all, and the words hit me hard, not because I'm surprised, but because I want to say yes more than I want my next breath.

Still, I try to do the responsible thing anyway.

"I said I would do that if there were no other complications," I remind her. "That isn't the case."

"I don't care about any of that," she insists. "I can keep anything that happens separate from working here and our agreement. Can you?"

She raises an eyebrow, doing her best to provoke me, and I have to tamp down the rush of desire tightening my jaw. "You don't need to worry about me. But I want you to be sure you're not saying this just because you're still broken-hearted about the asshole who cheated on you. If this is about revenge or proving something..."

"It isn't," she interrupts me before I can even finish my sentence. "This has nothing to do with Josh."

At the sound of his name, the kid's face flashes in front of my eyes again. Imagining him and Maxine together not only doesn't make sense in my head, it stirs something darker inside me too. Jealousy?

No, not quite.

Possessiveness.

He didn't deserve her, not when he didn't have a fucking clue what to do with her. I could make her forget all about him in one single night.

I don't say any of that out loud. "How do I know you're telling me the truth?" I ask instead.

Maxine shrugs, still holding my gaze almost defiantly. "You're going to have to trust me. Just like I'll have to trust you."

She has that much right. What I'm suggesting requires vulnerability on both sides. It requires total honesty, which means I should tell her about Sam and Josh. She should know *all* the reasons this might be a bad idea before we go too far down this road.

My mouth opens to fill her in, but before I can get the words out, someone knocks at my door. Maxine jumps in surprise, bumping her coffee mug that's perched on the edge of my desk. The cup tips, and the dark, hot liquid flows quickly across the papers I was showing her, heading straight towards me.

Maxine gasps in horror. "Shit! I'm so sorry. Let me..."

Her eyes dart wildly around my office, searching for something to mop up the spill, but there's nothing obvious in sight. Wincing, she pulls down the sleeve of her sweater and leans across the desk to block the liquid's path with her arm before it can spill into my lap.

In an instant, I'm on my feet, rounding the desk and pulling her back, yanking her arm out of the now-soaked sweater sleeve. "Are you crazy? It's hot."

I hold her arm up, checking for signs of scalding while Maxine bites her lip, obviously trying not to let me see she's in pain. "Your pictures..."

"I don't care about the fucking pictures. Are you hurt?"

She shakes her head but tears are starting to well in her eyes. She looks seconds away from breaking down, so I point towards the private bathroom attached to my office and soften my tone.

"Go run your arm under cool water. There's a first aid kit if you need it. Call me if you need help."

It's only when she steps away that I realize I've half-exposed her when I pulled her arm free from her sleeve, and she tugs the sweater down over herself as she hurries into the bathroom and closes the door.

From the door behind me, a quiet chuckle reaches my ears. "Well, that was quite a show. I only stopped by to say hi, Dad, but now, I have some questions."

Chapter Fourteen

~**Maxine**~

"Stupid, clumsy idiot."

I hiss the words under my breath as I run my sleeve under the cold stream of water in Reid's sink, frantically blotting at the spreading coffee stain. My soft and cozy sweater's already soaked through, the one my grandma knitted for me, red with little flecks of white yarn that mimic snow falling from a winter sky.

I love this damn sweater, but the potential loss of a piece of clothing pales in comparison to the spectacle I just made of myself.

Just as I worked up the nerve to tell Reid I wanted to move forward with his offer, feeling bold and brave and proud of myself, I promptly launched a mug of coffee across his desk, ruining his photos. Right in front of Reid and... I don't even know who else. Someone was at the door, an extra witness to my ineptitude, and now, any positive impression I might've made this week seems to be sliding down the drain along with the coffee-tinged water dripping through my sleeve.

I press paper towels against my arm, stuffing them up into the soaked fabric, and crack the bathroom door open. Maybe I can just sneak back to my desk with no one noticing me. Perhaps Reid left, or he'll be too distracted to stop me.

No such luck.

He's still standing exactly where I left him, and when I step into the room, he turns towards me. So does the person next to him, and I nearly stumble over my own feet.

The man has Reid's eyes: sharp and glacial-blue, ringed in dark lashes that are wasted on a man. A flicker of recognition registers in my brain even though I'm sure we haven't met before.

"Hey there." His voice is lighter than Reid's, and looser somehow. "You must be new."

My eyes flick to Reid whose jaw is locked tight, lips flattened into a hard, unreadable line.

Since he doesn't say anything, I find my own voice. "Yeah. Hi. I'm Max."

I don't offer my hand since I still have soggy paper towels sticking out of one sleeve, but the man crosses the room and offers his anyway.

"Jamie Larson." He flashes a smile that's pure mischief. "Nice to meet you."

Larson. The name drops into place like a puzzle piece. I remember it from the party invitation list and my conversation with Rebecca.

Jamie. *Reid's son.*

Well, that explains the eyes, and why he looks vaguely familiar.

My mind races to recalibrate as I shake his hand. He's not quite as tall as Reid, but built similarly: dark hair and broad shoulders, the kind of strength that comes from doing things with your hands. He's attractive and significantly younger than his father.

Obviously, Max.

What I mean is that he's probably right around my age.

But even as I take him in, some part of me is measuring him against Reid and finding him... lacking? No, just *different.* He doesn't have that coiled stillness and control that seems to wrap around Reid like an extra layer of clothing. Jamie feels more open, less restrained.

And somehow, less magnetic.

Still, I smile politely. "Nice to meet you too. I should get back to work. I'll leave you in peace."

As I turn to go, I catch Reid's jaw clenching tighter than ever. His lips have almost vanished, and I could swear he wants to say something but is holding himself back with Jamie standing there.

Jamie doesn't seem to notice. He gives me a wink and a smirk that might've made my stomach flutter on any other day. "Feel free to interrupt anytime."

This time, I don't smile back, because Reid is still in the room and *his* attention burns hotter than any flirty grin ever could.

With a small shred of dignity still intact, I make it back to my desk. Jamie heads off to chat with someone else, his easy laugh echoing down the hallway. It's nothing like Reid's low rumble of amusement on the rare occasions I've heard him laugh.

I try to focus on my screen, try to pretend I'm not half-drenched and mentally spiralling, until a sharp *thump* breaks through my thoughts. A piece of paper lands on my desk, pressed down by a long, firm finger.

I look up to find Reid there. "Read that." He taps the paper once more, then turns away. "Jamie, let's go."

Jamie reappears, still just as cheerful as before, and together they leave without another word.

Meanwhile, I stare at the paper like it might detonate. Is he firing me with a note? Rescinding his offer to teach me? No matter which way I look at it, I can't imagine it's anything positive.

Still, ignoring it doesn't do any good, so eventually, I suck it up and flip the paper over.

If you're serious about training, I'll give you a small introduction tonight.

You'll be ready at nine pm, wearing a skirt and heels.

If you change your mind, text me the name of a red fruit.

If I don't hear from you, I'll be outside your building to pick you up.

Nine o'clock sharp, Maxine.

Don't be late.

My pulse slams in my throat, and between my thighs, heat blooms.

I devour the words again, and again. Each time, they settle deeper into my skin, as if the ink itself is staining me.

He's still in.

The humiliation from earlier didn't scare him off. If anything, he's doubling down, and now, I'm crashing out all over again, not from shame but from anticipation.

What does 'small introduction' mean?

Where are we going?

What does he have planned that requires a skirt?

For half a second, the possibility of cancelling drifts across my consciousness, but it never takes hold. Why should it, when I'm getting exactly what I wanted?

Six more long hours of work stretch out in front of me, so I bury myself in Rebecca's year-end letter drafts, but no matter how hard I try to stay focused, it doesn't work. I can't stop picturing Reid's eyes, the set of his jaw, the pressure of his hand on my ass and the firm control in his voice.

Minutes disappear as I swim in the memories until I shake myself and refocus again.

After work, everything still feels hazy. I sleepwalk through grocery shopping and mailing holiday cards to my grandma and her friends. Out of habit, I smile politely at the cashier but I couldn't name a single thing I put in the basket.

Back in my apartment, I reach into the crisper drawer while making dinner and... *bam*. A memory of Josh slams into me: laughing beside me in this very kitchen when our relationship was new, his arm brushing mine, and how warm and easy it all felt.

It's so vivid, I half-turn, expecting to see him behind me. Of course there's no one there, and the expected pang of loss hits me. However, the edges are soft rather than jagged, and before the feeling even has a chance to linger, I glance at the sink and Reid's image rises instead. I can picture him there, ordering me to drink water, commanding a perfect stranger without a hint of apology.

Heat washes over me again and the ache returns, erasing any doubt about what I want. I'm definitely not doing this because of Josh. Reid doesn't have to worry about that.

After eating, I retreat to my bedroom where I try on every skirt I own, turning this way and that, bending over and watching myself in the mirror to check the angles. Eventually, I settle on a fitted black one that hits just above the knee, paired with thigh-high stockings and high-heeled black boots. It *is* December, after all. I can't go *too* skimpy.

As for underwear, the tiny scrap of fabric I slip on barely qualifies. It's just enough to be peeled away or yanked aside. I don't know what tonight will bring, but I want to be ready just in case.

With my clothes decided on, I move onto hair, then makeup. A shiny lip gloss comes last, followed by one final glance in the mirror.

When I'm satisfied and pull out my phone to check the time, I yelp in surprise.

8:57.

Fuck.

It'll take at least three minutes to get down the stairs in these heels.

My heart drums against my ribs as I grab my keys, and my heels clack a steady rhythm down the three flights of stairs. In the lobby, the air feels thick as I swallow in one last breath before bracing myself against the heavy front door and stepping out into the night.

Chapter Fifteen

~**Reid**~

That fucking skirt is going to kill me.

I knew telling her to wear it would be playing with fire, but nothing could've prepared me for the real thing. As Maxine slides into the passenger seat of my Lexus, the hem hikes up, exposing the smooth curve of her thigh and the soft, maddening line where her stockings end. A sliver of bare skin calls to me, beckoning me to get closer and see how it feels beneath my fingers.

Exhaling hard, I shut her door with a little more force than necessary. Frost forms on my breath as I circle the front of the car, dragging air into lungs that feel too tight.

You set the rules, I remind myself. *Now you just have to stick to them.*

When I get into the driver's seat, the warmth of the interior quickly drives away the outside chill. Maxine's scent, something light and clean with a citrus note, already weaves into the leather.

She glances around, taking everything in. "This is more what I pictured you driving."

The Lexus is for clients. Its job is to impress. The Chevy's my daily workhorse, the vehicle I think of as truly 'mine'. But Maxine's talking about the baby-blue Volkswagen she keyed, the one she didn't think a 'man like me' would drive.

Because I wouldn't.

But she doesn't know that yet, and that omission of truth coils around us like a snake, one I intend to kill tonight.

I'd actually been about to tell her earlier, in my office, before Jamie showed up. Watching him turn his considerable charm on Maxine played right into my jealous streak, as he knew it would. He was testing me, and when I didn't react, he accepted my explanation that he'd simply walked in on a meeting between me and a new employee.

And with a moment alone to think things over afterwards, I changed my mind about how and when to tell Maxine about Sam.

I *will* tell her tonight, but first, I want to let her experience the club. Even if she walks away afterwards, even if I'm not the one she wants to explore it with, I want her to know about this world and what it could mean for someone like her. Already, her happiness matters to me, even if it ends up having nothing to do with me.

So, I let her comment about the car slide and pull onto the street before changing the subject.

"Tonight has some ground rules. You won't speak to anyone unless I say you can. You won't leave my side without clearing it with me first. And if you want to leave at any point, we leave immediately."

She frowns as she takes that all in, turning in her seat to face me fully. "Where are we going? Is it dangerous?"

"Absolutely not. I will never put you in danger, Maxine. You're safe, always."

"Then why..."

I don't need to hear the rest of that question to know the answer. "Because I'm in charge."

A snort is her response, exactly as I expected. "Whenever someone says 'because I said so', it means they don't have a real reason."

"When *I* say it, it's because I've already decided and you don't need to worry about it."

"What if I want to..."

"...worry about it?" I interrupt again. "You want to be in charge? Make all the decisions? Carry the weight of control all the time?"

Silence follows that question, but rather than being uncomfortable or sullen, it's simply contemplative. She's truly thinking about what I'm saying, and I appreciate how open she's already shown herself to be. Even when she jumps to conclusions, like she did the night we met when she assumed I wanted her to work off her debt to me sexually, she doesn't dig in when confronted with an alternate viewpoint.

That quality is surprisingly rare, at least in my experience.

Outside, the streets seem to glow. Red and green traffic lights and red tail lights blend with the Christmas lights strung across shop awnings and around light poles, bleeding into snowy puddles and reflecting off windshields. The world looks soft and blurred, and not quite real.

Maxine's voice, when she speaks again, has also mellowed. "You never said where we're going. Do I get to know?"

"If you ask nicely," I reply, letting a smile tug at the corner of my mouth.

She bats her lashes with exaggerated innocence. "Reid, will you please tell me where we're going?"

"Smartass." Even as I fight a laugh, my fingers flex around the car's heated steering wheel, itching to get to work on showing her what happens when she teases me that way. "We're going to a private club for people who explore power dynamics. Where doms like me and bratty subs like you can be themselves."

Her breath catches. "Like... a sex club?"

There's no fear in the question. Perhaps a touch of nerves, but mostly, I just hear curiosity.

Her thighs also press together, just a little. I catch the movement from the corner of my eye and press my lips together to keep from groaning.

"Yes, but we're not having sex there. Not tonight."

"Oh."

That one soft syllable is all she says, exhaled so softly that I can't tell if it's relieved or disappointed.

"We're going so you can observe and learn. I want you focused on that, not worried about what might or might not happen between us. If you like what you see, then we'll talk about what happens next."

She doesn't respond, but she doesn't pull back either. That's good enough for now.

We reach the underground garage just a few minutes later. My keycard beeps against the reader, granting access to the club's private lot, and the security guard gives me a nod of recognition as we pass the booth.

I used to come more often. With my ex-wife, it provided an adults-only escape from the responsibilities of parenting, and a chance to indulge our particular preferences far away from curious little eyes and ears. We'd hire a sitter and spend the night focused on each other.

After my divorce, I came a few times on my own, trying to recapture the same excitement with a new partner, but nothing ever felt quite right. I'm not even sure how long it's been since I last visited; probably months since I thought about it, and even longer since I felt as excited about it as I do tonight.

After pulling into my reserved spot, I cut the engine. Maxine reaches for her door but I stop her with a hand on her knee. Her skin is warm through the stocking, and she stills instantly, something in her recognizing the signal before her mind does.

"I open your door. Always."

Her lips twitch like she wants to challenge me, but instead, she simply asks, "Why?"

"So I can make sure it's safe before you get in or out."

I lift my hand, just a little, as a test to see if she'll stay without it there. To her credit, she doesn't move.

After scanning the area, I walk around to her side. When I open the door and offer my hand, she takes it without hesitation, and as she steps out, the skirt shifts again, flashing more of that delicate strip of skin.

I pull her close, keeping my voice low and firm. "Remember: I'm in charge, but you're in control. You say the word, and we're out of here. No questions asked."

She swallows and nods, just once. "I'm ready."

I hope I am too. I told myself this was about showing her this world and giving her a choice, but I'd be lying if I said I didn't want her to choose me.

After all, there's a reason I haven't been able to walk away despite all the warning signs telling me this is a disaster waiting to happen. That little voice in the back of my head, the one that recognized something kindred in her that first night, keeps whispering at me not to let her go.

Together, we walk towards the thick steel vault door that leads into the club, her heels echoing in the cavernous garage, each click a countdown to the true start of the evening. Her fingers curl around mine, and I give them the lightest squeeze as I pull the door open for her.

"Welcome home, Maxine."

Chapter Sixteen

~**Maxine**~

Despite its size and heavy appearance, the steel door swings shut behind us with a soft *whoosh* that reminds me of the sliding doors on Josh's sci-fi TV shows. Which makes sense, in a way, because it feels like I'm stepping into a completely different world, one sealed off from the rules of life I thought I understood.

The entrance opens into a wide, elegant lobby that makes me blink twice. I don't know exactly what I expected when Reid said he was taking me to a sex club, but this isn't it. Nothing is dark or seedy or draped in red velvet. The walls are soft gray and cream, the space lit by sparkling chandeliers. Plush carpets hush the sound of footsteps. A reception desk with a coat check sits to our left, and down a few steps, a lounge area filled with low, leather-lined booths stretches out in all directions, warm and inviting.

Reid's hand finds the back of my neck, his fingers firm but not rough. "Do you want to go in?"

Does he really think I'm going to be scared off so easily? I haven't even seen anything yet. "You said in the car we can leave whenever I want. I'll tell you if I want to."

He huffs out an amused breath. "Noted."

With just a little pressure on my neck, he steers me towards the desk, where a beautiful, raven-haired woman in a Santa hat sits behind a sleek computer, flanked by a large man dressed in black.

The woman smiles as we approach while the man's blank stare gives nothing away.

"What a pleasure to see you, Reid." The way she says his name, familiar and appreciative, lands with a thud in the pit of my stomach. "And you brought a friend."

Her bright green eyes move to me, interested, assessing, and not bothering to pretend otherwise.

"Guest pass or membership application?"

I blink back at her, unsure what to say, but Reid answers for me. "Guest pass. Your coat, Maxine."

It's an order, given in his firm, no-nonsense tone, and with the two club employees watching us, I obey it without an argument, unzipping my winter coat and shrugging it off before handing it to him. Reid removes his own coat, revealing a charcoal-gray buttoned shirt stretching over his broad chest. He deposits both our coats at the coat check while the woman at the desk hands me a lanyard to wear with a red square attached to it.

"Have fun," she says as Reid moves us away, again with his hand on the back of my neck. The pressure serves as both an instruction and a comfort, and surprisingly, I don't hate it.

"What's this for?" I whisper as I hold up the red square.

He takes it from me and slips the lanyard over my head without breaking his stride. "It means you're unavailable. Guests can only play a scene with the person who brought them. Club rules."

I'm not sure exactly what 'scene' means in this context, but I have other, more pressing concerns. "Is that woman a friend of yours?"

Reid doesn't miss the jealous edge to my voice and addresses it head-on. "If you mean have I fucked her, then no. We played together once but the chemistry wasn't there. It didn't go any further."

Oh.

My stomach dips with desire, his directness not only reassuring me but turning me on as well. Hearing the word 'fucked' from his mouth sets my pulse thrumming deep between my legs, leaving me in no doubt about what my body wants even if I'm trying to keep a clear head.

As we move deeper into the room, I try not to stare. At least, not *too* much. I don't want to look naïve, even though I feel like a wide-eyed tourist in a place where everyone knows the language except for me.

Everywhere my eyes land, subtle and not-so-subtle displays of power dynamics are on full, unapologetic display. At one booth, a woman kneels at the feet of a man in a three-piece suit, her head bowed but her expression serene. In another, a shirtless man with his arms behind his back rests on his knees beneath a woman in a silky halter dress who sips her drink without so much as glancing down.

A low, murmured energy fills the room, full of tension and anticipation.

My gaze sweeps over the room until it reaches a section at the far end where a small group of people, mostly women, stand in a line, spaced apart but still close enough to form an obvious collective. Some shift from foot to foot while others stand perfectly still. A slow, queasy feeling twists in my stomach as I realize what I'm seeing.

"They're waiting for someone to pick them?" I whisper.

Reid's fingers press a little more firmly against my neck, his voice a quiet anchor in my ear. "Some submissives enjoy the ritual of being selected. Most are here with partners but a few come unattached. The club allows for both."

Though all the women are beautiful, one draws my attention effortlessly. She must be almost six feet tall, with a cascade of platinum curls and eyes that stay fixed on the ground even as a man walks a slow circle around her, inspecting her like a prize animal at the fair. The back of my neck prickles, a tingle spreading across my skin like static, and my jaw clenches instinctively as I watch, silently hoping she'll lift her head and challenge his presumption.

She doesn't move.

"You don't have to do that," Reid promises, reading my tension before I can even voice it. "Not unless you want to."

"I don't," I assert quickly.

His breath skates over my cheek as he chuckles. "I figured."

I take a slow breath and glance up at him. Those mesmerizing blue eyes are fixed on me, but there's no judgement in them. He's simply waiting to see how I'll respond.

The right words don't come easily but I try to express how I'm feeling anyway. "This feels like a dream. It's fascinating, but I don't know where I fit in."

"That's completely normal," he replies without a trace of disappointment. "Everybody's different, and I don't want you to pretend you fit in somewhere you don't. When something feels right, you'll know."

His response eases something jagged in my chest, a fear of rejection I didn't even fully realize was there. I don't want to be wrong here, not about myself and not about him.

With a few more steps, Reid leads me towards the bar. Couples nod in greeting as we pass, some with leashed partners in tow. One woman's collar glitters under the lights, a deep sapphire stone set into silver. Her leash is held by a woman in a tailored black suit who strokes her submissive's cheek with affection. It's actually kind of sweet.

Reid orders for both of us without asking. "Jack and Coke for me," he tells the bartender. "Sparkling water for her."

I want to retort that I can handle a drink of my own, but honestly, just being here has me feeling a little drunk already. Perhaps avoiding alcohol is the smarter move.

Beyond the end of the bar, a guarded hallway with a velvet rope and a steel door hints at something more private. I don't know what's behind it, but my heart beats a little faster at the possibility of finding out.

"You're doing well," he assures me as we find a table tucked into a semi-private alcove. "This place can be overwhelming at first. I've seen people bolt out the door at the first sign of a leash."

"I don't know what to do with my hands," I admit, laughing quietly as I set the glass down and fold my fingers in my lap. "Everyone looks so confident that it makes me feel awkward."

Reid leans in slightly, his piercing gaze giving me no room to hide. "You're not awkward and you don't have to do anything. Just pay attention. Ask questions if you want. Everything you see here tonight is a choice. Even the most extreme scenes start with consent."

I nod, tearing my eyes away from him to look out over the room again.

A woman walks by wearing nothing but a corset and heels, her partner trailing behind her with a hand possessively resting at her waist. There's no shame in her step; she looks... strong, oddly enough. In fact, she looks *radiant*. Like she knows *exactly* who she is.

I swallow against the lump rising in my throat.

Of course Reid notices. "What is it?"

"This is... confusing," I murmur, staring down at the bubbles in my glass. "I've always been the responsible one, and most of the time, I like that responsibility. I want to be taken seriously. But I also liked what you did to me in your office, and maybe I'd even like some of this and... well, it just doesn't make sense to me."

Reid doesn't respond right away, but I've already learned that his silence is never empty. He weighs his words more than any man I've met before. And when he does speak, it's always worth the wait.

"You can be strong and still want to let go. You can lead and still want someone to take the reins sometimes. There's no weakness in it, Maxine. It's about trust, just like you said in my office earlier."

The way he says my name, low and steady, makes my nerves sizzle.

"But what if I don't want *all* of this? What if I don't want to kneel or wait to be chosen or be leashed like a pet?"

"Then you don't want it," he replies, as if it's truly that simple. "Submission isn't one-size-fits-all. You'll only ever give what you want and what you *choose*, and the right dom for you is the one who respects and appreciates that."

His razor-sharp gaze watches every flicker of emotion in my expression as he speaks, not to catch me out but to make sure he doesn't miss anything. I've never had someone put so much effort into understanding me before.

I hope when he talks about 'the right dom', he means himself.

My pulse still fluttering, I take a drink and set my glass down again. "So, what happens next?"

He leans forward a little more, just enough that I can smell the woodsy depth of his cologne, and gestures towards the guarded door I noticed earlier. "When you're ready, I'll take you downstairs, where the real action is. We'll watch a scene. Just watch. If it's too much, we'll leave, but if you want more, we can talk about what comes next."

My nerves battle my curiosity as I draw in a deep breath. Something here pulls at me, but I can't say for certain what it is.

Maybe it's not even the world I'm drawn to. Maybe it's just Reid himself. Am I confusing the two?

There seems to be one way to find out for certain, so I meet Reid's eyes again and nod as confidently as I can.

"Okay. Show me."

Chapter Seventeen

~**Maxine**~

Lights beneath each step cast a soft, ethereal glow over the stairway as we descend, making it feel like something out of a dream.

Or maybe a nightmare, depending on your point of view.

My perspective lands somewhere in the middle.

Reid's hand stays warm at the back of my neck with each step until we reach a quieter, darker level of the club. The music down here is different: low and rhythmic, more pulse than melody. It vibrates deep in my body with a steady beat of anticipation.

Various rooms branch off from the main hallway, and Reid stops to have a murmured conversation with a man standing guard outside one of them. He points further down the hall, to the left, and Reid thanks him before we continue on. When we reach the door the guard indicated, Reid opens it and we step into a room that reminds me of one of my college lecture halls. Tiered seating slopes down to a central platform, all attention directed to that one spot.

My heart seems to skip a beat as I catch my first look at what everyone is watching. A single spotlight illuminates the woman standing with her arms stretched overhead, wrists cuffed to a thick silver chain that descends from the ceiling. Her skin glows under the light, smooth and bare except for a deep plum corset cinched around her waist that leaves her breasts and lower half exposed. Her legs are parted, her feet braced wide.

She looks like a goddess, ready to be worshipped.

Or punished?

Perhaps both.

Behind her stands a man in black pants and a tight gray shirt, similar to what Reid is wearing. His sleeves are rolled to the elbows, revealing muscled forearms, and he circles her slowly, dragging a flogger with long tails across her back. I only know the name of the implement because Janine brought one as a gag gift to a Christmas party one year. I never expected to actually see one being used, and the sound of the tails swishing softly across the woman's skin is almost hypnotic.

With a little pressure from his thumb against my neck, Reid guides me towards two of the cushioned chairs lining the back of the space. The room is far from full, but not empty either; other couples sit dotted around, watching the action. The music is just loud enough that we can talk without being overheard, though my throat feels a little too dry to speak yet.

The woman on stage lets out a soft moan as the tails of the flogger kiss her shoulders. Microphones dangling over her head pick up the sound, making it feel intimate despite the space separating us. The flogger's strokes aren't hard, almost a caress rather than a blow, and the way she arches into them tells me she craves it. Her body moves with the rhythm, breath syncing with each swish of the device. Her dom runs a hand down her back and between her thighs, and she shudders, hips tilting forward, greedy for more.

The whole room seems to hold its breath.

"She's not in pain?" I whisper.

"Not unless she wants to be," Reid replies quietly. "That's a suede flogger. It's meant to build sensation. He's warming her up."

"For what?"

He doesn't answer immediately.

Instead, the dom's fingers stroke between the woman's legs and she groans again, louder this time. He steps around to face her, tugs one of her nipples with a twist that makes her gasp, then whispers something I can't hear.

Her response, however, echoes through the room.

"Teasing bastard," she pants. "If you're going to make me beg, at least do something worth begging for."

I gasp in surprise and a ripple of laughter spreads through the room. She throws him a smirk that suggests she's not giving an inch despite being the one tied up, and my body hums in approval. *This*, I can relate to. Even the dom smiles faintly as he moves behind her again. His next stroke is firmer, sharp enough that she gasps.

But when she mutters, "Still too soft, you coward," he only chuckles and steps back.

From a table at the edge of the stage, he retrieves a remote and presses a button. A quiet mechanical hum fills the air, and her cuffs begin to lift, raising her onto her toes. Her body strains, muscles flexing, as the dom presses another button and another sound joins the hum.

A soft, buzzing sound that's unmistakably familiar.

"Is that..."

"A vibrator," Reid confirms. His eyes are on me rather than the woman, but I can't tear my gaze away from the front of the room.

The woman writhes against the stimulation, moaning through gritted teeth. "Don't you dare stop it this time, you motherfu..."

The buzzing cuts off.

A strangled cry leaves her throat as her head slams back with frustration. The room chuckles again, but it doesn't feel cruel. There's admiration in the sound, as if they appreciate the battle of wills we're witnessing, knowing that the end will be worth it.

"She agreed to all of this?"

"She has a safe word," Reid assures me. "If she uses it, everything stops."

I nod slowly, processing the situation. "She's cursing him out, but she wants him to keep going."

"Exactly. It's provocation, part of the game they're playing. She pushes him so he'll push her. That's their dynamic."

On stage, the dom reaches forward and thrusts a finger inside her. "You're soaked," he says loud enough for everyone to hear. "You want to come that badly?"

"Fuck you," she growls.

"Not yet," he replies calmly, taking a step back and turning the vibrator back on.

My thighs press together without thinking, as if the vibrator were edging *me* too. My entire body feels electric. That slow burn in my stomach is growing hotter and tighter with each passing second.

Beside me, Reid shifts slightly. His arm brushes mine, and I can feel the heat between us building as we both get turned on by the scene playing out in front of us.

Almost without thinking, my fingers curl against the fabric of my skirt. "Don't."

The word is quiet but hard as steel, and my head snaps to Reid in surprise. "What?"

"Don't touch yourself."

"I..." My voice cracks, both with embarrassment that he knew exactly what I wanted to do and with frustration at his command. My body continues to throb its need, even stronger now that I know Reid is aware of it. "I need to."

His eyes lock on mine, sharp enough to slice right through me. "No. You *want* to. You don't *need* to."

On stage, the vibrator switches off again and the woman screams in frustration.

I feel just the same.

My grip on the skirt tightens, inching the fabric up just a little, and Reid's eyes narrow. "Actions have consequences, Maxine. If you touch yourself now, that'll be the only satisfaction you get tonight. But if you can be good and wait until we leave, I'll do it for you. What's it going to be?"

A jolt of desire hits me at the mere possibility of Reid's hands on me. The throbbing between my legs is so strong, I might come simply from *thinking* about it. My clit aches for friction, my pussy begging to be filled, but I grit my teeth and force my fingers to relax, letting my skirt fall back into place.

"Good choice." He doesn't smile, but the flare of his nostrils gives me a hint that the idea excites him too. "Now, sit back and watch. Feel it, by all means, but don't touch."

With my pulse pounding in my ears, I turn my attention back to the stage. The woman still hangs there, tears of frustration and pleasure streaking her face. When her dom whispers something to her, she nods.

"Please," she begs at last, and with that word, he gives her what she wants.

The vibrator turns back on and he reaches down to press against it, driving it harder against her clit that must be aching and tender by now. She gasps and writhes beneath his touch, but she doesn't use her safe word. Doesn't ask him to stop.

Her body begins to tremble, the ecstasy of release on her face, and I don't think I've ever been as jealous of another person as I am right now, with my body teetering right on the edge too and my satisfaction still a long way off.

Chapter Eighteen

~Reid~

That couldn't have gone much better.

I wanted to show Maxine that submission could look different to what she imagined and what she saw upstairs. It could look like what happened between us in my office, and it could look like what we just watched together on that stage.

The scene was masterful. Calculated, teasing, and restrained in all the right ways, and Maxine responded exactly as I suspected she would.

Rather than scaring her, her arousal lit her up, and now she's practically vibrating with it.

The club door shuts behind us with a heavy click, sealing the warmth and sensuality inside. In the private garage, the chill slices through the air, making Maxine's hand tighten around mine as we walk back to the car, her heels once again clicking briskly on the concrete floor.

She doesn't speak, but she doesn't need to. Every line of her body pulses with tension. She's flushed, pupils still blown, every breath a shallow, impatient drag through parted lips.

The moment the car doors close, she turns to me. "You said if I was good and waited, you'd make me come."

Her voice is breathless, almost wild with need.

"I did," I reply evenly, turning the key. The engine hums to life beneath us. "And you were."

"So?" she presses, fidgeting in her seat like she's burning from the inside out. "I'm ready."

She's not wrong. She did wait, and I meant it when I said I'd reward her. I don't want to wait either. Hell, my cock's been hard since the first whimper left her lips during that scene downstairs.

But this moment matters too much to mess it up. I can't go any further until she knows the whole truth.

"I need to tell you something first."

Maxine's eyes narrow. "This isn't the time for a conversation, Reid."

"Yes, it is," I say calmly, backing the car out of the parking space and heading for the exit. "Because if we don't talk now, you're going to think I kept this from you on purpose."

"If it was something you planned to tell me, you could've done it earlier," she snaps.

An unpleasant twinge of guilt digs into my stomach, because she's right. I could've told her, and maybe I should have. But right or wrong, I had my reasons for the delay.

"After what happened in my office, I wanted you to experience the club without baggage attached. Now that you've seen what's on offer, we'll go to my house and talk there. Then, if you still want it, I'll give you what I promised."

With a groan, she presses the back of her head into the headrest. "You said I only had to wait until we left. We've left."

"You really want to argue semantics with me right now?"

The city has grown quieter while we were in the club, the streets emptier as the people of Chicago sleep in their beds. In the darkened store windows, Christmas displays glitter as the car's headlights catch on them.

"I want you to keep your promise," she mutters, frustration lining every word. "If you don't, I will."

"What's that supposed to mean?"

Before I can stop her, before I can even fully process what she's doing, Maxine leans back in her seat and parts her thighs. Her skirt rides high and her fingers disappear beneath the fabric.

My jaw locks, nostrils flaring as my eyes dart between the road ahead and the shape of her hand beneath her skirt. "Don't."

"I'm not asking for permission." Her other hand braces against the seat while she shifts, arching her hips just enough to give herself the access she needs.

My knuckles go white on the steering wheel. "Maxine."

Her eyes are locked on me when I glance over again. She moans softly, for my benefit, as her fingers slide deeper, her body finding a steady rhythm as she fucks herself right there in my passenger seat.

The smell of her arousal fills the cabin, heady, sweet, and maddening. Her breath fogs the passenger window as she works herself faster, the slick sound of her fingers drowning out every other sound.

She's daring me to pull the car over, drag her into the back seat, and take over. A younger version of me might have given in to the provocation, but I learned during my own training in this world that it lessened the ultimate satisfaction that came from staying in control and sticking to the rules, not only for me but for my sub too.

As much as she might push, Maxine wants the boundary. She needs it, the same as I do.

"You don't get to disobey me and expect it to go unpunished," I bite out. "Finish what you started, and make the most of it, because it's the only pleasure you're getting tonight."

A flicker of something close to regret crosses her face, her lashes fluttering, but she's too far gone to stop. Her breath shortens and breaks as her hips jerk once, hard, and her entire body goes still.

The sound of her release is so quiet, it feels more like an echo than a climax. Not at all how it would have sounded if I'd been the one coaxing it out of her.

As her breath slows, she sinks back into her seat and her hand slowly withdraws. Her cheeks are flushed, her chest rising and falling in uneven waves.

A heavy silence falls around us, and her gaze stays downwards.

By the time I pull into the garage and kill the engine, the air has cooled into something brittle, and not only because of the winter's night. Her hand fidgets in her lap, tugging her skirt down with shaking fingers, like the fabric might cover up what she did.

Too late for that.

She still doesn't look up at me when I open her car door and issue a simple order. "Inside. Now."

The clicking of her heels is quieter this time, and far less certain. She doesn't say a word as we reach the door to the house, and I don't speak again either.

I told her earlier that actions have consequences, and she's about to learn just how true that is.

Chapter Nineteen

~**Maxine**~

The quiet between us feels like static electricity, crackling with tension as we step inside Reid's house.

The house itself is *gorgeous.* It smells like cedar and something spicy; his cologne, maybe, or the lingering hint of whatever he uses to polish the furniture. Everything feels masculine but refined, from the clean architectural lines of the vaulted ceilings to the hardwood shine of the floors. Even from the entrance, I can tell the house is respected and well cared for, and a million times nicer than my apartment.

Reid shrugs off his coat and hangs it from a large hook on the wall, holding out his hand for mine when he's finished. My fingers fumble with the zipper as I undo it with my left hand, since the fingers on my right hand are still a little sticky from being inside myself a few minutes ago.

Now that the moment's passed, I can't believe what I did in the car. I've never touched myself in front of anyone before, and certainly never made myself come. Frustration mixed with need, overwhelming me until I lost all sense of decorum or common sense. I thought I'd tease him by making him watch, make him suffer since he made me wait, but I should have known better.

He has *way* more experience with all of this than I do, and he's going to get the last word.

"Bathroom," Reid says curtly, tipping his head towards an open door. "Go clean up."

I do as I'm told.

In the spotlessly clean bathroom, I catch sight of a woman I barely recognize in the mirror. Her cheeks are flushed red and her eyes are bright with... anticipation?

Yeah, that's what it is. I'm nervous about what he has in store for me but I'm not afraid. I know he won't truly hurt me, not in any way I don't want him to, and whatever pain does come, he'll make it worthwhile in the end. My heart understands all of this as it kicks against my ribs, the adrenaline making it pump so hard, I feel ready to run a marathon.

So, rather than coming up with an escape plan, I force myself to take a few deep breaths as I slip my wet panties off and stuff them into my purse, wipe my damp thighs, and clean off my hand. The masculine-smelling soap wouldn't be my first choice, but it smells like Reid, which holds its own appeal.

When I'm ready to face whatever comes next, I follow the light down the hall to the living room, and as I step inside, I can't entirely hold back my hum of approval.

Although it's big, the room feels cozy with warm-toned leather furniture and a fireplace with charred wood inside, suggesting it gets used regularly rather than being for show. Framed artwork hangs on the walls; not the kind of mass-produced prints I have in my place, but unique pieces that seem personal to the room and to the man. A set of photos of detailed woodwork catches my eye immediately and I wonder if that's Reid's own work on display.

On the mantle are framed photographs between chunks of carved wood, and I move closer to them out of instinct. Standing to the side, his arms crossed and eyes fixed on me, Reid makes no move to stop me.

In the first one, a younger version of Reid, still gorgeous but without the gray in his hair, stands in front of a lake with a young boy and girl. The kids are holding up small fish that they must have just caught. Although he's only about seven, the boy is clearly Jamie, already a miniature version of Reid. I suspect that makes the little blonde girl his daughter. She's pretty, with a wide grin and summer freckles. Everyone's beaming like it's the best day of their lives.

A perfect, happy family.

Next to it is a photo of Jamie in a football uniform, holding a trophy while Reid stands next to him. Given his size and physique, it doesn't surprise me that Jamie played, and I already know Reid's a football fan. He must have loved watching his son play.

The next picture makes me smile. Reid is even younger here than in the first photo, probably around my age. He stands outside the house we're in now, though it looks run-down and neglected, and he's wearing the breathtaking smile that nearly knocked me out the first time I saw it in person, looking so proud he could burst. I can't help smiling back at him.

Eagerly, I move on to the next one, loving each glimpse I'm getting into the life of the man I'm quickly becoming obsessed with, but as I take it in, my smile freezes.

Reid has his arm around a blonde woman in her robes at her college commencement. She holds her degree in front of her, her smile wide, and Reid sports the same proud but restrained smile he has in the picture with Jamie.

But it's the woman's face that stops me in my tracks.

I know that face.

But... how?

What?

Why?

Almost before I realize what I'm doing, I snatch the photo off the shelf, as if changing the angle might change what I'm seeing.

It doesn't.

The woman next to Reid is, without a doubt, Samantha. *Sam.* The woman who stole my boyfriend and turned my world upside down. *Josh's* Samantha.

What. The. Actual. Fuck?

I spin around to find Reid closer to me than before, his hands in his pockets, watching me carefully.

"Sam is my daughter," he states quietly, confirming my worst fears before they even have a chance to fully solidify in my head. "That's what I wanted to talk to you about."

A cold flush climbs up my spine and my stomach drops so fast it feels like missing a step in the dark.

"You... you knew?"

I don't elaborate, but I don't have to. He knows what I mean. He knew that my boyfriend cheated on me with his daughter, and he didn't say anything? All this time?

Suddenly, more pieces fall into place. *The car.* The fucking car! It *was* hers. I knew it was too much of a coincidence, and he made me feel terrible that I'd made such a horrible mistake.

"You lied to me about the car. You said it was yours."

A muscle ticks in Reid's cheek. "Technically, it is. She's the primary driver, but I own it. I was picking it up for her that night."

"Technically?" I repeat, my voice going shrill as the truth becomes more real with each passing second.

I've been falling for the father of Josh's new girlfriend. If they get married, he'll be Josh's *father-in-law.*

Oh my God.

"Maxine." Reid's deep voice stops my spiral, a warm hand finding my chin as his other one takes the picture from my hand. I didn't even realize how tightly I was holding onto it until I have to pry my fingers off it to let go. It clatters back onto the mantle behind me as he places the frame back down.

Pressure under my chin tilts my head up, making me meet his eyes.

"I know this isn't ideal. I certainly wouldn't have chosen it. But Sam and Josh don't have anything to do with you and me. I wanted you to know so that you wouldn't feel blindsided by it, but it only matters if we decide it matters."

His calm stillness helps, but doesn't entirely stop my spinning thoughts. I take a deep breath, trying to match his energy. "Why didn't you tell me before?"

His lips tighten into a grimace, just a small movement but enough to tell me he's asked himself the same question. "At first, I didn't think it really mattered. You were going to work off the damages and that would be the end of it. Then things between us began to develop, and it started to feel wrong not to say anything. After what happened in my office, I planned to tell you today, but Jamie showed up and I realized the office wasn't the best place for that conversation. Which brings us to now."

He makes it sound so reasonable, but he's leaving out one big thing. "What about the club?"

Again, his facial muscles tick, a little tell that he's not completely sure of himself. Most of the time, he's utterly in control, so when he isn't, it's noticeable. "I wanted you to know what's out there before things between us got even more complicated. If you decide this is too much, if you don't want to go any further, that's entirely your choice, but now at least you know what's possible. I'd like to say it was entirely selfless, but that'd be a lie. I got plenty out of watching you tonight."

Fuck. Even when I'm mad at him, his words and the intensity of his stare have the ability to spark a fire beneath my skin. And his explanation is so maddeningly rational, I almost want to scream. I can't deny the experience at the club and the way he made me feel shook something loose inside me, unlocking something I didn't know I needed.

That's crazy, isn't it? I should be completely turned off by him now that I know who his daughter is.

But he said it doesn't have anything to do with us unless we let it, and that makes sense to me too.

I don't know what the hell to think.

His expression softens even further as I stay silent, his stern, controlled posture slipping just a little. "Maybe I didn't tell you sooner because I didn't want you to look at me like I betrayed you. Like you're looking at me right now."

Damn it. His logic was sound, but that little glimpse of unexpected vulnerability is even more compelling.

"Have you told... *her*... about me?"

As strange as this situation is from my position, it would be just as weird for Sam. Weirder, even. My dad fucking my new boyfriend's ex? I might need therapy for that.

Okay, we're not technically fucking *yet*, but we both know that's where this is heading.

Or *was* heading, at least.

I was hoping it would get there tonight.

Reid blows out a breath through his nose. "No. I haven't told her anything about the car or meeting you. If it makes any difference, she claims she didn't know you existed when things started developing between her and Josh."

My lip curls in distaste before I can stop it. Hearing Reid defend her is *not* what I need right now.

He lets out a humourless laugh. "Doesn't help. Got it."

Strangely, I believe he *does* get it, and somehow, that makes me feel a tiny bit better.

"I don't know how to feel," I admit. "I'm glad you told me, though. You didn't have to."

It's no secret to either of us that I would have let him do whatever he wanted to me tonight. Hell, I practically begged him to do it back in the car. He could have gone along with it and never said a word about Sam and I would have been none the wiser.

The fact that he wanted to tell me first so I could go into this with my eyes open shows a level of respect and understanding that I know isn't typical of a lot of men out there.

Reid has a different view of it. "Yes, I did have to. This lifestyle, this type of relationship, is built on trust. It doesn't work without it. If we want to play together, you need to be able to trust me and vice versa. And since I do want you, Maxine, I had to tell you the truth. Simple as that."

Desire spikes low in my abdomen with those four words: *I do want you.* My mind flashes back to the club, to the couple we watched, to the argument in the car and Reid's promise of punishment.

I could walk away right now. He's giving me the freedom to do so, the power to make that choice.

But deep down, I don't want to.

It's messed up. I'm not going to deny that, but I've also never felt more alive, more seen, or more powerful than when I'm with him. Maybe I need that more than I need something neat and tidy.

Besides, there's a twisted kind of logic at work. She took my boyfriend?

Fine.

I'll fuck her dad.

My teeth dig into my lip as another shot of arousal floods my body. I don't know where the hell that thought came from or why it turns me on, but it does.

Time to be honest with myself: I'm not going anywhere.

Instead, I pose a new question: "What do I get when you mess up?"

Reid's brow furrows as he studies me. "What do you mean?"

"When I do something wrong, when I'm a brat, as you call it, you get to punish me. But you're the one who screwed up here, so what do I get?"

That right eyebrow of his raises, sending my pulse racing. "You want to negotiate?"

"I think I'm entitled to it."

I could swear the corners of his mouth twitch in amusement. "What do you want?"

That's easy. "I want the orgasm you promised me. You can punish me for disobeying you, but after, I want you to make me come."

Where this bold version of myself came from, I don't know, but I don't care either. I like her, and I can tell from the way Reid's eyes blaze that he does too. "Let's get started, then."

Chapter Twenty

~**Reid**~

Maxine stands in my living room, flushed and defiant, and it takes all of my considerable self-control to keep from smiling. I'm supposed to be annoyed with her for that little stunt of hers in the car, but the primary emotion I feel right now is *relief.*

Obviously, finding out that Sam's my daughter threw her for a loop, and I don't imagine for one second that it won't cause some issues going forward. But she could've walked away. A few minutes ago, it looked like she might. And yet, she's still here, ready and willing to move forward with... whatever this is between us.

It's too early to define it, but the fact that she stayed tells me she recognizes this pull between us as something special, the same as I do.

It's not *just* about the kink. The club showed her that there are other men out there who could do that for her.

She's here for *me*, and since I haven't been able to get her out of my head since the night we met, that's a fucking relief.

Now, we need to end this night on the right note and set the tone for everything else I hope will follow.

I take a step back from her, moving slowly and deliberately so that she follows me. And she does, as if gravity is pulling her towards me. When I reach the leather sofa, I take a seat in the centre of it, spreading my legs just a little to give my cock a bit of extra room. It's already hard at the idea of finally getting to lay my hands on her, and from the way her eyes dip to my lap, she notices it too.

Her chest rises with a heavy breath, her whole body tense with anticipation.

"Lie down on top of me," I instruct. "Ass up."

Those big brown eyes lock on mine, her natural instinct for defiance warring with her hunger to let go. When I offer a hand, she takes it and lets me guide her. Her stiffness melts away as I wrap an arm around her waist and shift her into place, holding her steady. With a long exhale, she relaxes into me, giving me her full weight.

My cock pulses with pleasure at the contact and I have to stifle my groan.

"Do you know why you're being punished?"

Her instinct is to fire back quickly, off the cuff, but I can almost feel her checking herself and considering how to answer before she speaks. "Because I touched myself in your car."

"And why shouldn't you have done that?"

"Because you told me to wait."

"Exactly," I murmur. "Because you disobeyed me."

My hand settles onto the curve of her ass, warmth penetrating through the fabric of her skirt.

"When you give me control, you're trusting me. When you defy me, you're undermining that trust. You're saying I don't know what you need. Is that true?"

I let my hand slide up and down over her skirt, the pressure slow and deliberate. A shiver skates up her spine.

"N-no," she stutters. "I think you do know."

She's damn right I do.

She tenses again when I lift the hem of her skirt, revealing the soft swell of her ass and... nothing else.

"Goddamn it," I mutter, more to myself than to her. "Don't tell me you were bare the whole night."

From this angle, I can't see her pussy, but it's obvious she has no underwear on. I didn't specify in my instructions to her that she should wear panties.

I didn't think I had to.

My cock swells even more at the sight of that bare flesh and I have to fight the urge to shift in my seat.

"I took them off when we got here," she replies, a little defensively. "You said to clean up. They're in my purse."

Is that better or worse? I don't fucking know. At least she wouldn't have accidentally flashed anyone in the club, but knowing that she stood in my bathroom and slipped her panties off before coming in here...

Fuck. Stay focused, Reid.

This woman gets under my skin in a way no one has in a very, very long time.

"We'll talk about underwear rules later," I promise. "For now, let's deal with your disobedience in the car."

My hand returns to her ass, her skin warm and soft beneath my fingers as I rub a circle there, and Maxine's hips shift instinctively.

I press my arm tighter across her back, pinning her in place.

"Stay still."

"Yes, Sir."

The title slips from her lips without hesitation, only slightly sarcastic, and fuck if that doesn't *also* go straight to my cock. I'm rock hard beneath her, and I know she feels it from the way she squirms and the way her breath catches when her stomach presses against me.

My palm smooths over the bare curve of her skin once more before it lifts.

The first smack lands with a sharp crack, reverberating through my hand and into her body, and she jerks beneath me with a gasp.

"Count them out," I order. "Show me you're paying attention."

Her breath comes short and shallow before she stammers, "O-one."

The next one lands on the opposite cheek, slightly harder.

"Two," she breathes, not moving this time.

I keep going, slow and rhythmic, building pressure as I let the sensation burn and spread and settle in her bones.

She's panting by the sixth, clenching around nothing by the eighth.

By ten, her thighs are trembling and her voice shakes as she says the number. Her ass is flushed pink, beautiful and hot to the touch.

I soothe the sting with a slow rub before letting my fingertips slip between her legs. It doesn't surprise me in the least to find wetness waiting there.

"God, Maxine," I murmur. "You're fucking dripping for me."

It's my last chance to stop this before we fully cross the line, before this becomes sexual rather than simply flirtatious, but I don't hesitate.

Slowly, my finger slides inside her.

Just one index finger, just a teaser, and her breath shudders out.

She whimpers, muscles twitching around my hand. "Please."

"Please what?"

"More. I want to come."

"Oh, I know you *want* to."

I curl my finger slightly, searching for that perfect spot, and when I find it, her body bows. Her hips press firmly into my lap, giving my cock just a little of the friction it's begging for, and her ass thrusts higher into the air.

"But do you *need* to?"

"Yes," she groans, slamming a palm against the sofa's leather surface. "I need to. Please, Reid."

She's fucking stunning like this, writhing with need and begging me for release. I haven't come in my pants in more than twenty years, but I swear I could tonight if I loosened my self-control just a little.

I add a second finger, pumping slow and deep, teasing her closer and closer. She's tight and warm and wet around me, and my body aches to be even deeper, to bury my cock in place of my fingers and claim her fully. My hips thrust up against her, letting her feel just how hard I am, and her thighs tighten around my hand. Her legs begin to tremble.

And just when she's there, *right* there, right on the knife's edge, I pull my hand out.

Maxine lets out a desperate, guttural cry, her hips lifting to chase the orgasm I denied her. Her breath catches on a sob of desperation. She wants it so badly, it's carved into every line of her face.

But she's not going to get it.

"No," I say firmly, my tone deep and final. "You don't get to come. Not yet. Not after you took it from me earlier. This time, you're going to wait. *That's* your punishment."

She whimpers again. "You promised."

"I did, and I always keep my promises. I just didn't say *when*. If you're going to negotiate, Maxine, be specific."

Her attempt to take control from me earlier was cute, but if she's going to try to top from the bottom with me, she'll learn very quickly it's a losing battle.

I pull her up into a seated position on my lap. Her eyes are wide, her lips parted and her cheeks flushed. Her skin is warm and her breath ragged.

In other words: she's utterly gorgeous.

My hand brushes through her hair, letting her rest against my chest, heartbeat to heartbeat.

"You did so well," I reassure her. "You let go. You let me take control and I know it's not easy."

She nods against me, still dazed and catching her breath, still fighting her frustration, but she *does* fight it. She doesn't argue any further.

"I'm going to take you home. Tomorrow, we'll talk over the phone and set some boundaries. We'll discuss limits and guidelines. And you're not going to make yourself come, even though I'm not going to be there to make sure you don't. You're going to resist, to prove to me that you can really handle this."

She lets out a broken laugh, not satisfied but resigned. "I haven't proven it already?"

I chuckle in return. "You're on the way. And if you do that for me, then I promise, the next time we see each other in person, I'm going to make you come so hard you forget your name."

Shivering against me, she lets out a sigh. "I think I've already forgotten."

"Oh, sweetheart," I murmur, brushing my lips against her temple. "You have no idea."

Chapter Twenty-One

~**Maxine**~

The next afternoon, my apartment feels quieter than usual. Snow falls outside my window, and inside, the very air seems to be holding its breath along with me, waiting for whatever comes next. The buzz of last night still lingers in my blood, and every shift of my hips draws my attention back to the place where Reid's hand left its mark.

It's not painful, exactly, but it makes it impossible to forget everything that happened... and everything that *didn't* happen.

When he walked me to my door after driving me home, I could barely keep my eyes open. The night had unravelled me, emotionally and physically, and I fell into bed without even a glance towards my drawer or the vibrator inside it.

This morning, I thought about it. The ache was still there, but the urgency had faded. When I imagined reaching for relief, it felt... wrong. Not because I didn't want it, but because I didn't want to deny myself, or him, what he'd promised me if I waited.

Would he know if I disobeyed him? I can't be sure, but the risk doesn't seem worth it.

I'll wait, because when I finally do come next, I want it to be at his hands.

The Bears game is about to start when my phone buzzes. Reid's name lights up the screen with a video call request and my stomach flutters. My crush on this man is only getting bigger the more I get to know him.

When I answer, he's sitting on his couch in the living room I now recognize, a worn, gray T-shirt stretched across his broad chest and stubble thicker than I've seen before.

I smile instantly, my chest warming as I take him in. "Hey."

"Hey, yourself," he rumbles in a relaxed, easy tone. "Game on?"

"Yup." I hold up my bowl of popcorn. "I'm even wearing my lucky socks."

Reid raises an eyebrow. "You have lucky Bears socks?"

I shift the camera and raise my foot to show him. "Technically, they're bear socks, not Bears. With actual bear faces."

I wiggle my toes for emphasis and Reid chuckles. "Not what I expected. You wear them every game?"

"Every single one since I bought them. It's tradition."

"Ever worn them to Soldier Field?"

"I've never been. Thanks for rubbing that in."

He smirks at my teasing complaint. "The first time I went, I was in my twenties, and now I have season tickets. You've still got time."

I let out a very unladylike squeak. "You have *season tickets*?!"

His eyes twinkle. "For fifteen years now. I hardly ever miss a home game."

"I'm so happy for you," I deadpan, and Reid chuckles again. He's in a good mood today and so am I, now that I'm talking to him. It seems like a good time to try to find out a little more about the man who's taken up permanent residence in my head, so I start at the beginning. "Did you grow up around here?"

"No, I grew up in Nashville. The one in Illinois, not the one in Tennessee."

I blink at him through the screen. "I didn't know there was a Nashville in Illinois."

"Most don't," he replies wryly. "It's a small town with a couple of auto parts plants. My dad worked at one of them. He was a small-town guy, through and through, and even as a die-hard Bears fan, it never crossed his mind to take a trip up to the city to see them in person. He never complains when I take him now though."

"You don't seem like a small-town guy," I venture, and Reid nods in agreement, tossing a handful of something into his mouth.

"Staying there was never part of my plan. They're good people, but when I got into carpentry and construction, I knew I'd never be able to do the kinds of projects I wanted to work on in towns like that."

"What kinds of projects are those?"

The tug upwards on his mouth suggests he approves of the question. "Ambitious ones with big money behind them."

Projects like the Stamer Hotel, I suspect.

"So, I ended up here," he summarizes.

There's so much more I want to know, but I can't help jumping ahead to the part I'm most curious about. "Was your wife from Nashville too?"

Reid's expression doesn't harden like I feared it might if he thought I was being too nosy. Instead, his smile turns sardonic.

"Fiona? No. Definitely not."

Fiona. The ex-Mrs Larson has a name and I have to fight down the urge to immediately try to find a picture of her online. With how good-looking both Jamie and Sam are, of course she'll be gorgeous. Why put myself through the torture?

When I stay quiet, Reid continues.

"She was the daughter of one of my first clients here in the city. It was pretty reckless, really. Getting involved with her nearly cost me a job I badly needed. Her father was furious when he found out we were together."

My jealousy spikes but I do my best to control it. On the screen in the background, the game kicks off, and I use the break in our conversation to compose myself. When the play ends, my focus returns to Reid. "Sounds pretty romantic."

He shrugs again. "Depends on your definition of romantic, I suppose. Seems I have a habit of getting involved with women I shouldn't."

"Like me, you mean?"

His blue eyes lock on mine through the screen, and a shiver of electricity works its way down my spine. "Yes. Like you. You know as well as I do why this isn't a good idea, Maxine. And yet, here we are."

We're both distracted when the Bears fumble the ball on the next play.

"Unbelievable," I mutter.

"They're testing us," Reid says dryly.

"Every damn week," I agree with a laugh, and take a sip of my drink to try to build up my bravery for the next question I want to ask. Before I can talk myself out of it, I blurt out the words. "Was Fiona a brat too?"

Those blue eyes sear into me through the screen, his focus fully on me. "What do you think?"

I haven't really given it a lot of thought until this moment, so I talk through my reasoning out loud as I think it over. "Well, I suppose it depends when you figured out what you were into. If you knew before you got married, you wouldn't have married someone who wasn't compatible with you. But if you didn't know until later, it might be the reason that you split up."

Reid's eyebrows lift just a little. "That's pretty sound logic. In our case, I already knew when I met her."

I brace for the jealousy I expect to hit with that response, but it doesn't really materialize. I had no illusions that I was the first woman he's done this with, so being jealous about it doesn't make sense.

"How did you find out that you liked it?" I ask next. If Reid hadn't shown up in my life, I might have never discovered this side of myself at all, so I'm curious how he came to know so much about it.

"Through a friend. He has a similar kink, and he suspected I could benefit from some exploration. He recommended his trainer to me."

"So, you took, like, a course?"

Reid chuckles at my bewildered tone. "In a way. Not like any course you've ever been on, I'm sure."

I can't argue with that.

Before I can decide where to take my interrogation next, Reid turns the tables on me. "What about you? Where'd you grow up?"

My life isn't nearly as interesting, but I try to match his candour. "Aurora. Close enough that we could come into the city whenever we wanted, but we never did. My parents are the most cautious people on the planet, and in their eyes, downtown Chicago is a series of disasters waiting to happen."

Reid snorts. "What do they think of you living here?"

"I think they try to forget about it as much as possible. They've never really been involved in my life except to tell me when they think I'm making a mistake."

"Like what?" he asks, sounding like he genuinely wants to know.

"Well, growing up, I wanted to be an artist. I used to draw constantly. I even won a competition at a local art camp once. But my parents wanted me to focus on something realistic and reliable instead."

The muscles in his jaw tighten as he glances away at the TV screen before his eyes come back to me. "So what did you do?"

"I compromised. I went to college for graphic design instead, which sounded creative enough to satisfy me, and practical enough to make them happy. But, after I graduated, jobs were scarce and they made me feel so irresponsible for not working that I took a temp job to pay the bills. Turns out I was pretty good at it, so I got promoted, and now, four years later..."

I shrug, hating how pathetic it sounds next to Reid's achievements.

He doesn't judge though, nodding as he considers what I've said. "And where did Josh fit in?"

"We met at college. He was a safe choice too. Predictable, or at least I used to think so."

My parents still don't know that Josh and I broke up and they're going to be devastated. From the questions they've been asking, I think they're expecting a proposal, not a breakup. Christmas isn't going to be fun this year, but at this point, I'm done relying on their advice.

I find myself stating that determination out loud, even though he didn't ask. "My life has been focused on playing it safe, and I don't have much to show for it. On the other hand, the time we've spent together definitely doesn't feel safe, but I think that's why I like it."

Reid nods like he knows exactly what I mean. "I can't make any guarantees about how this will turn out, but it sounds like we both want to give this a chance. We should talk about a contract."

"Contract?" I repeat slowly. It feels like I missed something, even though I've been fully engaged in this conversation. "What kind of contract?"

Reid winces, his eyes darting off-screen, and I look up to see that the other team has just scored a touchdown. Normally, I'd be screaming at the TV, but although it's disappointing, I'm a little distracted at the moment.

"It's common in the early stages of a relationship like this to lay out limits and expectations. It helps provide some security in what can be an emotionally-heightened time. Think of it as a safety net. That should please your cautious parents."

A laugh bursts out of me at the idea that *anything* about this situation will please my parents. I can't even think about them and Reid at the same time, they belong to such completely different worlds.

Reid flashes me just a glimpse of his heart-stopping smile. "It's just a framework to start from. Nothing's set in stone. If you want to change something, or I do, then we'll talk about it. We'll adjust. Communication is vital. When we stop talking, it stops working."

"Is that what happened with your wife?"

The words are out of my mouth before I think them through and my heart nearly stops at the intense way Reid's eyes lock onto mine.

"You really don't have a filter, do you?"

The question feels rhetorical, so I don't answer. I force myself to hold his gaze, waiting for his response.

Finally, he sighs. "There's more to it, but the short answer is that she cheated on me. That's why we broke up."

I'm momentarily stunned into silence. *She* cheated? How does someone like *Reid* get cheated on? This woman must be insane.

Reid's words rush back to me from the first night we met, standing in my kitchen just a few feet away from where I now sit, when I told him that my boyfriend cheated on me and he met that declaration with sympathy rather than condescension.

Nobody deserves that, he said.

Apparently, he was speaking from experience. And even though it must have been terrible for him, it gives us something in common despite the differences in our ages or career success.

"I'm sorry, Reid."

He grunts in acknowledgement but obviously doesn't want to dwell on it. "What the hell was that call?"

We both watch the TV as they replay the pass interference penalty, giving the other team a first down. It's not looking good for the Bears, but again, I'm not nearly as upset as I would normally be.

"So, how do we make a contract?"

The smile of approval he gives me nearly makes me melt. "Let's keep it really simple to start with. Rule number one applies to us both: no messing around with anyone else as long as the contract stands."

I have no problem agreeing to that. There's no room for anyone else in my head besides Reid anyway. "Okay."

"Do you want to use protection during sex?" he says next. "I've had a vasectomy and I'm tested regularly, but it's your call."

"You had a vasectomy?" The words come out in a higher pitch than I intended, fuelled by surprise.

Reid isn't fazed by the question or my reaction. "Yes. We were done having kids and I didn't see why my partner should have to change her body when it was much simpler for me to do it. It's reversible, if I ever wanted to reverse it. Why wouldn't I?"

Every single word he says is true, but I can't imagine Josh *ever* agreeing to that. Just one more difference between them.

I force my thoughts back to the actual topic at hand. "Skipping the condoms sounds good to me. I'm already on the pill, so I guess we'd be doubly covered. And I haven't been tested in a while, but I should probably go anyway."

I leave the words *since my boyfriend cheated on me* unsaid, but based on the way he grimaces, I know he hears them.

"I'll send you my doctor's details," he promises. "They'll make room for you on short notice. Make an appointment whenever you like and I'll look after it."

He'll pay, he means, and though part of me wants to protest that I can do it myself, we both know that I'm already working for him because I can't afford to pay for the damage to Sam's car. "Thank you," I say instead.

After typing something into his phone, Reid returns to the subject of the contract.

"Next, you need to pick a safe word. If at any time you want to stop something we're doing, use that word and it stops immediately."

I rack my brain for a word I would never say in a sexy situation, and the bowl in my lap seems like as good a word as any. "Popcorn?"

"Perfect. And if you're unable to speak for any reason, hit the closest surface to you twice with the back of your hand. I'll see it."

The question is almost out of my mouth to ask why I wouldn't be able to speak when an image of me on my knees in front of Reid pops into my head, and a shot of pure lust hits me instead.

"There's one other thing I'd like to try," Reid adds, and if I didn't know better, I'd almost think he was nervous as his tongue darts out to wet his lips. "I like my control to extend beyond just the time that we're together. In small ways."

That sounds intriguing. "Like what?"

"Like your underwear, for example. I'd like to choose it for you each day."

A small part of me rebels against the idea of giving anyone control over something so personal, but a larger part thrills to the idea of Reid being so intimately involved in my day-to-day life. "How would that work?"

"Each night, you can send me pictures of two different choices. I'll select one of them, and that's the one you'll wear."

So, each day he'll know exactly what I have on beneath my clothes, whether he's going to see it or not. There's something sweet about that, as well as sexy. It doesn't take long for me to give in. "I can agree to that."

The smile that flashes across his face is genuine and utterly charming. "Good. I think that's enough for now. Something to get us started."

A knock at my door interrupts us before I can respond, and I jump in surprise. Nobody ever just stops by my apartment. For a moment, I panic that it might be Josh, but on the screen, Reid smirks.

"That'll be your delivery."

My brows lift. "What delivery?"

"You'll see. Go."

I scramble off the couch, phone still in hand, and open the door. A courier hands me a large but slim, rectangular box with a black ribbon and my name written in bold silver script. I've never seen anything so beautiful and I'm burning with curiosity as I carry it back to the sofa.

"What is this?"

He doesn't even give me a hint. "Open it."

Gently, I pull the ribbon loose and use my nail to slice through the label. Tissue paper greets me as I pull back the flaps of the box, rustling as I move it out of the way. When I finally reach the box's contents, I gasp.

Inside is the most gorgeous dress I've ever seen: deep emerald silk with a structured bodice and delicate straps. It looks like it was made to drape along every curve, including some I'm not even sure I have. It's in my size too, though I'm sure I never told him what size I am.

I'm completely speechless.

"There's a holiday party tomorrow night," Reid says casually, like this is an everyday occurrence for him. "I want you there, wearing that."

My heart does something strange and fluttery, like it wants to hide and leap out of my chest at the same time.

"But... I'm working tomorrow," is the first thing I can think of to say.

"You are," he agrees. "And this is a work party. It'll count towards your hours."

He's taking me to a work party? I'm not sure if that makes me his date, his employee, or his possession, but whatever it is, *I want it.*

And if we're seeing each other tomorrow, he'll have to keep his promise and make me come. My thighs clench at the thought, my body humming in anticipation.

Looking back down at the dress, I smile. "Guess I better shave my legs."

His chuckle is low and wicked. "You better shave more than that."

Fuck.

The next 24 hours are going to be torture in the best possible way.

Chapter Twenty-Two

~**Reid**~

The ballroom glows with warm light and polished silver, holiday garlands are strung across archways, and the scent of pine and champagne hangs in the air. I've attended this particular party for the last fifteen years, ever since Bear Construction became big enough to earn invitations to the city's premier architecture events. Usually, it's just another night of small talk, corporate ass-kissing, and scanning for potential clients, but tonight feels different.

Because tonight, Maxine's here with me.

The crowd parts as we make our way inside, men and women alike turning to get a look at the woman at my side. I don't blame them, since I had to do a double take earlier when she climbed out of the car.

Her curly hair has been swept up, leaving only a few teasing tendrils hanging loose along the elegant line of her neck. Her make-up is heavier than usual, more dramatic in a way that suits the occasion perfectly, and it somehow makes those big, brown eyes of hers appear even bigger than usual.

Although I'd wanted to pick her up myself, I got held up at the building site where I spent the day and barely had time to change into my tux before heading straight to the hotel. So I sent a taxi over for her, promising I'd be there to meet her when she arrived.

In spite of that promise, her shoulders were stiff with tension as she exited the taxi, and I winced in self-reproach. I hated that I couldn't soothe her nerves sooner, but as it was, I wasted no time in striding over to her, and when she turned and saw me coming, the tightness around her mouth melted into a relieved smile that stoked every protective fire inside me.

My hand found the small of her back. "Come inside. Let me get a look at you."

In the warmth of the lobby, she shed her heavy winter coat, and my heart damn near stopped. The dress looked even better than I imagined, and I had spent an indecent amount of time imagining it over the last 24 hours. It clung to her, framing her curves like a piece of art. For what felt like a full minute, I couldn't move, couldn't even think as my eyes roamed over her, devouring every inch.

Eventually, Maxine squirmed beneath my inspection. "Do you like it? I've never worn anything like it before."

"You could wear it every day for a year and I'd still be starved for the sight of you." I offered my arm. "Come inside before I forget this party exists."

The blush that crept up her cheeks only added to the effect she had on me, and now, the rest of the room is getting their first look at the beauty at my side.

"Mr Larson." We haven't quite reached the bar when we're intercepted by two developers I've been in discussions with about a new condo project. "It's good to see you."

Although the man's words are addressed to me, his eyes are already on Maxine.

"I don't believe we've met."

He offers her his hand and Maxine's eyes flit to me, looking for direction. That small gesture, the instinctiveness of it, recognizing that I'm the one in charge and I'll protect her, pleases me in a deeply primal way.

When I give a subtle nod, she shakes his hand while I introduce them.

"This is Maxine, she works at Bear Construction. Maxine, this is Leon and Grant. They're about to hire us to build their new condo."

The two men laugh good-naturedly as Grant offers his hand to her next. "Not a done deal just yet, but definitely a possibility."

We make small talk for a few minutes, and while Maxine doesn't say much, she's polite and engaged, poised and present. There's no need for attention or hogging the spotlight, but she doesn't shy away either. The pride I feel watching her sits like an ember in my chest, burning slowly with a spreading warmth.

I bring employees to parties with me on occasion, so having her here tonight isn't exactly an external declaration of our personal relationship, but it's still significant to me. Even though she signed the contract I sent her last night, we still have a lot to figure out about how this connection between us is going to play out. Is it purely sexual, or could we fit into each other's lives in a broader way, despite the differences between us?

Tonight is a test of that as much as anything.

When the developers step away to refresh their drinks, I turn to her, keeping my voice low enough that nobody will overhear.

"You're doing well."

Maxine's eyes flick to mine, gleaming with something between challenge and pride. "You mean I haven't spilled anything or insulted anyone. Yet."

I let out a quiet chuckle. "True, but I also meant that you're waiting very patiently for your reward."

She hasn't forgotten about it; I knew that for sure when I got the email from my doctor's office confirming that Maxine went for her sexual health tests today and they emailed her both her own results and mine, as I requested. Moreover, she's learning that when I say I'll do something, I do it, and that includes keeping my word about her reward.

As soon as the word is out of my mouth, her body shifts, her thighs pressing together. The movement is subtle, but I don't miss it and my body responds in return. "How do you know I didn't already take care of myself?"

The way she asks makes it clear she didn't, even if I couldn't already tell from the way she's carrying herself. "I just know."

"Can we get a smile here?"

A photographer standing just a few feet away pulls our attention, and Maxine naturally moves closer to me as the camera clicks. He gives us a nod and smiles before moving on.

When we're alone again, Maxine turns back to me. "How long do you usually stay at these things?"

I can't help smirking. "We just got here, and you're already eager to get somewhere more private?"

Her eyes narrow but it doesn't lessen the heat in her gaze. "You're the one who brought it up."

I did, and honestly, I can't wait either. We need to stay for now, but it doesn't mean we can't engage in some foreplay in the meantime.

I lean in as if I'm adjusting something on the back of her dress, even though she's already perfect. "If I'm going to make you come later, your panties will only get in the way. Go to the restroom and take them off. Give them to me when you get back."

Her breath flutters in surprise, but given the reward I've promised, she doesn't argue. While I head to the bar to get us some drinks, she excuses herself. My gaze follows her out of the room and it's not the only one. She's definitely making an impression here tonight but they're not going to get to do more than look, not when she's here with me.

By the time she gets back, I have two glasses of champagne and am deep in conversation with an older, very wealthy woman whose house I worked on a few years ago. I introduce Maxine to her, handing her one of the glasses.

Her other hand remains balled at her side, her pulse visible in her neck as she does her best to smile naturally. The conversation continues as I let my arm brush against Maxine's, giving her a silent instruction.

When my hand lowers to hers, she shoves the fabric into my empty palm as she nods along to what the woman says, her pupils dilated with adrenaline.

Casually, I slide the panties into my pocket before anyone notices.

When someone else approaches to speak to the woman, we say our goodbyes and move further into the room.

Maxine exhales a deep breath. "I was so sure she was going to notice."

"And it turned you on, didn't it?"

I already know the answer, but it makes me smile when she whispers, "Yes."

"Good. Now, you're going to keep smiling and charming everyone, pretending like you're not dripping wet under that dress, until I'm ready to do something about it."

Her eyes flash with defiance, but her lust is stronger, so obedience ultimately wins out.

"Yes, Sir," she mutters.

Chapter Twenty-Three

~**Maxine**~

The longer we stay at the party, the more unbearable it gets.

At first, I manage pretty well. I sip champagne, smile politely, and nod when I should. But I'm already wet when I return from the restroom without my panties, and it only gets worse.

Reid barely touches me, but his presence at my back, the heat of his breath when he leans close to speak, and the casual brush of his fingers on the small of my spine all ignite every nerve ending until I'm ready to burst into flames.

While he guides me into conversations with developers, suppliers, architects, their names go in one ear and out the other. He looks cool and controlled while I'm flushed, throbbing, and completely out of my depth.

I want to squirm but don't. I want to beg but won't.

Instead, I cling to the rules and the promise he made: if I'm good, I'll be rewarded.

"Breathe," Reid murmurs in my ear as I laugh stiffly at some stranger's joke. "You're doing so well."

I almost whimper.

The final straw is when his hand ghosts over my bare shoulder under the pretense of fixing a stray hair. His thumb brushes against my skin, branding me with a glancing touch. To anyone else, it would look completely innocent, but I'm so on edge, my knees nearly buckle.

Reid gives me a knowing smirk before turning to the people we're talking to. "I just remembered I need to make a call. Please excuse us."

With his hand at the small of my back, guiding me through the crowd the way he did at the club, he leads us to the ballroom door where he pulls aside one of the hotel employees.

"Is there a private room where my colleague and I can make a quick phone call?"

The woman nods and leads us down the hall to a small conference room with neutral carpet, a round table, four chairs, and, most importantly, a lock.

"I'll need to lock up when you're done. Will ten minutes be enough?"

Reid's expression doesn't waver. "More than enough. Thank you."

The door clicks shut behind her and Reid slides the deadbolt into place.

When he turns back to me, his smile feels almost predatory, and I've never wanted to be prey so badly in my life.

"I knew you could behave when you really wanted to. You did everything I asked you to."

A retort jumps to the tip of my tongue but dies just as quickly when Reid steps close enough that I can feel the heat radiating off him. My eyes lock onto his mouth, achingly aware that he hasn't kissed me yet. He's spanked me, multiple times, and had his fingers inside me, but my lips haven't been touched.

"I've been dying to see just how wet you are," he rasps. "Show me."

The words alone send another ripple of heat through me and I nod, almost forgetting how to breathe.

Before I can move, his strong hands are at my waist. In one smooth motion, he drags the silk of my dress up around my hips and lifts me onto the table. The air kisses my soaked skin, making me shudder.

He props one leg onto a chair, then the other, spreading me wide and leaving me completely exposed. The cool wood under my ass and the vulnerability of the position contrast with the distant sound of party chatter down the hall, giving the whole situation a surreal, almost dreamlike quality.

This is insane.

And I'm loving every second of it.

"Fucking perfect," is Reid's verdict when he takes a step back to examine me, delivered in a rumble that sounds even lower than usual.

Another shot of need blasts through my veins. "I swear to God, if you don't get over here and touch me, I'm going to..."

The threat dies on a gasp as his large hand palms my pussy, two fingers sliding deep inside with devastating ease, and I nearly sob in relief. My hands claw at the table edge, knuckles white as his thumb circles my clit with ruthless precision.

"You're going to what?" Reid teases. "Come? Not without my permission, I hope?"

I can't answer. I'm shaking too hard, my hips grinding helplessly into his hand.

His free hand clamps onto the back of my neck, pinning me gently in place and keeping me grounded as the pleasure mounts. My breathing turns ragged, thighs trembling violently and his fingers thrust and circle inside me, stroking that perfect place that makes my vision blur.

If he pulls his hand out again like he did the other night, I might actually die.

"Please... please, Reid... I need to come..."

The words tumble out, half-moan, half-desperation, and Reid leans in, hot breath feathering my ear.

"Then come, Maxine."

The orgasm detonates through me like a volcano erupting. For a few terrifying, glorious seconds, I lose myself entirely, my body convulsing around his fingers. I barely hear my own broken cry, but I have a feeling it wasn't discreet.

As the waves slowly subside, Reid strokes me through the aftershocks, his touch turning soft and tender until I slump boneless against his chest. Only the warmth of his palm keeps me tethered to reality.

"Good girl," he murmurs, and I shiver as his hand withdraws. "Worth the wait, wasn't it?"

He sounds so smug that I'd love to bring him down a peg or two, but I can't lie.

That was the best orgasm of my entire life.

"When do I get to return the favour?" I ask, my eyes trailing down to the bulge pressing against the zipper of his tailored pants. Ever since he asked me about condoms yesterday, I've been thinking about his cock far more than is probably healthy.

Reid chuckles. "Not here, and not tonight, but if you continue to behave, you might get that chance."

"You make it sound like you'd be doing *me* a favour," I complain. Any other man I've known would have whipped his dick out at the first suggestion I wanted to make him come.

Reid, however, is dead serious. "My cock is a privilege you have to earn and we're not quite there yet. But tonight was a good start."

A fucking *privilege*? The brat in me is screaming to tell him where to shove his 'privilege', but the needy Max really wants that dick. If he could make me come like that with just his fingers, what would it be like with him buried deep inside me?

Weighing the pros and cons, I keep my mouth shut.

Reid helps me off the table, using the panties he still has in his pocket to wipe his hand and the moisture left behind on the table while I straighten out my dress. My legs wobble, betraying just how wrecked I am.

"Do you want to go back to the party, or are you ready to go home?" he asks.

I know he doesn't have to give me the choice; he could tell me we're staying and I'd stay. But with how intense that just was, I'm drained, and I think he knows it. "I'd like to go home, please."

"Of course." Reid presses his lips to my temple once more, still the closest we've gotten to an actual kiss, and opens the door for me. "Let's go."

Chapter Twenty-Four

~**Reid**~

A piercing whine fills the air in my workshop as I power on the table saw. Carefully, I work the wood into place, my hands steady as it meets the blade. There's a throaty, rasping snarl as steel bites into walnut until it yields.

It's a beautiful wood but stubborn as hell. You have to learn its language before you shape it, check for fault lines or knots before you cut, or you'll ruin it forever.

Kind of like the relationship I'm trying to shape with Maxine.

The image of her sprawled across that meeting room table last night flashes vivid and sharp across my mind as I power down the saw. The way she came apart under my hand and the quiet tremble of her legs afterward are burned into my memory. I could barely sleep afterwards, replaying the scene over and over in my mind.

Since my divorce, there have been women I've enjoyed spending time with socially. There have been women who enjoy the same kink I do. But there hasn't been a woman who naturally fits both categories, and the more time I spend with Maxine, the more I believe this could be something real and beautiful, just like this piece of wood.

The first night we met, she struck me as passionate but principled, someone who felt things deeply enough to key the car of someone who'd done her wrong, but whose sense of right and wrong compelled her to make amends when caught in the act. Since then, I've been impressed by her work ethic, her openness, and the bravery she's shown by diving into new experiences with me. That's without even talking about our sexual compatibility, which feels close to combusting every time we're together.

If circumstances were different, I'd have claimed her already, but her inexperience, her age, and the messy connection to Sam are all factors I can't ignore. So, I move slowly, checking for cracks before I commit, knowing one wrong move could splinter everything.

I'm sanding down the piece when someone knocks on the workshop door.

"Come in," I call out.

The door opens and Josh stands awkwardly at the threshold, taking in the cluttered benches, the curls of sawdust drifting across the floor, and the sharp implements lining the walls. He tugs nervously at the sleeves of his coat.

Sam called me at work yesterday, turning up the pressure to keep my promise and schedule a follow-up meeting about the app. So, I told her he could come to my backyard workshop, knowing that it gives me the home-field advantage.

It might not be fair, but I don't mind making him sweat. It's the least he deserves.

"Is this a good time, Mr Larson?" he asks. "I can come back if you're busy."

As much as I'd like to get rid of him, I'm going to have to talk to him eventually. Might as well get it over with. "No, it's fine. Come on in. We can talk while I finish off this piece."

I pull off my goggles as Josh gingerly steps inside, trying to avoid the sawdust that litters the floor.

I fight the urge to roll my eyes. "You know anything about wood, Josh?"

He blinks, looking almost as confused as if I spoke in another language. "Not really. My dad was more of a car guy."

"You didn't take woodshop in school?" I press.

A quick shake of his head tells me no. "I did coding instead, which turned out to be useful in app development, so..."

He trails off with an awkward laugh that I let hang in the air for a few seconds before reaching down and picking up the piece I just cut, one of the pieces I'm preparing for a built-in library we're building in the new year.

"This is walnut. Strong, dense, and a bastard to work with if you don't know how to handle it."

I run my hand down the grain of the wood before grabbing a nearby hand plane and gesturing to him.

"Come here."

Reluctantly, Josh steps forward and I press the worn handle of the tool into his soft hands.

"You can't force it. If you go against the grain, you ruin the piece. You have to listen to it and let it tell you where it wants to go."

Circling him, I position the tool over the wood and press his hand forward, shaving off a thin curl of wood. The sharp, sweet smell of freshly planed walnut fills the air.

"It's the same thing with people. You want someone to trust you? You need to show them respect. Treat them the way you'd want to be treated."

Josh shifts uncomfortably, still clutching the plane. "I... I suppose that's true."

I take the tool back before he hurts himself with it and set it on the workbench with a soft thud. "That's why I wanted to talk to you. If I'm going to invest in an app you're in charge of, I need to know I can trust you."

Josh straightens, some of that nervous energy giving way to forced confidence. "I know you don't know me very well, sir, and I realize dating Sam while asking for your investment complicates things. But I think you'll find..."

I hold up a hand to silence him. "We're not talking about Sam. For now, let's stick to the app. If you want me to even consider investing, you're going to need to prove you deserve that level of trust."

Josh nods quickly, looking relieved to be staying on the topic of business, which feels like safer ground.

Yeah, you think that, kid.

"Of course. That's why I'm here: to answer any questions you have after reviewing the pitch."

"Let's get into it, then. First, I don't buy your monetization model. You're too reliant on ad revenue, and you have no meaningful partnerships or user retention strategies. The market you're entering is oversaturated. If you think your only competitive edge is 'no one else has done this *exactly* the same way', that's a red flag."

His mouth opens, but I cut him off again.

"Second, your risk mitigation plans are weak. Your safeguards for illegal use like drugs, sex work, and gun sales, are vague at best. That's not good enough. If you can't guarantee me ironclad compliance, I won't put my name anywhere near it."

Josh's face has started to pale. "We're working through some of those concerns after you raised them in the meeting. Our lead engineer..."

"I don't care what your engineer says. I need to see it spelled out, in writing. I've spent twenty-five years in an industry where one overlooked detail can kill people, and I'm not interested in anything that doesn't have a full blueprint."

I pause, letting the weight of my words settle before I deliver the final blow.

"Finally, and most importantly, I don't trust you."

His expression crumbles, all his confidence vanishing. "But you don't even know me."

"Exactly. You're dating my daughter, apparently, but the first time you met me, you asked for money. Not to get to know me, not to talk about Sam, but for an investment. That tells me you prioritize your goals over respect for the people around you."

Josh's gaze drops to the floor, his cheeks flushed with embarrassment and frustration as if it's only just now occurring to him that he might have screwed up.

He doesn't know the half of it.

"What can I do to change your mind, Mr Larson? I care about Sam and I care about this project. You can trust me with both of them, I promise. What can I do to prove that to you?"

Nothing is what I'd like to say, but I know Sam. She won't let it go if I shut this down outright. I'll have to at least give him a chance, but I intend to make him earn every inch.

"First, I want a revised proposal. A full rewrite of your pitch deck with detailed contingencies, financial projections with stress testing, and a real compliance plan. Not theoretical bullshit but actual legal consultation."

He nods hurriedly. "I can do that."

"Second, I want personal character references. Two of them. One from someone you've worked with for at least three years."

His head keeps bobbing in agreement. "Sure. And the other one?"

"From an ex-girlfriend."

It's an unusual request, to be sure, and Josh freezes mid-nod. "A... what?"

I stare him down, not blinking. "You heard me. I assume Sam isn't the first woman you've ever dated."

He flushes deeper. "No, but... why an ex?"

"Because no one knows how you treat people better than someone who doesn't owe you anything anymore. If you're the decent, stable partner you claim to be, it shouldn't be a problem."

I let the implication hang there while Josh swallows, his face now so pale, I think he might actually pass out.

Finally, he nods once more and gives me a quiet promise. "It's not a problem."

"Good." I reach for the plane again, dismissing him without saying so. "I'd like to get this settled before Christmas, so I'll expect to hear from you soon."

Josh hesitates for a second, as if he wants to say something else but ultimately decides better of it. He slips out the door, the faint crunch of his shoes on the gravel path drifting back to me before the door closes.

I brush my hand across the grain of the walnut again, tracing the natural imperfections with my thumb. It's going to be beautiful when I'm done with it.

Chapter Twenty-Five

~**Maxine**~

Tamara's apartment looks like Santa's workshop... if the workshop were run by a tyrannical, perfectionist elf.

The dining table in her tiny apartment has been turned into a present-wrapping production line, with wrapping paper, tape and decorations lined up precisely. I snagged the spot closest to the open window, since Tamara insists we wear Christmas sweaters for the occasion but her apartment is always overheated. Her unit thermostat doesn't work, leaving her at the whims of whoever's in charge of the building's central heating.

"You need to move," we've told her more than once, but Tamara always waves us off.

"I've done the math and it's best for me to stay put until I can afford the down payment on a permanent place. Moving isn't logical."

It might not be logical, but it would certainly be more comfortable. Instead, I sit there sweating before an icy blast of air comes through the window, giving me a chill until the heat warms me up again.

"Don't even think about cutting the paper before measuring twice," she says, eyeing Ellie with a look of warning as we work. "And always use the matching ribbon."

"You terrify me." Ellie grins as she obediently lines up a glittery gold bow to her reindeer-print paper. "What about gift bags?"

"Anyone who uses them is dead to me."

I choke on a laugh and snip a piece of twine with the tiny scissors she provided from a special box labelled 'wrapping supplies only'. The tree behind us glows with multi-coloured lights, and a Christmas playlist hums from her speaker, currently crooning an aggressively cheerful version of "Let It Snow."

"Thanks again for helping," Tamara says, her tone warming. "The men in the office are happy enough to give money, but no one ever wants to help with the actual gifts."

For the past three years, Tamara has organized a gift drive at the investment firm where she works. And for the past three years, we've helped her wrap them. Janine and Willow helped the first year too, but Tamara found their wrapping skills lacking. I suspect she went back after they left and re-wrapped every gift.

Now, they help her with the shopping and Ellie and I do the wrapping. It works out better for everyone.

"It's really good of you to take this on," I tell her. "We're just happy to be your sidekicks."

She beams and passes me another box. "Sidekicks who keep their edges tight."

"Right."

Ellie and I share a smile as we fall into a rhythm of folding and taping, everyone focused on their tasks while Bing Crosby sings about going home for Christmas.

It's Ellie who finally breaks the lull.

"So, Max, are you going to tell us what's going on with mystery man or what? You haven't stopped smiling all night. Spill."

Tamara's eyebrows lift with interest over her glasses. "Yes. I'm curious about what's happened since Friday night because something clearly has."

I roll a scrap of ribbon between my fingers, trying not to grin any wider than I already am. "It's... intense."

Ellie leans forward, eyes gleaming. "Is that your way of saying he spanked you again?"

And so much more. Honestly, just the memory of last night's orgasm is enough to set off a thrumming vibration deep in my core, but I'm not sure exactly how much to share.

There's one thing I know they'll go crazy over, though.

"He actually took me to a sex club."

"What?" Ellie shrieks so loudly that Tamara rips the piece of wrapping paper she was cutting. With a look of pure defeat, she puts it to the side and starts over. "Chicago actually has sex clubs?"

I hadn't known it either, but Tamara isn't surprised. "Based on the population size and the percentage of people in general who enjoy such experiences, I would guess there are several of them. Just because we haven't been to one doesn't mean they don't exist."

"Thanks, professor." Ellie rolls her eyes before leaning in again. "What was it like?"

"Honestly, it was both tamer than I expected and also way wilder at the same time. Does that make sense?"

"No," they both answer in unison, setting off a round of giggles around the table.

"Well, I'm not sure how else to describe it. We didn't do anything there, we just went to watch so I could see what it was like. But he's a regular, I guess. Like I said: things with him are kind of intense. Nothing like any of the guys I've dated before, but not in a bad way. Not at all. It's just different. I *feel* different when we're together. A little bolder, because he makes me feel safe to be more fully myself. I know that probably sounds weird but..."

"It doesn't," Ellie quickly assures me. "Well, I mean, the sex club stuff is definitely different, but feeling safe in a relationship is what you want. It's what you *should* have. Didn't you feel safe with Josh?"

I cast my memory back, trying to recapture the feeling of being with him, but it's already growing fuzzy. Four years together, and just a couple of weeks after it ends, I'm struggling to remember.

"It's not that I felt *un*safe. Just... unseen, I guess. I think I spent years being who he needed instead of who I was. Like, why was I always the one planning what we did every day? Paying our bills and making our appointments? I did it because it needed to get done and he wouldn't do it unless I nagged him. Reid's not like that. He thrives on being in charge, and it takes a lot of the pressure off, you know?"

Ellie's nodding along, but Tamara zeroes in on one word in particular. "Reid? Is that his name?"

Shit. I wasn't going to share that just yet, especially since I haven't figured out how to tell them about him being Sam's dad. They're going to freak out over that news, rightly so, and I'm not sure I'm ready to deal with it just yet.

So, my stomach drops when Ellie's lips purse into a thoughtful frown. "That's funny. Brad was just talking about a guy named Reid the other day and I thought about how I'd never met anyone named Reid. Now, they're everywhere."

"Oh?" I try not to sound too interested. "Who was he talking about?"

Her lips pull into a grimace. "I hate to bring her up, but apparently, he's Sam's dad. I guess they're trying to get him to invest in the app they're developing. By the way, I told Brad he should fire Josh for being a cheating asshole, but he says that's not technically against the terms of his contract."

She looks so put out, I have to smile. "It's okay, Ellie. I know you can't avoid Josh when he's working with Brad. I don't want you to feel like you're stuck in the middle."

"Oh, I'm 100% on your side," she promises. "It's Brad who's working with both of them. This weekend is the company Christmas party and I'm dreading going there and having to talk to them both. I'll be biting my tongue the whole time."

I know the Christmas party she's talking about. It's been on my calendar at home for months and I already knew what dress I'd be wearing for it. The thought stings, but only a little. My thoughts are still on Reid instead.

"Does Brad think Sam's dad will invest?"

Ellie shrugs. "He's not sure. They did a pitch for him in the office the other day and Brad said Josh was really nervous beforehand and even more nervous after. I guess this Reid isn't the warm and fuzzy type."

What? Reid met Josh? I try not to react to that news but my heart has started to pound. Why didn't he tell me? How did it go? Did they talk about me?

I have so many questions and I'm not even sure I want to know the answers.

"Sounds like Max's Reid isn't the warm and fuzzy type either," Tamara chimes in. "But that seems to be what she wants."

Grateful for the pivot away from Josh, I give her a mischievous smile. "Warm and fuzzy is nice every now and then, but I think I prefer hot and hard."

Ellie cackles while Tamara shakes her head, busying herself with her next present.

"When do we get to meet him?" Ellie asks when she stops laughing.

That's a good question. "It's still really new. I've met some people he knows, but only as an employee of his, nothing more. I met his son, actually."

They both stop what they're doing and stare at me. "He has a son?"

I nod, grabbing a piece of tape so I don't have to look at them. "And a daughter. They're about my age, so it might get a little awkward."

"Shit," Ellie breathes. "I'd say so."

"This seems quite unorthodox," Tamara points out. "He's your boss and he has grown kids and he goes to sex clubs. Are you sure it's what you want?"

That, at least, is an easy question to answer. "I'm sure. I just hope he feels the same about me."

"It doesn't have to be all or nothing right away," Ellie adds. "You're allowed to just enjoy it for what it is right now. You just got out of a relationship. Don't rush into anything."

Outside, snow starts to fall in slow, lazy spirals past the window, and Tamara declares a break for hot chocolate.

The conversation moves on to Christmas plans and the gifts we still need to buy, but Reid never fully leaves my mind. Ellie's right that we don't have to put a label on things right away, but I'm not so sure that it doesn't have to be all-or-nothing.

Reid seems like an all-or-nothing kind of guy, and when it comes to him, I'm greedy enough to want it all.

Chapter Twenty-Six

I should have gone home an hour ago. City lights sparkle outside my office window, while inside, half the floor is dark. Only a few people are working on this Thursday evening in December, but Maxine is one of them, and that's why I'm still here too.

We haven't seen each other since the party on Monday. We've texted in the meantime; quite a lot, actually. Her nightly underwear selection process has quickly become my favourite part of the day. At first, she sent me two options laid out on her bed. Last night, though, she sent a mirror selfie in each pair.

I damn near cracked my phone screen gripping it too hard.

Knowing exactly what she looks like beneath her clothes at this very moment makes it difficult to concentrate, but it's a challenge I relish.

And then she stands and stretches, arms over her head and back arching slightly, and my thoughts instantly derail. I can imagine that arch in a different position, on a different surface, and blood immediately heads south.

She heads towards the break room, and I give it thirty seconds before following her.

When I enter, she's standing by the coffee machine, stirring sugar into a mug of freshly-brewed coffee. She doesn't look up when I walk in, but the corner of her mouth curves.

"Strange that you need a refill the same time I do."

I step closer, keeping enough distance that it looks innocent but close enough that my voice only travels to her ears.

"Every time you pass my office, I get a craving for something wet. Must be a coincidence."

Her eyes flick towards me, glinting with amusement. "You might want to pace yourself. You wouldn't want to be up all night."

She sips her coffee slowly, her tongue briefly wetting her lips as my gaze traces every motion.

"You're playing with fire," I warn her.

She leans back against the counter, utterly unrepentant. "Maybe it's worth getting a little burned."

Someone clears their throat behind us, and we break apart instantly. Maxine hurries out with her cup and I grab a mug from the cabinet, feigning a need for a drink of my own.

Half an hour later, I'm back in my office when Rebecca knocks and walks in without waiting. "You have a minute?"

"Of course."

After closing the door behind her, she drops into the chair across from my desk, her expression unreadable. That never bodes well.

"I saw the picture," she begins.

"What picture?"

"The one from the Christmas party. The one the event photographer posted online of you and Maxine."

Ah. *That* picture. Maxine in that emerald dress, eyes sparkling and body tucked in close beside mine. I downloaded the damn thing the moment I saw it.

Rebecca's waiting for a response, so I keep my reply simple. "It's not the first time I've taken an employee to an event with me."

"Longtime employees, yes. She's a temp."

Good point. I try another angle. "I didn't feel like going alone and she was available. She represented the company well."

"Reid, don't bullshit me. You and I have worked together too long for that."

Since I don't want to lie to her any further, I don't say anything at all. I haven't asked Maxine if she wants our personal relationship to be public knowledge and I won't put her in a potentially uncomfortable situation without discussing it with her first.

Seeing I'm not going to answer, Rebecca exhales, glancing out the window over my shoulder. "Look, you're a grown man and you don't answer to me. I just hope you know what you're doing."

On that point, I can reassure her. "I do."

"Really? Because if Fiona sees that photo..."

The sound of my ex-wife's name sets my teeth on edge. I've been avoiding her calls, hoping if I ignore her long enough, she'll give up on hounding me about using the island house for Christmas.

So far, it's not working, and Rebecca's absolutely right that Fiona would crash out over the idea of me and Maxine, even if she has no right to.

"Fiona will see what she wants to see. She usually does."

Rebecca simply shakes her head. She's known Fiona for a long time and she knows I'm right. "And you're sure this isn't some kind of midlife crisis?"

I almost choke on a sputtered cough of surprise. "It isn't, but thanks for the reminder that I'm probably due for one."

That earns me a smile, the tension in the room easing just a little. I lean forward, a signal she recognizes means that I'm serious.

"Listen, I'm not going to insult your intelligence and pretend nothing's going on. And I can't guarantee it won't blow up in my face. However, I do promise I'll keep any drama out of the office and away from the business. You can go on your vacation and rest easy on that front."

She studies me for a moment longer before standing. "For what it's worth, I hope it *doesn't* blow up in your face. She doesn't seem entirely useless."

Coming from Rebecca, that's high praise.

The office grows quieter as people leave for the night, and just as I'm debating whether to send Maxine a text to ask if she needs a ride home, she knocks at my door.

"I'm finished for the night. Do you have a few minutes to talk?"

As usual, we're on the same page. "Yes, but I'm dying to get out of here. How about I take you home and we talk there?"

Excitement sparks in her eyes, just as I hoped it would. "Alright, but just so you know, 'talk' isn't a euphemism. There really is something I want to talk about."

"Understood."

Twenty minutes later, we're at her apartment. I haven't been here since the night we met, but I feel like I know it, and the woman living here, much better than I did then. She has a small Christmas tree in the corner and a few cards displayed on the table by the door. I get the distinct scent of peppermint candy canes from somewhere, though I can't see any.

Maxine sets her bag down and gestures towards the couch. "You want something to drink?"

"No, thank you. It's late and we both have work tomorrow. I won't stay too long. What did you want to talk about?"

We sit, but she doesn't speak right away. Her fingers twist in her lap in a rare sign of nerves.

"You met with Josh."

It's not a question, but I answer anyway. "I did. Did he tell you?"

She scoffs. "No. I haven't heard from him at all."

Interesting. Apparently, he hasn't asked her for a reference yet, then.

"Brad's girlfriend told me," she explains. "She doesn't know about us. I mean, she doesn't know that you're Sam's dad, but she told me that Josh met with 'Sam's dad'. Why didn't you tell me?"

"Mostly because I don't want to waste our time together talking about him. Also, I didn't find him that interesting."

A smile flashes across her face, brief and beautiful, before disappearing.

"Have you told Sam about me yet?"

I had a feeling this conversation was heading in that direction and I lean forward, elbows on my knees so I can meet her gaze directly. "No. I didn't know if you wanted me to. Do you?"

"I don't know," is her immediate response, and I can tell it's an honest one.

Maxine pulls her feet up onto the couch, wrapping her arms loosely around her knees. She's chewing at her lower lip, another nervous tell. I can practically hear the wheels turning in her mind but she's not getting anywhere.

And this kind of situation, the times when my partner is unsure about something or struggling to make a decision, is what being a dom is all about. I'm here so that she doesn't have to feel unsure. I'm here to take that burden from her.

I ease back into my seat, watching her. "Talk to me."

"I just..." She shrugs, hugging herself tighter. "Sometimes, it's hard to wrap my head around the fact that Sam is your daughter."

"Because of Josh or because she's your age?"

She winces. "Both. I mean, if my dad started dating someone my age, I would find it weird. Not that we're dating, but..."

There it is. That's the raw edge, the part of this that's making her so uncertain, so I address it with two simple words.

"Aren't we?"

Her lips part in surprise and she blinks at me with those big brown eyes, a move I find irresistible even though she has no idea how it affects me.

Maybe it's *because* she has no idea how it affects me that I find it so irresistible.

"Look, I'm not a fan of labels but I understand how the world works. Labels make things easier, especially for people on the outside looking in. And I know this is complicated. I know you don't want to be reckless by jumping into something too fast, or to be vulnerable when you just had your heart broken."

Her blinking becomes more rapid, almost like she's holding back tears, so I press on.

"But you *are* being vulnerable, Maxine. You're trying new things. You're letting me see you, the real you. That's brave, and I won't betray the trust you're giving me. I want you to feel completely safe and secure in this."

"The contract helps," she admits. "Sometimes, I think I dreamed you up, but it's right there in black and white."

That's ridiculously adorable.

"Well, that contract says we're exclusive," I remind her. "I'm not seeing anyone else, socially or sexually, and I don't care what we call it. If you want to say we're dating, then we're dating."

Her expression changes multiple times as she processes that, finally settling on a small smile. "Just like that?"

"Just like that. And if you want it to be public, I have no problem telling anyone, including Sam. If you'd rather not make it public yet, I can wait. It's up to you."

It won't come without consequences for me, particularly where Fiona's involved, and who knows what Sam's reaction will be? Rebecca was understanding but others around the office might be less charitable. Still, I'll deal with whatever comes. That's what I signed up for when I signed that contract.

Maxine blows out a breath, the tension easing from her shoulders. "I thought you were the one in control."

I lean forward again, lowering my voice. "I am. And don't you forget it."

The shiver that races down her spine is incredibly satisfying, and I lean back with a smirk.

"However, being with me isn't about following rules for the sake of it. It's about finding the freedom that comes when you know someone's watching your back. And I have your back, whatever you decide."

A slow nod follows that declaration. "Alright, I'll think about it and let you know."

It's still not an answer, but the fear is gone. She knows that whichever way she decides will be the right answer.

"Good. I'm glad you felt comfortable talking to me about this. In fact, I think that deserves a reward."

Instantly, the atmosphere in the room shifts, the air around us getting thicker as anticipation rushes in.

Maxine's arms tighten around her knees again, and her eyes dance as she leans in closer.

"What kind of reward?"

Chapter Twenty-Seven

~**Maxine**~

It's a strange thing to feel completely safe with someone I barely know, even when he's undressing me with his eyes.

Or maybe it's not strange at all.

Maybe it's exactly what I've been missing.

My parents taught me safety came from avoiding conflict or danger or even difficult emotions, but Reid doesn't ask me to avoid anything. He asks me to face it, explore it and confront it, and promises that when I do, he'll be right there to catch me.

Josh never made me feel that way. When we had difficult conversations, he'd let me take the lead and then let me take the fall. If I brought up our future, our goals, anything that mattered, he'd shrug and say, "Whatever you want to do."

As if that was empowering. Like pushing the burden onto me wasn't a kind of cowardice.

And if the consequences sucked? Well, that was on me, too.

When Reid asks me to choose, it feels different. The decision is mine, but the follow-up will be his. With him, I don't feel like I'm doing it alone, and even now, with my nerves still fluttering from our talk, I feel steadier than I should.

Steady enough to ask him exactly what kind of reward he has in mind.

He holds out his hand. "Come here and find out."

I take the outstretched hand without a second's hesitation.

Reid pulls me to my feet while he remains sitting. The light from the Christmas tree casts a soft, warm glow over the room, the colours flickering against the side of his handsome face as I stare down at him. It seems impossible that I've only known him for a matter of weeks. He's completely consumed my thoughts since then.

He's consumed *me*.

"You were brave tonight." His voice is so low and smooth, I want to wrap myself up in it. "That kind of honesty matters to me."

His hands slide up the back of my thighs, his fingertips brushing the hem of my skirt. Knowing I would see him tonight, knowing he likes me in a skirt, I wore it just for him.

"You want your reward now?"

My lungs squeeze so tight, I can only nod.

"Words, Maxine."

I force myself to take a breath. "Yes, Sir."

"Good girl."

It's ridiculous how fast those words go straight to the base of my spine.

"Take off your panties."

Reaching beneath my skirt, I ease my tights down first, carefully stepping out of them. In the apartment that sat empty all day, the air is cool against my skin but the heat of Reid's gaze makes up for it. The panties come next, and he takes them from me, folding them and slipping them into his pocket.

"Now, I'm going to taste every inch of you until you can't remember what you were worried about."

My lips part, but no sound comes out as he leans forward and lifts my skirt, exposing me inch by inch. With me standing between his knees, he's eye-level with my pussy when it comes into view.

"Fuck, you're beautiful."

His mouth is hot when it meets my inner thigh, and the first kiss nearly turns me to jelly. His hands anchor my hips as he trails his mouth closer to my centre, nuzzling and teasing until I'm squirming.

I want to beg him to go faster, but I'm afraid that if I do, he'll only make me wait longer, so I press my lips tightly together and force myself to be patient.

After what feels like an eternity of exquisite torture, his tongue finally finds my clit.

Fuck, yes. My head drops back with a moan as the whole room spins around me.

Nothing about it is rushed or rough. He licks me with deliberate care, his tongue slowly dragging across every nerve ending. His hands circle to my ass, tilting my hips forward so he can bury his face even deeper while his tongue keeps swirling, circling and pressing, building a rhythm that drives me mad.

"Reid," I gasp, gripping his shoulders for balance.

He hums in response, and the vibration sends another hot wave of desire straight through me. His slow, steady pace is both infuriating and intoxicating. Rather than getting me off quickly, he seems determined to make me feel every single moment, and honestly, if this is my reward for being honest about my fears, I'm never keeping a thing to myself ever again.

Despite his leisurely pace, the edge sneaks up fast, and I arch into him, chasing it. To my relief, he doesn't stop. His fingers dig into my skin to keep me still, his mouth never faltering.

"Please..." My voice is breathless. "Please, I need..."

My whole body tenses, waiting for his permission and dreading his denial. Every single inch of me is alive with hope and need.

"Go ahead, sweetheart," he murmurs.

The orgasm crashes through me, and I bite back a cry as my body trembles against him. Only his firm grip holds me in place, and the warmth of his mouth as he works me through every last wave keeps me grounded.

When I can't stay standing a moment more, he pulls me down onto his lap. When he did this the other night, it surprised me, but now, it feels completely comfortable and natural. His hand strokes my back, steadying me with his surprisingly gentle touch.

Gradually, the haze of my orgasm lifts and I become acutely aware of his stiff cock pressing against my thigh. Eyes still half-closed, I lift my head. "Let me take care of you."

My hand trails towards his belt but he catches my wrist before I reach it.

"No. You don't get to decide when or how. When it's time, I'll let you know."

There's steel in his response, and heat flushes through me, half arousal and half frustration.

"But..."

He gives my wrist a gentle squeeze before pressing a kiss to my temple.

"I want you, Maxine. Badly. But you don't dictate the pace with me. That's not how this works."

The ache in my core starts to rebuild just from the gravelly firmness of his voice. *Damn him.*

He helps me off his lap back onto the couch next to him and smooths my skirt back into place, every motion precise.

"I'll see you tomorrow," he says, brushing a thumb over my cheek.

Calm and collected, he heads out the door without another word while I'm left limp on the couch, my muscles still wobbly from pleasure.

Part of me wants to scream in frustration, but the other part, the part that craves the push and pull, only wants more.

God help me, when it comes to him, I want everything.

Chapter Twenty-Eight

~Reid~

Maxine arrives at the office the next night dressed like she's looking for trouble. Normally, her clothing is neat and professional, but tonight, she's wearing a low-cut black top and a short red skirt that suggest she plans to head out on the town afterwards. Completing the look is a Santa hat cocked jauntily to the side.

Her long legs are bare, her heels unapologetically high, and the look in her eyes tells me she knows exactly what she's doing. One glimpse of her in that skirt and I can practically taste her on my tongue again.

She knew Rebecca wouldn't be in tonight since she's leaving on her vacation tomorrow, so there's no one to disapprove of her outfit. In fact, the men who *are* in the office haven't stopped stealing glances since she walked in. I don't think any of them are about to complain.

I'm two steps from dragging her into my office the moment I see her, but I manage to hold myself back. How far will she take this? How far will I let her? Who's going to blink first?

An hour into her shift, she stops by my office with some fabricated excuse about printer settings, bending far too low over my desk and flashing the lace trim of her bra when she reaches for a pen. Naturally, I recognize the bra since I picked it out for her from the photos she sent me last night, and her perfume lingers in the air long after she leaves.

I'm wrestling with exactly how and when to lay down the law when Jamie appears in my doorway.

"Hey, Dad." He strolls in with his usual casual, relaxed energy that, for the life of me, I don't know where he got it from. Definitely not from me, and not from his mother, either.

"I thought you were on site today."

"I was, but I needed to grab some things from my office. And since I'm here, Mom asked me to tell you to call her. She says you're ignoring her messages."

Of course I am. I don't know how many more times I can tell her that no, she cannot use the island house for Christmas. I'm intending to go there, and I own the fucking place. She took a lot in the divorce settlement, but not that. Why she thinks she has any right to even ask to use it is beyond me.

And now, she's using our son as a go-between, which sets my jaw on edge.

"If your mother wants to talk to me that badly, she can do it herself. You're not her messenger."

Jamie holds up his hands. "I told her the same thing. Just passing it on."

"When are you leaving for the holidays?"

Jamie has his own plans for Christmas with a group of his friends, jetting off to some tropical destination where they'll drink the holiday away, probably with a lot of pretty women at their sides. I don't begrudge him any of it; he works hard and he's unattached, so he deserves to have some fun.

"Next Wednesday, but I'll see you at the Stamer party tomorrow before I go. I'm not missing that one."

No, I'm sure he won't. The Stamer Hotels Christmas party is always one of the best parties of the year, in the city's nicest hotel. This year, Jamie wrangled an invite for himself too, along with the one for me.

He heads to his office to pick up whatever he came to get, but on his way out, he stops at Maxine's desk.

"Nice hat," I hear him say, his voice carrying through the quiet office. "And nice drawing."

Through the open door, I can see her glance up at him, the hat nearly tumbling off her head at the sudden movement. "Oh. It's nothing. I was just doodling."

"Doesn't look like nothing." He leans over to pick something up off her desk, getting a little too close to her for my comfort. "Is this my dad?"

What? I lean forward, as if I could see it for myself from where I'm sitting.

"It's good," Jamie states. "I mean, *really* good. What other talents are you hiding?"

His eyes drop briefly to her chest before flicking back up, and a fierce possessiveness blooms deep in my gut. I'm out of my chair before I even think about it.

"Maxine. My office. Now."

Her eyes widen as her head snaps in my direction, and her lips part slightly in a breathy way that shoots straight to my dick.

Jamie glances back over his shoulder at me before rolling his eyes. "Don't let him boss you around."

"He *is* the boss," Maxine points out, and knowing that she's not just talking about our professional relationship sends another surge of heat straight to my groin.

They say goodbye and Maxine walks over to my office in those damn heels, closing the door behind her before turning to face me.

I pace behind my desk for a few seconds, tightening my grip on my self-control before I address her.

"What exactly are you trying to prove?"

She bites her bottom lip, feigning innocence. "What do you mean?"

"Don't play dumb. The skirt. The shirt. The hat."

I point to each item in turn, and her hand reaches up to pull the fur-lined trim further down her forehead. "Do you like it? I thought it would be festive since it's almost Christmas."

"Maxine." Her name is a warning, and I can tell by the way her eyes widen that she gets the message. Her stance turns a little more defensive, her fingers pressing together at her sides, and she drops the pretense.

"You said last night that you want me, but you're still holding back."

What I didn't tell her last night is that it's part of her training. As we're establishing our boundaries and routines, I need to know that I can control myself around her, even when she doesn't make it easy. And *fuck*, she's not making it easy right now.

"So you thought that provoking me by dressing this way was a good idea? What did you hope to achieve?"

Defiance flashes in her eyes, that spark that appeals to me so damn much. "Honestly? I hoped you'd let me suck your cock under your desk."

The straightforward answer hits me like a punch, the raw desire in her voice a powerful turn-on.

I can't let her get away with this though. We're in a delicate stage of the training right now, a stage that will set the tone of our entire relationship going forward, and she needs to know that pushing me like this isn't the way to get what she wants.

Not even when it's what I want too.

I'd deny myself to teach her a lesson, but maybe I don't have to. Maybe I just have to deny her getting *exactly* what she wants.

"Is that what you think you deserve for being a brat? A reward?"

She says nothing, but her eyes shine with an anticipation that suggests that's exactly what she expects.

I circle the desk, grip her chin and tilt her face up to mine. "Bathroom. Now."

Without hesitation, she turns and heads to my private ensuite, walking ahead of me with her hips swaying. I lock my office door, just in case, and once the bathroom door is closed behind us too, Maxine drops to her knees immediately. From this angle, I have a perfect view of her breasts, barely contained within the shirt she's wearing.

Lips parted, she gazes up at me hungrily, still mistakenly believing that she's getting her way.

I let her think it just a little longer as I unbuckle my belt, unzip my pants and pull my cock free. It swells immediately, already hard from the look of her in that outfit and the way she's been teasing me all night. It hardens even further from the way her eyes widen as she gets her first look at me.

I've seen enough other men in the club to know that I'm an average length but my cock is thick. It'll satisfy her well enough when we get to that point, but we're not getting there tonight.

In fact, she's not getting anywhere near it tonight. Instead of moving towards her, I lean back against the sink.

"You don't get to taste it. You don't even get to touch. You wanted to see what you were missing so badly? You can watch."

Her breath catches as I begin to stroke myself slowly and deliberately, keeping my eyes locked on her. She squirms, thighs pressing together and lips parting wider, and her right hand drifts towards her skirt.

"No. Keep your hands behind your back. You don't get to come from this."

Although she whimpers in frustration, she obeys. Clasping her hands behind her back only pushes her chest out even more, and fuck if she doesn't look spectacular this way, kneeling for me, flushed and needy, trusting and vulnerable, and taking her punishment just like she should. The primal pleasure that gives me only intensifies the physical sensation.

I take my time, dragging it out until my hand begins to chafe along my shaft. Spitting hard into my palm, I increase the pace, even though the sight of Maxine's gaze fixed on my cock like she's hypnotized by it is nearly enough to make me come on its own.

Eventually, my breathing turns harsh, the release starting to crest, and I step forward.

"Look at me."

Her gaze flicks upwards to my face, her pupils blown in those big brown eyes and a desperate need written across her whole face.

With a loud groan, I come. Strings of it land on her cheek, her chin, and her collarbone, and she pants in surprise while I drag out every last twitch of pleasure.

That's the first time I've let myself come since our night at the club together, and as good as it was, I know I can't deny myself that long again, not if we keep spending time together like we have been. The next time, she'll be the one doing it.

Still watching her closely, I tuck myself back into my pants. To her credit, Maxine doesn't move as she awaits my instructions.

"You can clean yourself up now. If we were at the club, I'd make you walk out that way, but in the office, it's not quite appropriate."

Her cheeks flush even harder, as if the idea of wearing my cum home isn't an entirely unpleasant one.

"I'm not sure that was a punishment," she admits as she grabs a washcloth and wets it in the sink before running it over her skin. "It might have been the hottest thing I've ever seen."

"The hottest thing you've ever seen... yet," I correct, and her thighs clench together again in a way that satisfies me enormously.

Her posture is proud as I walk her back to her desk, and damn if I don't admire that. She pushes me, but when I draw the line, she accepts it and keeps coming back for more. That deserves a reward, and I don't intend to be stingy.

"I'm heading out now, but the Stamer holiday party is tomorrow night. I want you there with me."

Her eyes light up. "Really? I've always wanted to see what the hotel is like inside."

"Yes, really. You did me proud at the other party, and I'm sure you will for this one too. Jamie will be there, though, so you'll need to be on your best behaviour if you don't want any gossip. Do you want me to tell him you're there as my date, or as my employee?"

She considers that for a moment before answering. "Employee, I think. For now, anyway."

I'm not too surprised. We only had the conversation last night and she's been at work all day, first in her day job and now here. I didn't expect her to come to a decision quite yet. "Fine. I'll send you something to wear."

"Can't I wear the same dress from the other night? It's gorgeous."

"It is, but you can't be seen in the same dress twice in one week."

She lets out a bubbling laugh that makes me want to laugh too. "Says who?"

"Says me. I know what I want you to wear, and you'll do what I say, won't you?"

Mischief lurks in those big brown eyes, but she doesn't disagree. "Yes, Sir."

Those two simple words are enough to make me want to take her right back to my office, but I force myself to move towards the front door instead. "Goodnight, Maxine. See you tomorrow."

"Yes, Sir," she repeats in a tone that suggests she knows exactly what she's doing to me and doesn't feel guilty about it at all.

Chapter Twenty-Nine

~**Maxine**~

When I sent out a text asking if anyone wanted to help me get ready for the Stamer Hotel Christmas party, I didn't expect Janine and Willow to show up with snacks, makeup kits, and a curling wand set.

I'm not complaining, though. Their energy is infectious, and after a week of adapting to my new normal with Reid, a week full of intense conversation and mind-blowing orgasms, I need the dose of reality.

"You're basically living the dream," Janine says, holding up a shimmering eyeshadow compact as she surveys my face. After I got out of the shower, I bundled up in my bathrobe while they worked on my hair. Now, we've moved on to makeup. "He buys you dresses, takes you to parties, fools around with you at work... do you even realize how hot that is?"

Willow flops onto the bed beside my garment bag and unzips it with a flourish. "Let's talk about this dress again. I want to live in this fabric."

She's exaggerating, but only a little. When the velvety crimson dress arrived by courier that afternoon, I might have moaned when I first brushed my fingers over it.

"Can you imagine someone just sending you a custom dress like this?" she continues, stroking my dress like it's an exotic animal. "I'd marry him on the spot."

"He hasn't *asked* me to marry him," I point out, even though the idea makes me swoon just a little.

"Not yet," Janine replies, giving Willow a wink in the mirror. "But at this rate, I expect a proposal by New Year's."

My attempt to glare at them fails, and the three of us erupt into laughter. It's such a far cry from the atmosphere when they were consoling me over Josh, I can hardly believe it's only been a few weeks. *Josh who?*

As Janine works on my eyeliner, Willow fingers the delicate strap of the bra lying on the bed beside the dress.

"Have you definitely decided on this one?"

Might as well tell them this part too. "Actually, Reid decided on it. Every night, I'm supposed to send him two choices and he tells me which one to wear."

Willow's eyes go wide. "I don't know if that's hot or controlling."

"Both," Janine says without missing a beat. "But most of all, it's fucking sexy. The man has opinions, he knows what he wants, and he gets it."

I shrug, trying to seem like it's not a big deal even though I've already grown to love the ritual of it. "It's actually kind of freeing not having to overthink what he might like. He already knows what works."

Willow grins, eyes gleaming with mischief. "You ever think about wearing the one he *didn't* pick? Just to see what he'd do?"

The thought has definitely crossed my mind, and my stomach flutters as I imagine it again. "I haven't tried it yet."

"I dare you," Willow whispers dramatically.

"You're going to get her in trouble," Janine admonishes Willow before turning to me with a grin. "But I kind of want you to do it too. How does this look?"

We all admire the results of Janine's skill, and I hesitate for all of five seconds before going over to the dresser and picking out the black lace panties and bra that Reid *didn't* choose. My hands tremble as I slip them on, wondering if he'll notice and what he'll do if he does.

"You guys are terrible influences," I tell them as they high-five each other with a laugh.

When we're finally done, I barely recognize myself in the mirror. The deep red dress hugs my curves like it was poured on, my hair is styled into big, lazy curls rather than my natural tighter ones, spilling onto my bare shoulders and the halter-top neckline, and the heels I've paired with the outfit make my legs look about a mile long.

As much as I liked the green dress I wore on Monday, this one looks even better. I've never looked or felt this glamorous.

Right on cue, the buzzer from downstairs goes off almost as soon as we finish.

My heart immediately thuds against my ribs. "That's him."

Both of my friends run to my window, which overlooks the street in front of the building. "Oh my God," Willow gasps. "He's in a tux."

"An actual tux," Janine confirms, elbowing in beside her.

They press their faces to the glass like they're spying on a celebrity, which, to be fair, kind of checks out when I go to take a peek for myself. Reid gives off a movie star vibe as he leans against his car.

"I hate you," Janine says dreamily.

"*Please* tell me he has some equally hot friends," Willow adds, looking me over one more time before giving my ass an approving swat. "Go get him."

I leave them to let themselves out, unable to keep from grinning as I make my way downstairs. I'm trying to think of something witty to say when I reach the front door, but as soon as I'm outside, I hear shouts from above.

"Have fun!"

"Be safe!"

"Don't do anything we wouldn't do!"

One of them lets out a loud cat-call as I look up to see my friends waving out the now-open window.

Reid's lips twitch as he opens the car door for me. "Friends of yours?"

"Not for long," I mutter. "They're so embarrassing."

"Don't worry." He helps me into the car and shuts the door before circling around to the driver's side. It's the same car that we took to the club the other night, and I feel even more glamorous than ever in the front seat. Reid brushes a few snowflakes off his tux jacket as he gets in beside me. He smells like cedar even more than usual, as if he's just been working with it, and something else lingers beneath it, spiced and warm. "Never be ashamed of having people in your life who care about you. It means you're doing something right."

The words settle into me with surprising warmth. It's such a simple thing, but generous at the same time. Josh used to complain when my friends were too loud or if I spent too much time with them. In just a few words, Reid showed he respects them.

I've walked by the Stamer Hotel before, but when we pull up to it tonight, it looks more like a palace than a hotel. Italian lights wind around every railing and wreaths frame the enormous arched entryway, and valet attendants in long black coats rush to take our car as we come to a stop.

"Are you going to take your coat in?" Reid asks.

The question catches me off guard. "I... well, yes. It's freezing."

He reaches for his door handle. "Leave it. Let's make an entrance."

Obediently, I shrug it off while he circles the car, and when he opens my door and helps me out, a blast of winter air hits my bare shoulders. My teeth chatter immediately.

"Trust me," he murmurs.

I do trust him, so I take his arm, shivering against him as we climb the wide stone steps. As I press my thighs together, I'm reminded of my small disobedience with the underwear, and another shiver goes through me, though this one stems from the thought of what Reid might do when he finds out.

If he finds out.

As soon as we enter the building, though, all thoughts of the cold or anything else disappear.

The interior is bathed in golden light, the ceilings cathedral-high with garlands twinkling from every surface. Live music floats down from somewhere above us, and I can already see the shimmer of chandeliers and the glitter of gowns and tuxedos on the mezzanine. A grand staircase curves upward like something out of a storybook.

I feel like Cinderella stepping into the ball.

"Wow," I whisper.

Reid leans down to brush his lips against my ear. "Wait until you see the ballroom."

I barely nod, too stunned by everything to reply.

The doorman directs us towards the staircase, and we climb it slowly, Reid's hand steady on my back. Every head seems to turn as we pass. Maybe because we're an unexpected couple, or maybe just because Reid looks so damn good in a tux. Either way, I can feel the weight of every glance, and even though being the centre of attention should terrify me, it doesn't.

I'm proud to be here with him, and no matter what happens tonight, I know it's going to be unforgettable.

Chapter Thirty

~Reid~

Maxine's hand is light on my arm as we enter the ballroom, but the tension in her posture tells me she's a little more nervous than she lets on. Can't say I blame her; the first time I came to this party, I felt my small-town roots were branded on my face. Everyone seemed so elegant and sophisticated, but I faked it until I could blend in, and based on how she carried herself at the other party we attended together, I already know Maxine will do the same.

She looks incredible in the crimson dress I sent her, even better than I imagined when I picked it out. Heads turn as we cross the room, and I know it's not because of me. She owns the room without even trying.

The first person who approaches us, however, is a familiar one.

"Wow," Jamie drawls, appearing at our side with a drink in hand. His tux is similar to mine, probably since he still shops at the same stores I do, but unlike me, he's here on his own. That leaves him free to size up my companion without needing to hide his interest. "So... is Maxine still just an employee, or are we finally admitting there's something more going on here?"

Maxine's cheeks flush but I keep my expression neutral. "You're making assumptions, Jamie."

"No, I'm making observations. There's a difference."

He makes a show of leaning over to Maxine, close to her, but 'whispering' loud enough that I can still hear him.

"For what it's worth, I think you can do better."

"Jamie," I warn.

He lifts his hands. "Kidding. Mostly." His smile is easy, but I can see the curiosity behind it. He really does want to know how serious this is, and as much as I want to tell him the truth and make it clear that this isn't just a flirtation or fling, Maxine hasn't told me yet how public she's ready to be.

Until then, it's not my news to share.

We're spared from having to answer when a voice cuts through the low hum of the ballroom.

"Well, well, Reid. Is this why you've been ignoring my calls?"

Fuck.

My jaw sets as I slowly turn to face Fiona, my ex-wife. She's standing just a few feet away, dressed in a silver gown, blonde hair sparkling beneath the lights above, and a flute of champagne dangling from one hand like she's considering throwing it in my face.

Fiona's a beautiful woman. She always was, but the attraction that used to burn so strongly between us doesn't even flicker at the sight of her. All I see now is the pain she caused and the trust she broke.

She gives Maxine a once-over that would wither lesser women while still addressing me. "Couldn't resist the cliché, could you? Trading me in for someone young and stupid enough to say yes to anything so you could dress her up like your little doll. How sad."

My hand itches to tighten around Fiona's wrist and steer her away from Maxine, but we're surrounded by half the city's power players. Losing my temper here wouldn't just damage my dignity, it could embarrass Maxine, and I won't allow that.

Before I can decide how to respond, Maxine takes my arm, offering Fiona a sweet smile. "I can tell Reid didn't pick out *your* dress. Desperate and bitter isn't his style."

Jamie sputters into his drink, coughing as he tries not to laugh aloud. I press a hand to Maxine's lower back, partly in support and partly to make sure she doesn't throw anything. I've seen what that temper can do when someone crosses her.

Fiona raises her brows, lips curling with disdain. "Classy. Your parents must be so proud."

Before either of us can reply, another voice joins the conversation, bright and utterly disarming.

"Reid Larson. It's been a long time."

We all turn to see a handsome man in his 30s with dark hair and green eyes, wearing a perfectly-cut suit. Next to him stands a beautiful blonde with a warm smile, oblivious to the frost in the air between us.

It takes a second for recognition to register, but eventually, I put it together.

"Noah Stamer." I extend my hand to the owner of the hotel, who shakes it firmly. "I didn't realize we had the top dog here tonight."

Stamer Hotels has hundreds of properties around the world. I've never seen Noah, or his father before him, at any of the Christmas parties here in Chicago.

He laughs off the title. "I had some business here and we never turn down a party. This is my wife, Olivia."

I offer her my hand while Noah explains our connection to her.

"I met Reid when we were renovating the west wing. His company created the woodwork for the interiors that your mom designed. Reid did the carving himself and I remember watching him work. The man has magic in his hands."

Olivia's blue eyes sparkle in amusement. "Does he?" Her gaze slides to my side, to where Maxine stands. "I might need to get a second opinion."

Maxine glances at Fiona, her lips curling into a smirk. "Oh, I definitely agree."

Fiona's mouth tightens like she's biting back something sharp, and for a second, I think she might actually hold her tongue, at least in front of strangers.

"I'm flattered you remember. This is..."

No such luck. As soon as I start to introduce Maxine, Fiona takes a sip of her champagne, then stumbles forward, quite deliberately, sloshing the remaining contents of her glass across Maxine's chest.

"Oh!" she exclaims, all false surprise. "How clumsy of me."

Maxine gasps in shock, but Olivia doesn't hesitate.

"Not to worry. I'm an expert in champagne emergencies. Come with me, we'll get you sorted out."

She side-eyes a knowing glance at Fiona before sweeping Maxine away with the kind of elegant efficiency that leads me to believe she really has had to clean up these kinds of messes before, even if they don't always involve champagne.

"Seriously, Mom?" Jamie mutters, shooting her a glare before holding out his hand to Noah. "I'm Jamie Larson, Reid's son. Do you think there's some bourbon around here somewhere?"

"I'm sure there is," Noah replies smoothly, giving me a nod of acknowledgement. "Nice to see you, Reid. Enjoy your evening."

Just like that, Fiona and I are alone and any pretense at civil discussion vanishes.

"You're making a fool of yourself, Reid. I thought you were better than this."

"That's funny, I remember saying something similar to you a few years ago."

She stiffens the way she always does when I bring up her infidelity. "Don't pretend this is about that."

"Then let's talk about what it is about." I step closer, lowering my voice. "You don't get to play the betrayed ex-wife when you're the one who left, and you sure as hell don't get to tell me who I can and can't be with now."

Of course that doesn't stop her. She was never one to back down. "She's half your age."

"Do you think that's news to me? That I didn't notice?"

"She's your daughter's age," she hisses. "It's inappropriate."

"But fucking my best friend was completely appropriate? Just making sure I get this straight."

"How long do you plan on throwing that in my face?"

"As long as you keep thinking you have any place in my life anymore. And while we're on that subject, you're not using the island house for Christmas. It's mine, I'll be going there, and if I'd been considering changing my mind, this little performance tonight would have convinced me not to. Why the hell are you even here?"

Right on cue, a man appears beside her, and my throat tightens. He's older than the last time I saw him, the day I fired my former best friend and cut him out of my life completely. Since then, he not only moved my ex-wife into his house, he started his own construction firm, attempting to undercut us to steal our clients.

Connor doesn't meet my eye as he takes Fiona by the arm. "Are you finished? There are some people I'd like to introduce you to."

"We're finished," I confirm, my tone flat. "She's all yours."

Fiona's eyes narrow on me. "You're really going to go sit in that house by yourself for Christmas? Just to spite me?"

"It has nothing to do with you, and neither does my personal life. Move on, Fiona."

Her laugh is harsh. "I'm not the one making a fool of myself with a date who's half my age."

She always has to have the last word, so I don't bother to respond again. Connor tugs on her arm and they turn to leave while I exhale a deep breath. That wasn't the start to the night I wanted, but on the bright side, it can only get better from here.

Time to find Maxine and get the evening back on track.

Chapter Thirty-One

~**Maxine**~

The restroom is as elegant as the rest of the hotel, with gleaming marble and soft lighting, but I flinch when we reach the mirror. Champagne has soaked the bodice of my dress, leaving the fabric matted and my skin sticky.

"It was so soft and perfect," I groan, staring at the damp velvet. "Now it's ruined."

"Nonsense," Olivia says, grabbing a few of the heavy paper towels sitting on the counter and beginning to blot at the spill. "It'll be good as new when we're done. She's not going to win that easily."

I can't help laughing, surprised that Olivia could so clearly see that Fiona did it on purpose even when she doesn't know any of us. For someone with her last name on hotels all over the world, she seems really down-to-earth. She has a natural gracefulness that comes from confidence without being stiff or formal in any way.

I have a feeling Olivia is exactly the kind of woman Fiona *thinks* she is.

She wets a couple of paper towels and hands them to me so I can wash my skin while she keeps working at the dress.

"Thanks for helping me. You really didn't have to."

Olivia lifts her eyes to meet mine in the mirror, a smile on her lips. "Honestly, that was the most exciting thing that's happened at one of these parties in years. Let me guess: she's the ex?"

"That's it. And apparently, she doesn't think I'm a suitable replacement."

Olivia snorts. "We don't know each other, so you can take this or leave it, but I know what it's like when other people have an opinion about your relationship. My philosophy is that you can't please everyone so you might as well please yourself. The only thing that matters is how *you* feel about it."

I hesitate for a moment, unsure how much to share, but quickly decide on: *screw it*. She's already figured out the situation, so what do I have to hide?

"The relationship is really new but I'm falling for him. Pretty hard, actually."

She hums thoughtfully. "Have you told *him* that?"

"Not exactly. It feels too soon."

Olivia shrugs, wetting another towel and adding a drop of hand soap to it before starting to dab the stain with it. "Who says when 'too soon' is? When something's special, the usual rules don't apply."

"Was that how it was with you and Noah? You just knew?"

I wince as soon as the words come out, not sure if they're too personal for someone I just met, but Olivia only laughs.

"Well, we've known each other my whole life, so our situation was a little different. But nothing would have happened if we hadn't both taken some risks. You know what they say: you'll regret the chances you don't take more than the ones you do."

I let out a dry laugh. "My parents would absolutely disagree with you on that."

"And has following their advice made you happy?"

Thinking back to the way I always played it safe, with school, with work, and with Josh, my answer is a resounding, "No."

"Then maybe it's time to try something different."

She wets one last paper towel, telling me to rinse out the soap as much as I can. It looks better already; there's still a darker spot where we've wet it, but it blends in a little more, and hopefully, as it dries, it'll clear up even further.

More than that, Olivia's words are a balm on the anger and frustration I felt at Fiona's comments. Olivia's right: it doesn't matter *what* Fiona thinks, or what anyone else thinks either. Things with Reid feel *right* in a way I've never experienced before, and I'm not going to let anyone else ruin it.

We return to the ballroom a few minutes later, and I spot Reid standing near the windows with a glass of water in his hand, his jaw tense. The moment he sees me, his expression shifts; relief first, then heat, like he's assessing me for damage and already fantasizing about revenge.

Or maybe fantasizing about something else, given the way his eyes linger over my body as they trail up and down.

"I'll leave you to it," Olivia says with a wink, giving my shoulder a squeeze before she heads back into the crowd.

Reid walks towards me as I head towards him, the two of us meeting in the middle.

"Hey," I say gently as I reach him. "Are you okay?"

His brow furrows, like the question doesn't make sense to him. "You're the one who got doused in champagne. Shouldn't I be asking you that?"

"I'm fine," I assure him before glancing around and lowering my voice, just to be sure we're not overheard. "It's just that... I haven't seen Josh yet since we broke up, but I know it'll get under my skin when I do. And I figured Fiona might make you feel the same."

Reid stares at me for a moment before giving a slow nod. "That's very insightful."

"Don't sound so surprised," I scoff. "I'm not entirely oblivious."

"No, you're not at all." He looks out at the crowd for a beat, weighing his response. When he does speak, I can hear the truth and the vulnerability in his words. "Honestly, seeing her does throw me, but not because I miss her or want her back. It's like I don't recognize her anymore. She's not the person I fell in love with, and I don't know if she changed, or if I did."

"Maybe it's both," I offer. "Maybe you both grew but in different directions."

His mouth curves faintly. "You might be right."

As I reach for a fresh flute of champagne from a passing waiter, the neckline of my dress shifts, and I see his gaze drop and darken. Glancing down, I see the problem: the lace edging of my bra peeks out just enough to betray me.

"Maxine."

I blink innocently. "Yes?"

"That's not the bra I picked out for you."

My heart beat turns erratic, but I try to play it off with a teasing smile. "Oh. Well, I didn't think it worked as well with the neckline."

He steps closer, steel settling in his tone. "It worked perfectly with the neckline. If you were wearing it, I wouldn't have seen it. That's *why* I picked it."

My stomach flips and heat pools deep inside, but before I can come up with a retort, he pulls his phone from his pocket.

"What are you doing?"

He taps something on the screen, calmly and methodically. "Setting a reminder."

"For?"

He slips the phone away again and meets my gaze. "For your punishment."

The words curl around my spine, a promise and a threat all at once, and I don't care that we're surrounded by strangers and sparkling lights. My thighs press together instinctively, chasing friction that won't come, at least not here and not yet.

The worst part is that he knows exactly what he's doing to me by saying he's going to punish me but not saying when or how. The anticipation will drive me crazy.

I sip my drink, trying to steady my voice. "Your ex-wife throwing her champagne on me wasn't punishment enough?"

"That was between you and her. This is about you and me."

His voice drops so low on the word 'me' that my body throbs in response. I have no idea what he's planning, but I don't care. I want the punishment, and I want whatever comes after it.

As magical as this party is, I suddenly can't wait to leave.

Chapter Thirty-Two

~**Reid**~

The rest of the party passes in a blur of laughter, conversation, and lingering, heat-filled glances with my beautiful companion. Maxine holds her own, charming everyone we speak to. I introduce her as my employee, which is technically still true, but anyone watching us for more than thirty seconds would know there's more going on. The way she leans in when I speak, the way her hand grazes my arm when she laughs, and the way her eyes flick to me when she has the floor, like she's checking to see if I'm watching, all give us away.

She doesn't need to check anyway. I'm *always* watching.

As she laughs at something one of my clients says, I lean in close enough for only her to hear, my lips brushing the shell of her ear. "Every time you laugh like that, little brat, all I can think about is how good your moans will sound later."

Colour blooms high on her cheeks, but she doesn't pull away. If anything, she draws closer, showing me how much she's craving it.

By the time we say our goodbyes, Maxine is practically vibrating with anticipation. Her heels on the marble floor as we head for the exit beat a steady rhythm, ticking down to her punishment. In the lobby, I drape my tuxedo jacket over her shoulders while we wait for the valet.

"I'm sorry we didn't get a chance to talk to the Stamers more," she says, glancing back at the staircase. "They were nice."

I'm glad she thinks so. "Actually, I made plans with them tomorrow, so we'll see them then."

Her mouth drops open as she stares up at me. "What plans? When did this happen?"

"I spoke to Noah while you were in the restroom. The third time, I think. Maybe the fourth."

She rolls her eyes at my teasing. "Were you going to ask me if I *wanted* to do something with them?"

"No."

The abrupt answer stops her short and her head tilts to the side as she eyes me curiously. "What if I already had plans?"

"Then you could have decided which you preferred to do, but I assumed since you didn't mention any plans and there's a Bears game tomorrow afternoon, you were going to be sitting at home on your couch."

I know that I've hit the nail on the head when she has no snappy comeback for me.

In the car, Maxine is silent as I drive us back to my house through the snowflakes drifting lazily from the night sky around us. I didn't ask if she wanted to come over and she didn't ask me why I'm not taking her home.

I break the quiet when we're just a few blocks away. "I know you're wondering what your punishment will be."

From the corner of my eye, I can see her throat working as she swallows. "Yes, Sir."

The way she slips into this more submissive tone when she knows she deserves what's coming is so fucking perfect. And it comes completely naturally to her. I didn't have to teach her any of it.

During our time at the party, I had some time to think about the way I want to approach this, and I lay it out for her now. "I have a feeling that you decided to disobey tonight just to get a rise out of me. To see what I'd do."

Her arms cross over her chest, but she doesn't deny it.

Like I thought.

"So, since you're in the mood to feel out our boundaries, I'm going to give you a choice."

That earns me a glance. "What kind of choice?"

"Option one: you can sleep in the guest room tonight, alone. No pain but also no pleasure. Nothing. That would be your punishment."

Her fingers dig into her arms, her discomfort with that idea abundantly clear.

"Or," I continue, "option two: you can accept a spanking, with an instrument of my choosing, and then you can sleep in my bed. With me."

She's quiet for a long moment, pretending to debate it, and I wait patiently. She was never going to choose the guest room, and we both know it.

"I'll take the spanking."

In the freshly-fallen snow, the house looks even more warm and welcoming than usual, and I hope Maxine sees it that way too. We park in the garage and her hand reaches for the door handle.

"You really want to do that?" I ask in a tone that makes it clear I wouldn't recommend it.

Her eyes roll but her hand pulls back and she waits for me to come and open the door for her.

Inside, I let her use the bathroom while I wash my hands in the kitchen, my blood pumping in excitement. Bringing her back here tonight was always the plan but I didn't know exactly what it would look like. Her punishment adds a structure to the night I appreciate, a way for us to ease into this new step. While I have a minute to myself, I take a few deep breaths to clear my head and leave all thoughts of Fiona and the party and everything else behind. When we're alone together, it has to be about us and nothing else.

Maxine appears in the doorway, her stockinged feet quiet on the hardwood. Her eyes are bright, looking just as ready for this as I am.

"Are you hungry? Thirsty? Do you want anything before we begin?"

Her head shakes immediately. "No. I'm fine."

I hold out a hand to her, both an offer and a command, and she steps forward to take it without hesitation. Together, we walk down the hall to the master bedroom.

The large room looks out over the backyard with a door leading directly onto the deck. With a press of a button by the door, the window shades all close, sealing us away from the outside world.

Next to me, Maxine looks around the room with curiosity and, unless I'm mistaken, a hint of disappointment. "This is really nice," she offers.

"But?" I prompt.

"But..." Her face scrunches in uncertainty. "It's pretty normal. I guess I was expecting something more like the club. Something..."

Before she can finish, I pull her across the room to the door that leads to the adjoining room. Originally a large walk-in closet, I've repurposed it into my own miniature playroom. When I flip the light on, Maxine's jaw drops.

"Something like this?"

The walls are a deep charcoal gray, the lighting warm and soft. In one corner stands a sleek, padded bench with adjustable supports, and along the far wall, a polished cabinet displays the various tools I can choose from for tonight's punishment.

Maxine steps inside slowly, her eyes trailing over the bench, the straps, and the neatly organized tools in the cabinet.

"Did you use any of this with Fiona?"

The jealousy in her voice is a little unexpected, but it doesn't upset me. If anything, I'm pleased that she's feeling possessive, and I can reassure her truthfully.

"Everything in here is new. After she left, I cleared the house. Gave the bed to charity and replaced everything."

I walk to the cabinet and pull out a leather paddle, the perfect toy for a beginner. It's sleek, firm, and has just enough give to sting without bruising.

"In fact, you'll be the first to use anything in this room. Usually, I play at the club. I haven't had any relationships serious enough to bring back here."

Until now are the unspoken words that linger in the air between us, and I can see the tension ease from Maxine's shoulders as she exhales.

I'm glad she's feeling comfortable, but I don't want her to get *too* relaxed. Not when we still have her disobedience to deal with.

"Strip."

The order is quiet but firm, and Maxine's hands move immediately, unzipping her dress and letting it fall in a pool at her feet. The black lace she wore instead of the set I picked out clings to her, but with one lift of my eyebrow, she slides the panties down too and reaches behind her back to undo her bra.

It joins the rest of the clothes on the floor, and she stands before me completely naked, eyes wide but her gaze unflinching.

She's ready to take what I have to give her, and it turns me on more than she could possibly know.

"Onto the bench, on your knees and elbows. Grip the handles."

It's abundantly clear from the way she hesitates that she's never used a spanking bench before, but it doesn't stop her from doing her best to obey. I only have to adjust her posture slightly, positioning her ass in the perfect spot and bringing her elbows forward so I can strap her arms down.

The sight of her like this, bared and bound for me, sends a jolt of heat through me so fierce I have to grit my teeth. I press the heel of my hand against my cock to relieve the edge. She's not ready for all I want to do to her, but we're getting close. *So fucking close.*

I drag my fingertips down her spine and her skin puckers beneath my touch, leaving a trail of goosebumps that makes her shiver.

"You're going to count for me," I instruct. "I don't want any other words out of those bratty lips. Only the numbers. Understood?"

She starts to answer me before catching herself, just in time. She settles for a nod instead.

"Good. Are you ready?"

Another nod, and I plant my feet as I position myself alongside her beautiful body.

The first strike lands with a satisfying smack that echoes through the room.

"One," Maxine gasps, but the tremble in her voice stems from arousal, not fear. Her thighs clench around the bench and my cock pulses in response.

Fuck, this is going to be fun.

Chapter Thirty-Three

~**Maxine**~

The paddle definitely feels different than Reid's hand.

It lands with a sharp *crack*, feeling like it hits my whole cheek at once, and the sting spreads across my skin in a hot bloom. My breath hisses, and I squeeze the leather edges of the bench tighter to anchor myself.

"One." The number gets stuck halfway through my throat, but I push it the rest of the way before inhaling a deep breath.

Reid's quiet praise, just a low murmured, "Good girl", makes my body shiver in a way that has nothing to do with the cool air on my naked skin.

Crack.

It comes down on the other side, sharing the attention equally across my body as I stutter out, "T-two."

The ache is real, but it's also a relief. The alternative Reid offered of being left in a cold, empty guest bed without his touch or presence would have been far worse. I knew what I was doing when I put on the wrong underwear. I knew it could very well end this way, and I made the choice.

There's pain, yes, but there's also fire, an intense desire that builds each time we play out this dynamic. And that desire, that feeling of being wanted and *seen*, is addictive.

Reid doesn't speak again between blows. Sometimes, they come quickly, in a fast, staccato rhythm: *three, four, five.* Then he waits, measuring his next move, while my body sits on the edge, anticipating and dreading and craving the next one. As much as I want to beg for him to hurry, I keep my mouth shut.

"Ten."

When the final strike falls, the silence that follows seems to ring in my ears. I'm panting, my skin damp with sweat. Every nerve in my body is on fire, and yet, I've never felt more alive.

Reid's hand moves over my lower back in slow, grounding strokes. Achingly slowly, it moves higher, and higher, until he steps in front of me and the air seems to shift. My head snaps up at the sound of his zipper.

He crouches down just enough to take my chin in his hand, lifting my face until our eyes meet. His grip is possessive rather than harsh.

"You did well." His voice is rough and sexy as hell. "Do you think you've earned my cock now?"

I nod so eagerly that if I weren't strapped down, the movement might have shaken me off the bench.

My enthusiasm makes Reid chuckle. "Let's start with just a little taste."

He doesn't keep me waiting. With calm certainty, he shifts his touch from my jaw to the back of my head, threading his fingers through the base of my hair and anchoring me there as he pulls his cock free from his pants.

Up close, it's even more enticing than it was back in his office bathroom when he made me watch. Now, I can see each vein and ridge, and every *thick* inch. I don't have a lot to compare it to, but it's by far the thickest cock I've ever seen. My pussy clenches at the thought of having it inside me, a throbbing need pulsing deep in my core.

That doesn't seem to be his plan, though. At least, not right now. Instead, he fists it at the base, one hand on his cock and the other still holding my head up, as he brings the tip to my mouth.

My lips part immediately, my eyes finding Reid's steely blue gaze as he pushes the head of his cock forward. My tongue slides along the underside, licking him as best I can with the rest of my body immobile. The taste is so overwhelmingly *male* and also uniquely him, a little musky with a hint of whatever body wash he uses. I want to commit the taste to memory, to remember this moment forever and the way it makes me feel.

Because even though I'm still bound, completely at his mercy, I don't feel small. I feel *safe*. If someone walked into the room right now, it might not look like I have any choice in what's happening, but I trust him completely with the choice I've already made.

Reid groans as he pushes in deeper. "Such a perfect mouth, Maxine. I knew that sassy tongue would be good for more than one thing."

I *would* show him just how sassy I can be, except I can't, because my mouth is full of him. He pushes even deeper, my lips stretching wide around his girth until there's no more room. Until I can't breathe.

My eyes find his again, this time with a touch of panic, and he can read every thought in my expression.

"You're doing so well. Breathe through your nose. If you need to stop, remember you can hit the bench with the back of your hand twice. That's your safe word anytime you can't speak."

Right. I'd forgotten, but knowing that I have that option available helps me to relax. My fingers, which had closed around the edge of the bench, loosen and I inhale deeply through my nose.

Slowly, he pulls completely back out, a string of saliva draping between the head of his cock and my lips as he withdraws. I quickly swallow, lick my lips, and open my mouth again.

"Just like that," he praises before pushing in again.

With each controlled thrust, he seems to get even bigger. He fills my mouth, over and over again, hitting the back of my throat and testing my limits, and when I can take him almost all the way in without gagging, he begins moving in earnest.

That firm hand still in my hair, Reid fucks my mouth, and I can do nothing but kneel there, strapped to the bench, and take it.

"Fuck, that's perfect," he growls, his eyes losing their usual intense focus as he nears his climax. Tears have gathered in the corners of my eyes but I force them to stay open, not wanting to miss the moment he falls apart, the brief moment where he loses control.

Before long, I get what I'm after. His hips jerk forward erratically, his movement stuttering, and he lets out a panted, heavy breath. His cock swells even more inside my mouth, pulsing against my tongue, and his salty, warm cum coats the back of my throat. Instantly, he pulls out, letting me breathe as I swallow it down.

Fucking hell.

My knees are shaking, my whole body trembling. I've just been tied down, spanked and fucked in the mouth, and I'm throbbing with need.

"Reid, I need…"

He leans down to press a kiss to my forehead before removing his hand from my hair. "I know what you need, sweetheart."

He disappears from view, and I expect to feel the restraints loosening, to be guided down off the bench, but instead, firm hands grip my hips, adjusting my position, and a soft hum starts up behind me. Before my brain can process the sound, something firm and vibrating presses against my clit.

"Oh, God!"

My hips buck instinctively, but it doesn't do much since I'm still strapped down, helpless against whatever he wants to give me.

The vibrations are relentless, perfectly targeted, and with how turned on I already am, it doesn't take long. *God*, it doesn't take long at all before I'm coming undone.

The pressure doesn't stop as my body convulses, though, and I whimper out his name. "Reid."

"Use your safe word if you need it," is his only reply as the toy presses hard against me.

Popcorn, I remind myself in my head, but I don't say it out loud. Not when pleasure is already building again.

One orgasm rolls into another, then another, until my throat is sore from moaning and I can't tell if it's pleasure or pain I'm feeling. Is this a reward, or further punishment?

Maybe it's both, feeding off each other.

When he finally switches the toy off and loosens the straps, my body falls limp against the bench. All the adrenaline built up inside me crashes, and to my utter horror, I burst into tears.

What the hell?

Why I'm crying, I have no fucking idea. I loved everything we just did, and I loved that he wanted to do it with me. I've never cried after sex before, and the idea that Reid might think I didn't enjoy it only makes the tears come harder.

Strong arms lift me gently, cradling me against his chest. "It's okay, sweetheart. You did perfectly. That was a lot, but I'm so proud of you."

His words help to ease my fear but still, the tears don't stop as he carries me out of the playroom and into the adjoining bedroom, laying me carefully on his bed like I'm made of something precious.

"I'll be right back. Don't move."

As if I want to.

As if I could.

He returns very quickly, like he promised, and the tenderness in his touch as he wipes the tears from my cheeks with his thumb is almost unbearable.

"Drink this."

A glass of water appears at my lips, and I obediently take as big a sip as I can manage. A peeled banana comes next, bite-size pieces hand-fed to me. When I've stopped trembling, he rolls me gently onto my stomach. The snap of a tube penetrates my haze, and his warm hand rubs a cool gel into the tender skin of my ass. Aloe, I think, based on the smell, and the relief is immediate even as the soreness lingers.

Eventually, my muscles start to slacken and my eyelids droop. Reid climbs into bed beside me, stripped down to his underwear, and wraps himself around me like a shield.

"You're okay," he murmurs, kissing my temple. "I've got you."

And he does. In every way that counts, I'm utterly his.

Chapter Thirty-Four

~**Reid**~

The cold air bites at my skin as I push through the final stretch of my morning run. Chicago in December isn't exactly ideal running weather, but I needed the clarity that only movement and fresh air can bring.

The house was quiet and warm when I slipped out an hour ago, Maxine still curled in my bed, her breathing soft and even. After everything we did last night, she deserved the extra sleep.

I left a note for her on the bedside table:

> If I'm not here when you wake up, help yourself to coffee and anything you want to eat. There are some clothes in the top drawer of the dresser that are your size. I'll be back soon.

Images from the past few weeks flicker through my mind with each step. Every time we're together, I'm more certain that this isn't a passing fascination. This is the kind of foundation we can build on, something solid and true.

But she's still getting over Josh, and as much as I want to move forward, I can't push her. While I've had years to come to terms with being cheated on, she's only had weeks.

So when I woke up this morning, saw her in my bed, and felt the insane urge to ask her to move in today, I figured going for a run instead was the better idea. Although I'm becoming surer about her by the day, pushing too fast before she's ready could bring the whole thing tumbling down, and I don't want to think about the damage it would do to either of us.

A rush of warmth greets me as I step back through the front door of the house a few minutes later. "Hello?" I call out, not too loudly in case Maxine is still sleeping.

"In the kitchen!" a voice calls back, and my hand freezes on the zipper of my coat.

That is *not* Maxine's voice, and my heart pounds as I kick my shoes off and stride down the hallway to the kitchen door.

"Sam?"

My daughter stands by the island, holding a mug of coffee. Her hair's pulled up in a messy bun, a few tendrils hanging down over the shoulders of her red and white Christmas sweater. With the morning sun streaming in the window behind her, she looks almost angelic.

Seeing that Maxine isn't with her, I force a calm I don't entirely feel. Chances are that Maxine's still in bed, so disaster could still be averted if I get Sam out of here quickly. "What are you doing here?"

She eyes my running apparel suspiciously. "I thought you put the home gym in so you didn't have to go running outside any more. Isn't it dangerous to exercise outside in the cold?"

"I'm not *that* old," I remind her drily, walking over to the coffee machine to get myself a cup. "And that doesn't have anything to do with why you're here."

Her grip on her own mug tightens, a sure sign that she's nervous about whatever's about to come out of her mouth. "I want to talk to you about the stuff you asked Josh to do."

Of course. I should have known he'd complain to Sam about it and try to weasel his way out of getting the reference. It doesn't surprise me in the fucking least.

Before I can say anything out loud, though, there's a sudden, sharp intake of breath behind me. Sam and I both turn, and my stomach sinks.

Maxine is frozen in the doorway, barefoot and wide-eyed. She's wearing the hoodie I left for her, a Bear Construction one, and some black yoga pants. Her hair is damp and almost straight; she must have just come from the shower, and her hair must curl as it dries.

Learning little things like that about her makes my fucking day.

Unfortunately, I have no time to dwell on it as Sam turns back to me, her eyes just as wide as Maxine's and swimming with confusion. "Who is that?"

A dangerous question, considering Maxine still hasn't told me how she wants to approach the situation with Sam and Josh. On the plus side, Sam doesn't seem to recognize her. Maybe because Maxine looks different with her hair like this, or maybe simply because Josh hasn't shown her pictures of his ex.

For some reason, that thought irritates me.

My eyes meet Maxine's across the space between us, a war waging across her expressive face, and though it's not exactly a direction, it tells me everything I need to know.

She's not ready for the truth to come out just yet.

And now that I know what she needs, I'll handle this for her.

"This is my date for the Stamer Hotel Christmas party last night."

I keep the explanation simple, not mentioning her name. I don't want to lie because the truth *will* come out eventually. Maxine isn't going anywhere.

Sam's eyes flick back and forth between us, confusion quickly replaced by understanding and something else, halfway between disapproval and hurt.

"Last night? She stayed here? So you're..."

She can't seem to force the words out, but we all know what she means. *Are we sleeping together?*

"Yes," I say simply.

Sam glances towards Maxine again in disbelief, and Maxine takes a step back into the hall. "I... I should give you guys some space."

"Are bacon and eggs good for brunch?" I ask, like it's utterly normal for us to be spending the morning together.

"Sure. Thanks." With that, she turns and disappears back down the hallway, back towards my bedroom, leaving me with my dumbstruck daughter.

"How old is she?" Sam hisses as soon as we hear the bedroom door close.

It shouldn't disappoint me that she decided to ask that question first, but I still hoped she wouldn't immediately jump to it.

"Old enough to make her own decisions," I reply evenly, reaching into the cupboard for an extra mug.

"Does Mom know about this?" comes next.

"Considering she was also at the party last night, yes, she knows. Not that it's any of her business. And Jamie knows too, before you ask. It's not a secret."

"So, you told everyone except me?" This time, the hurt in her voice tugs at my heart. I didn't mean for it to come across that way. "And you're actually, like, *dating* her? For real?"

"Yes. For real." I grab a frying pan and put it on the stove, each movement slow and deliberate so she doesn't think I'm ashamed or nervous. Because I'm not either. "It's new, and I haven't been hiding it from you. Every time we talk lately, it's been about the app and your new boyfriend, so it just hasn't come up."

That brings us back to the reason she came here in the first place, but that no longer seems to interest her.

She stews on things a little longer while I lay some bacon in the pan, instinctively moving Sam a little further away as the fat begins to sizzle and spit.

"I didn't think you were the kind of man who would do this," she finally says, and sometimes, I can hear her mother so clearly in her words, it's like Fiona's standing right there beside her.

Turning to face her fully, I fix her with a stare she can't hide from. "Dating someone younger than me, or older than me, for that matter, is not any kind of moral failing. We're both adults. Neither of us are in a relationship."

She squirms beneath my gaze at the reminder that her current relationship didn't start quite so freely.

"If we choose to be involved with each other, it's our own business and no one else's. I think you'll like her if you get to know her, and I hope you will, because I expect her to be part of my life going forward. I would have liked the chance to introduce you properly, but given the circumstances, I think maybe it's best that you leave and we can try again another time."

Her mouth opens as if she wants to make a rebuttal but quickly snaps shut again. "Fine," is the only reply I get before she turns on her heel and heads towards the garage.

She walks out without slamming the door, at least, which I suppose is a good sign.

Still, it could have gone better too. I exhale slowly as I finish cooking our quick late-morning meal, pushing out any stress so I don't carry it into my interactions with Maxine.

"You can come out now," I call down the hall when I'm back in control. "We're alone."

The door creaks open, and a few seconds later, she's back in the doorway.

"I'm sorry," she says immediately. "I didn't mean to complicate things."

"Things are already complicated, and you didn't do anything wrong. She still doesn't know who you are, but I think we should tell her soon."

Her teeth drag over her lower lip. "I guess so. She just looked so... shocked."

I place her mug down on the table and pull out her chair. "She'll get over it. It was a surprise, that's all."

Maxine slides into the chair, still looking a little uneasy. When her ass hits the chair, she winces, and the reminder of last night refocuses me.

"Aside from Sam, how are you feeling?"

Knowing exactly why I'm asking, she gives me her first true smile of the morning. "I'm good. And with this coffee, I'll be even better."

We eat together, chatting about the party and the people we met there, the conversation refreshingly comfortable after the unexpected intrusion. When we're finishing up, she nudges my foot under the table.

"Are you going to tell me what we're doing with the Stamers today?"

I'm going to have to if we don't want to be late. "Better. I'll show you. Stay here."

Leaving her at the table, I get up and head to the entryway closet where I've stowed a gift I bought earlier this week. When I return to the kitchen, however, Maxine is at the sink, rinsing off our dishes.

"What part of 'stay here' didn't you understand?"

She sweeps an arm out, indicating the kitchen. "I'm still here, aren't I?"

"I meant: stay at the table."

"Well, you should have said that then." She wrinkles her nose at me in the most fucking adorable way, and I'm relieved to see that she's not going to let the encounter with Sam throw off the rest of the day. This is the confident, sassy Maxine I want this morning.

"I'll say it now, then: sit your ass back down. When I want you to clean up, I'll tell you so. Otherwise, assume you don't have to."

"But I can..." she starts to protest.

"No. You'll do what I want you to do, and right now, that involves taking it easy. Sit. Your. Ass. Back. Down."

She obeys with an exaggerated sigh. "So bossy."

I drop the gift bag onto the table in front of her, one eyebrow raised. "I trust this will make up for it."

Her brow furrows so intensely, I begin to wonder if no one has bought her a present before. "What's this?"

"It helps if you open it and look inside."

She rolls her eyes before peeking inside, and a second later, I wince as she lets out a high-pitched squeal.

"Oh my God! Really?"

The navy blue Bears jersey with her favourite linebacker's number from the team's golden years appears as she whips it out of the bag.

Above it sits an embroidered name, the stitching crisp and new. Not the linebacker's name, though, and not hers either.

"Larson?" Her eyebrows arch as she glances up at me. "Is this yours?"

I shake my head. "I think you'll find it fits you much better than it fits me."

She still doesn't get it. "But why does it have your name on it?"

"Because I want everyone at Soldier Field to know that you're there with me."

Her jaw drops, her lips moving like she's trying to speak but no sound comes out. Finally, she swallows and tries again. "We're... we're going to the game? In person?"

That's what she took out of my statement? I'm not sure whether to be charmed or offended.

"Yes, we're going to the game. I was going to take you anyway, but Noah invited us to join him and Olivia in their box, so we'll watch the game from there. We won't have time to go to your apartment, so I figured you needed something to wear."

Maxine's gaze drops to the jersey, staring at it like it might disappear at any second.

"Reid, this is... I can't... this is too much."

She has to be kidding me. "It's just a shirt, Maxine."

"No, it isn't. It's thoughtful, and personal, and... damn it, you're going to make me cry."

Moisture really is starting to gather in her eyes, making it perfectly clear that Josh never put any actual effort into buying her gifts.

I make a mental note to find out what he gets Sam for Christmas.

Offering her my hand, I pull her up from her chair. "Go get changed. I'm going to have a shower and then we'll head out."

Pressing the jersey to her chest like it's something sacred, Maxine beams up at me. "I'm so excited, Reid. Thank you."

As she disappears down the hall, I lean back against the table and let out a long, slow breath. I'm excited too, but the truth is, Sam's reaction stung more than I let on. My relationship with my daughter is one of the most important things in my life, and though it's no fault of Maxine's, it's felt shaky ever since I met Maxine and found out about Sam and Josh.

Hopefully, we can find a way back to the way things were before. Hopefully, it won't be too awkward when she finds out that Maxine is Josh's ex.

Hopefully, I won't have to make a choice between them, because it would fucking break my heart either way.

Chapter Thirty-Five

~**Maxine**~

The jersey fits perfectly.

I smooth it over my hips, smiling as I catch my reflection in the bedroom mirror. Technically, Reid was right: it's just a shirt, but it also might be the most thoughtful gift I've ever received. The dresses were more extravagant, but this shows just how well he already knows me. He remembered my favourite player, and he knew I'd want to wear a jersey to the game.

And then there's his last name on the back.

If someone had asked me a month ago if I wanted a man to make a public declaration that I belonged to him, I would have laughed in their face. *Nobody owns me,* I would have said. I can actually hear myself saying it.

But when Reid's the one who wants to claim ownership, for some reason I just melt, and honestly, who the hell can blame me?

Then there's the drawer for me in his dresser. He wasn't kidding about having clothes in my size. The top drawer is full of neatly folded yoga pants, jeans, t-shirts, soft sweaters, a few matching sets of underwear, and even a cozy flannel robe.

Fiona and Sam are both thinner and shorter than me, so there's no chance that these are their cast-offs. He bought them just for me, and my heart does a funny little skip in my chest as I pick out a pair of black jeans to go with my jersey. Who *does* this?

It's the same in the ensuite bathroom that I use while he showers in the main one. Everywhere I look are examples of his attentiveness. A brand-new toothbrush still in its packaging. A comb and a brush and a satin scrunchie, along with a few drugstore makeup basics, all shades that actually work for my skin tone.

And he's taking me to a Bears game. *In person*!

If it wasn't for Sam showing up unexpectedly, I'd say this is the best day of my life. Even with her interruption, it's a strong contender, and I do my best to push any worry about Sam or Josh or anything else out of my mind as I finish getting ready.

Reid's waiting back in the kitchen in jeans and a jersey of his own, and honestly, I think it suits him even better than the tux last night. I could climb this man like a tree right now if we didn't need to leave.

When he sees me, he gives a low whistle, confirming that the feeling is mutual. "I've never seen a jersey look that good before."

"Because it has your name on it?" I tease, turning around to flash the back at him.

His eyes gleam with satisfaction. "That certainly doesn't hurt. Let's go show you off."

Yes, please.

The drive to Soldier Field is slow with game-day traffic, but I barely notice. We chat about the game, the opposing team and what our Bears need to do to win. Though we're in agreement on most things, we also get into a passionate argument over whether our tight ends this year are overrated or just need to be utilized better. We're still discussing it when Reid pulls into the designated parking area for season ticket holders.

Before we can even make it inside, Reid's phone buzzes with a message.

"Noah's sending someone to bring us up," he explains.

Of course. Who *doesn't* get a personal escort into the stadium?

How is this my life?

A suited staff member meets us at the gate and leads us up to the luxury suite reserved for Stamer Hotels, where Noah and Olivia greet us like old friends. Olivia's dressed like she walked straight out of a style blog in a chic coat, perfect lipstick, and absolutely effortless charm.

"Look at you!" she says, pulling me into a hug. "I love the jersey."

I beam back at her. "Thank you. It's new. It was a gift."

"A good one, it seems," she says with a knowing glance at Reid.

Inside the box, we find food, drinks, and sweeping views of the field. It's all gleaming and warm and comfortable. Almost *too* comfortable, actually. It doesn't feel all that different from watching at home, except I don't have to make the snacks.

We chat for a while before the game, mostly about holiday plans. They live in New York and are heading back there tonight. "We have four kids," Olivia says when I ask, and when my jaw drops, she laughs. "It's chaos but I love it. Especially at Christmas time, it's so special to see the holiday through their eyes. It's like being a kid all over again."

"Enjoy it while they're young," Reid offers. "They grow up fast."

There's a wistfulness when he says it that I haven't heard before, and a twinge of discomfort twists at my stomach at the thought of Sam, waking up on Christmas mornings with Reid when she was a kid. Now, she's waking up next to Josh.

I take a swig of my beer to push the thought down.

"What about you, Maxine?" Noah asks. "Is Christmas a big deal in your family?"

"Not really. I have a sister but she's married and they live closer to his family now. My parents don't really see the point of decorating when it all has to come down again a few weeks later. So it's kind of just another day."

Olivia's horrified gasp almost makes me jump. "That's close to sacrilege in our family."

Noah chuckles as he presses a kiss to her temple. "I can honestly say that for the Stamers, Christmas is *never* just another day."

The announcer's voice booms over the loudspeakers, introducing the teams, and I race to the window for a better look. I still can't quite believe I'm here, but the glass between me and the roar of the crowd quickly frustrates me.

"Where are your usual seats?" I ask Reid, who's come to stand next to me.

He points to a section near the 40-yard line, lower level. "Right down there."

The yearning I'm feeling must be apparent on my face because he reaches into his pocket and pulls out his two regular tickets.

"I want to chat with Noah about an upcoming project, but why don't you and Olivia go sit down there for the first half?"

I snatch them from his hand, leaving him huffing in amusement behind me as I sprint over to her.

Outside, the cold air stings, but I don't mind. It feels *real*, and the energy of the crowd soon warms us anyway. We jump up during key plays, cheering and chanting like we've been doing this our whole lives.

"Are you even a Bears fan?" I ask her during a break in the play.

She shrugs. "I don't really have a team. I just like to watch."

I envy her for that when our quarterback throws an interception that results in a touchdown, putting us 10 points down at the end of the first quarter. Not caring so much about the outcome would make the losses easier, but it wouldn't be nearly as much fun when we win.

"Did you enjoy the rest of the party?" she asks a few minutes later.

"I did. Thank you again for your help, and for your advice. I'm going to work on not caring what other people think, though I think I failed that test this morning."

Her pretty blue eyes turn to me with genuine concern. "What happened this morning?"

Between plays, I explain the whole situation, about Sam and Josh and the secrets Reid's keeping for me. For some reason, telling a complete stranger about it comes easier than talking about it to anyone else.

Olivia blows out a long breath when I finish, the warm air curling up above her as it meets the December chill. "That's tough, but I think you have to tell her. Don't let her find out on her own, and the longer you keep it a secret, the harder it will be to come clean."

She's right, I know she is, but that doesn't mean I like it. Almost without thinking, I speak straight from the heart. "I'm worried that she'll make him choose, and he'll choose her over me, just like Josh did."

Where the hell did that come from?

The thought hadn't even consciously crossed my mind before, but now that it's out there, it makes sense. The same woman who broke up my last relationship has the potential to torpedo this one too, and the worst part is, she has more of a claim to Reid's heart than I do. I can't even argue with it.

Olivia wraps a supportive arm around me. "I know it's cliché, but if he does, then he wasn't worth your time to begin with. And I don't believe it'll come to that. If she loves her dad, she'll want him to be happy. It might sting at first, but trust me, secrets sting worse. When Noah and I were young, he kept something from me and I found out in the most awkward way possible. We didn't speak for a year afterwards."

"Seriously?" They're so obviously in love with each other now, it's hard to imagine, but Olivia nods.

"She'll come around if she sees you care about him, and you can help by respecting her enough not to keep her in the dark."

That's an interesting way of looking at it, and I have to remind myself that as awkward as this situation is for me, it'll be just as bad for her. Maybe I have to stop thinking of her as a one-dimensional homewrecker and try to deal with her as a real person instead.

Around us, the crowd starts to cheer, and my eyes dart down to the field, wondering what I missed. Nothing's happening, though, and it's not until Olivia grabs my arm and points up to the screen that I realize the cameras are on us.

Laughing, we both wave and cheer, and even though he's still up in the box, I can practically feel Reid's approval and pride.

At half-time, we head back to the box, and to my delight, Reid thanks the Stamers for having us but makes our excuses so we can head back down to the seats together for the second half.

The game is a close one and we're on the edge of our seats most of the time, too caught up in the action to talk about anything important.

But during one break, Reid glances over at me before saying, "If you don't want to go home for Christmas, you could spend it with me."

Just like that, like it's no big deal, and my heart skips a beat at the thought of several days with him, uninterrupted by work and other commitments.

Just as quickly, the feeling sours as another thought crosses my mind. "Who else will be there?"

Hanging out with Jamie might be okay, but spending Christmas with Sam or, God forbid, Fiona, sounds like hell.

Reid quickly shakes his head. "No one. Jamie's travelling, Sam's with her mom this year, and I'm heading up to the island house alone."

I don't know what the 'island house' is, along with a million other things I still have to discover about Reid, but the word 'alone' supersedes anything else. He really wants us to spend the whole holiday together, by ourselves?

"I'd love that. I can cancel on my parents, they won't really care, and I'd have so much more fun with you."

His hand finds mine between the seats, our gloved fingers lacing together. "Perfect. So, how about we enjoy the break and then, when we're back, we can talk to Sam?"

He watches me carefully, looking for any clue that I'm uncomfortable with the idea, but after what Olivia said, I agree it's the right thing to do. "Sure. As soon as we're back."

I don't know how Sam will react. Maybe it'll be fine, or maybe it'll be just as bad as I fear. But sitting there, watching my favourite team with this man who came into my life like a dream, right when I needed him, I have to believe it'll turn out okay.

Chapter Thirty-Six

~Reid~

It comes down to the last play of the game.

The stadium is electric, the cold air buzzing with tension as the final seconds tick off the clock. The Bears are down by four with the ball on the opposing team's 15-yard line. I've watched hundreds of games in this stadium over the years but I don't remember the last time I was this invested. Maybe it's because Maxine's beside me, curled into my side as we stand, everyone in the stands too tense to stay sitting. Her fingers are tight around mine and I can feel her holding her breath, just like I am.

The snap is clean. The quarterback drops back and searches for an opening, the offensive line doing their best to keep the pressure off. One of the tight ends, one of the ones we'd been arguing about in the car on the way over here, gets clear in the end zone and the quarterback fires a bullet to him in the corner.

Touchdown.

Maxine screams, both hands flying up in victory and eyes wide with disbelief as the whole crowd erupts. Her joy is radiant, and for a second, I forget to breathe. Satisfaction fills up my chest, so strong it feels like it might crack open. For just a moment, nothing exists outside of the two of us, wrapped in our team's reflected triumph.

Breathless and glowing, she turns to me, wraps her arms around my neck, and reaches up to kiss me.

And just like that, everything else comes crashing back in.

Kissing is a step I'm not ready to take yet, so before our lips can connect, I drop my head, bury my face in her neck and hug her tight.

It's a decent diversion, I think, but when we separate, Maxine's smile has faltered. She looks like someone pulled the plug on the energy she'd been exuding a moment earlier, and though she tries to cover it up by turning back to the field, still clapping and cheering, I can tell she's disappointed.

Fuck.

"Do you want to take a look at the store on our way out?" I ask when the cheering fades and the crowd begins to disperse, ecstatic in our near-Christmas win.

"No." She doesn't meet my eyes as she walks past me. "I'm ready to get home. I have some things to do before work tomorrow."

I don't think she's lying, exactly, but I also don't think she's telling me the truth.

The drive to her apartment is mostly silent, tension winding tighter with each mile. The city lights flash across her face, illuminating the growing hurt in her expression. I hate that I put it there, and I'm not at all surprised when she confronts me about it as soon as we reach her apartment.

"Why didn't you kiss me at the game, Reid?"

I open my mouth to answer but she barrels on before I get a chance.

"Why haven't you *ever* kissed me? Is it because this is only about sex for you?"

I fix her with a hard stare as I stand by her front door. I'm not staying for long, *can't* stay for long since I have things to do too, but I'm not leaving with this hanging in the air between us.

"Don't say things you don't actually believe. Playing dumb isn't going to fix anything."

Fire flares in her big brown eyes. "So it's 'dumb' to want my boyfriend to kiss me?"

She's picking a fight on purpose, channelling her hurt into anger, so I keep my reply steady but firm. "You're deliberately misinterpreting me, but yes, it's dumb to say I'm only here for sex after the time we've just spent together. I could've kept things simple if that's all I wanted. Why would I have planned this whole day when I already had you in my bed this morning?"

"A day that you ruined by refusing to kiss me when any normal boyfriend would have," she retorts, and my jaw clenches, both because she's refusing to see my point and because she has a valid one too.

"I didn't mean for it to feel like a rejection. Kiss or not, you know this is more than physical. I've made that pretty fucking clear."

"You've made it clear that you enjoy bossing me around," she shoots back. "That's what you want, right? Someone young and naive who will do whatever you say and not ask questions."

Now, she sounds just like Fiona at the party last night. The things my ex-wife said must have gotten under her skin even if she pretended they didn't, and I'm not about to let that doubt fester a minute longer than necessary.

"I don't want someone who'll give me control because she doesn't know any better or because she doesn't have any choice. I want someone strong and smart, someone who'll let me take charge because she trusts me to make us both happy. I want to work for it. I want you to demand my best because you deserve it. And when I give it to you, I want you to fucking take it."

Her arms wrap around herself as I'm speaking, her eyes blinking to hold back her emotion. Silence falls after the last word, the air thick and heavy around us.

When she speaks again, the anger has shifted back into hurt. "Then why won't you kiss me?"

This time, she actually pauses to let me answer, so I try my best to be honest with her.

"To me, kissing is the most intimate thing you can do with another person. Other people might have a different perspective, but it's how I feel. I never kiss the people I play with at the club. In fact, since Fiona, I haven't kissed anyone."

I don't tell her about that last kiss, how Fiona threw herself at me when I came home unexpectedly during the day to try to distract me so I wouldn't notice Connor sneaking out of our bedroom. We were supposed to be working a job together, but he'd called in sick, and she shoved her tongue down my throat after just using it on his dick.

Maxine doesn't need to know all of that right now, but she deserves an explanation for my hesitation.

"I don't want to do that with you until I know for sure that you're over him."

Those words clearly aren't what she expected, and Maxine blinks up at me in surprise.

"Him? You mean Josh?"

"Who else would I mean?"

Her nose wrinkles like she's smelled something foul. "I've told you that this has nothing to do with Josh. You don't believe me?"

"I believe you *want* to be over him," I say carefully. "But I also think you haven't fully dealt with it. You've been hurt. Everything you thought your life would look like is gone, and this is something new and different, and I just want to be certain that it's really what you want and not a rebellion or a distraction."

A beat passes, the quiet sharp enough to cut through.

"You think I'm *using* you?" she finally whispers.

I wouldn't have phrased it that way. "Not intentionally, and maybe not at all. But as long as you're hurting, you're not fully free, and that scares me."

"*Scares* you?" she repeats the word like she's never heard it before. "What are you afraid of?"

She wants me to say it? Fuck it, I'll say it then.

"I'm afraid that you're going to break my heart, Maxine."

Sometimes, I think I should have said those kinds of things out loud to Fiona more often. Sometimes, people mistake my grip on control for a lack of emotion, but that couldn't be further from the truth. I feel things; of course I fucking do. And right now, I feel like I could give myself completely to this woman only for it to blow up in my face.

That's what's holding me back, and with the words finally out there, Maxine's eyes go wider than I've ever seen them. She stares at me for a long moment, and another, before swallowing.

"I don't know what else to do to prove to you that I'm ready," she finally says. The anger is gone, and most of the hurt too. Now, there's just confusion and a little bit of sadness.

"I don't know either, but when it happens, we'll both feel it. Look, I'm leaving for the island house on Wednesday morning and I'd still love for you to come with me. Why don't we take a little break for the next couple of days, and I'll pick you up on Wednesday?"

She starts to protest but I shake my head.

"This isn't a punishment. Just a couple of days of space, some time to reflect, and I'll see you Wednesday morning."

She looks down at the jersey she was so proud to wear this morning, her fingers brushing the hem. I can tell she doesn't love the idea, but deep down, I think she knows it's for the best. "Alright. I'll see you Wednesday."

I press a kiss to her forehead before saying goodbye, and force myself to head out the door before I give in to the urge to slide my lips those few short inches down to her mouth.

Hopefully, it'll be the last time I have to fight it. Because once I kiss her, there'll be no turning back.

Chapter Thirty-Seven

~Maxine~

I can't stop replaying it in my head.

There are plenty of candidates for things that I could be fixating on, from the uncomfortable silence in the car on the way home to the argument we had in my apartment or the way my voice cracked when I asked him why he'd never kissed me.

But what I can't wrap my head around is what Reid said in response. *I'm afraid that you're going to break my heart, Maxine.*

He looked right at me when he said it, a fragile offering from a man I've only ever seen as unbending and strong. I don't know what stunned me more: that he admitted he was scared, or that he thinks I have the power to hurt him like that. That I matter *that* much to someone like him.

Because if the disciplined, guarded, intimidatingly-in-control Reid Larson feels that kind of vulnerability around me, what does that say about us?

What does it say about *me?*

I've been curled on my couch since I got home, my laptop open but forgotten, candles flickering on the coffee table, and my half-drunk tea gone cold. I keep running a finger over the stitching on the back of the Bears jersey he gave me, now spread out over my lap, his surname printed there in bold letters like he wanted to brand me with it.

I want to believe I'm free of Josh and that the way I feel for Reid isn't any kind of rebound, but Reid has a point. I haven't really faced Josh.

I went from living with him and seeing him almost every day for four years, to nothing at the drop of a hat. I don't want him back, I'm sure of that, but maybe Reid's right and there are wounds I've left to fester, keeping them buried rather than letting them heal.

I *want* to be done with it, but wanting and being are not the same.

In need of advice, I send out a message to my group chat.

> Emergency summit? Who's available for a call?

Responses come quickly, but everyone's busy. Willow's out shopping, Tamara is elbow-deep in cookies, Ellie's at Brad's parents, and Janine's with her grandma. Everyone's sorry, offering love and "you okay??"s, but with just a few days until Christmas, no one can talk.

I tell them it's fine and toss my phone aside with a frustrated groan. Now what?

A few seconds later, my phone buzzes again. Hopeful that someone's changed their mind, I lean over to pick it back up. Instead of any of my friends, though, Josh's name flashes across the screen for the first time since he moved out.

> Hey. I saw you at the Bears game today on TV.

My heart hammers as I stare at the words. Was Sam watching with him? Did she see her dad, and did they figure it all out?

Before I can panic too much, another message appears.

> Not sure who the girl you were with is, but I'm glad you got to go. I know you always wanted to.

The *girl*. He means Olivia, and I exhale a deep breath. *Right.* We were on the big screen together, and it must have been shown on the broadcast too. That's pretty cool, actually.

With my worst fears put to rest, I reread the two messages. They're suspiciously nice. I don't hear anything from him for weeks, and now this? What prompted him to reach out to me today?

Luckily, I don't have to wonder for long about that either.

> I need to ask a favor.

There it is. He wants something from me. Why am I even surprised?

However, since I need something from him too, I bite my tongue and send a message back.

> I need to talk to you too. Can you come to the bar down the street tonight?

Josh's reply shoots down any hopes of a quick resolution.

> Actually, I'm out of town now until after Christmas.

Memories of past Christmases with his family hit me out of nowhere, bittersweet moments now that I know how things end, and I wonder what his parents thought when he broke the news that we'd broken up. Were they disappointed, or do they like Sam better too?

The sting in that thought takes me by surprise.

Maybe I *do* have more unresolved feelings about this than I realized, so I decide to poke on the bruise and see how bad it hurts.

> Tell your family Merry Christmas from me.

A little sore, but not too bad. I think that was quite mature of me, all things considered.

Josh's response quickly puts a stop to any momentum I might have been building.

> I'm not with them but I'll tell them when I talk to them.

He's out of town but he's not with his parents? That must mean he's with Sam, and Reid said Sam was spending the holiday with Fiona. An image of Fiona fawning over Josh when she was so vile to me makes my stomach turn.

Fuck, maybe I'm really not as over it as I thought.

> Can I just give you a call?

I stare at the message for a long time, thumbs hovering, unsure of how to answer. I don't think a call will work. I want to look him in the eye when I let go of everything. I think it would do me good.

Finally, I tap out a reply.

> Let's talk after the holidays. I'll message you.

His reply comes much quicker.

> That's fair. Merry Christmas, Max.

I don't respond, because I don't know what kind of reply feels true.

Do I want him to have a good Christmas? Not really.

Does that mean I'm not over him?

I don't know what to think.

Setting my phone down, I press the heels of my hands into my eyes. My head is buzzing and my chest feels heavy. I wanted clarity and instead, I got more ambiguity. Just enough to stir everything up again.

At least now I know that Reid was right about me needing to face this. It won't be settled by Wednesday, but I feel like I made a little progress. That has to count for something.

Looking around my living room, I suddenly feel the need to *do* something, and that's when I remember the drawing I made in the office the other day, the one that Jamie caught me doodling. It wasn't anything special, just a quick sketch of Reid's face, but it felt good to be creating again.

It takes me a few minutes to dig through the bedroom closet and find the drawing pads and small, framed canvases I haven't touched in years, not since Josh asked me to move them out of the living room to make room for his gaming system. My pencils are a little dusty but they still work, and as soon as I take one in my hand, ideas start to flow.

I'm a little too rusty to do a proper portrait, but something else soon takes shape, inspired by my work at Bear Construction and all those beautiful Christmas party invitations I went through on my first shift there.

Before long, I'm transferring the design onto a canvas, sketching it out in confident strokes that surprise even myself. In fact, I like it so much I might just give it to Reid as a Christmas present. From what I've seen, he doesn't lack for anything, so something personal might be the best way to go, just like the jersey was personal for me.

Most of all, it'll show him that even when we're not together, he's still on my mind.

If this time apart is a test to make sure I'll stick it out even when things get vulnerable and uncomfortable, he'll find that I'm more than equal to it.

And somehow, I hope he'll understand that although I'm afraid too, I'm not going anywhere.

Chapter Thirty-Eight

~Reid~

By the time I pull up in front of Maxine's building on Wednesday morning, the sun hasn't even cleared the horizon. A dusting of new snow muffles the city streets, and a few windows in her building still glow with strings of Christmas lights left on overnight, blinking softly like they're waiting for the day to begin.

We weren't going to leave so early for the 6-hour drive, but the weather forecast predicts a storm moving in this evening and I don't want to risk running into it. Even in my work truck, driving through heavy snow is no fun.

Besides, the early start doesn't bother me. I've been looking forward to this trip more than I probably should admit, especially after two days of radio silence between us.

I've barely turned the truck off before she pushes her way through the front door of her building, a weekend bag slung over her shoulder, bundled up in a heavy coat and a knit hat that makes her eyes look even bigger than usual.

"I thought I might have to come up and wake you," I tell her as I get out and take the bag from her. She steps to move past me, but I wrap an arm around her, pulling her into a hug. Her hair smells of fresh flowers, and I inhale deeply to get my fix. Fuck, I missed her. It might have only been two days, but they were some of the longest days of my life.

Maxine leans into the embrace, the tension melting from her shoulders as her body slots in perfectly against mine. "I barely slept. I couldn't wait to see you."

That's music to my ears.

After opening her door for her, taking her coat, and tossing her bag in the back with mine, I slide back into the driver's seat and pull away from the curb. There's traffic, but at this time of day, most of it will be coming into the city, not going out. We should be in the clear.

We barely make it to the end of the block before she blurts out, "I made contact with Josh. Well, he made contact with me, actually."

My grip on the wheel tightens instinctively. Not out of jealousy or any bullshit like that, but because I don't trust him not to make things harder for her.

He probably got in touch because he still needs to get me that reference. He was supposed to have already sent it to me, but Sam called me up on Monday to ask for an extension. That's probably what originally brought her to my house on Sunday too.

"It's difficult to pin people down because of the holidays," she claimed. "Can he get it to you after Christmas?"

I could have pointed out that he should have been the one making the call, or that I knew for a fact that he hadn't even attempted to reach Maxine yet, but it was the first conversation we had after she found Maxine in the house on Sunday and I didn't want to pick a fight.

"Fine," I agreed. "I'm going to be out of town for a few days myself."

"I heard," she said, her tone making it clear that she'd heard it from her mother. "Merry Christmas, Dad."

"Merry Christmas, Sam. I'll call you when I'm back."

Now, when Maxine tells me Josh got in touch with her, I dig, just a little. "What did he want?"

"To talk. I told him I want to talk too, but apparently, he's out of town. We're going to arrange something when I get back. So I did try, but nothing has changed since Sunday."

Disappointment lines each word, as if she thinks she's failed, but I don't see it that way at all. "A lot of things get put on hold for the holidays, and there's nothing else you can do about it now. So, let's forget all about it and just enjoy ourselves for the next few days. No Josh, no Sam, no Fiona. Just you and me. Does that sound alright?"

A relieved smile spreads across her face. "It sounds perfect."

We fall into a comfortable silence as we merge onto the highway, and once we hit the open road, Maxine glances over at me again.

"So, where exactly is this mysterious island house?"

I raise an eyebrow. "You decided to wait until *now* to ask?"

"I was a little distracted before," she retorts, her arms crossing just beneath her breasts.

The action pushes them up, stretching out her red Christmas sweater even further, and distracting me for a second too long. With a grunt, I force my attention back to the road.

"Besides, why do I need to know?" she adds. "Aren't you taking care of everything?"

I take back what I said earlier. *That* is fucking music to my ears.

"I am. You don't need to worry about anything, but if you'd like to know, I'll tell you. It's on Mackinac Island in Michigan."

Her lack of response makes it clear the words mean nothing to her, so I explain further.

"The whole island is a national historic site. Gorgeous old houses. I got hired to do a job up there twenty years ago, when Bear Construction was new, and I fell in love with the place. Fiona came to visit and she liked it too."

Maxine's expression tightens just slightly, but if I'm going to share stories from my past, they're going to occasionally include Fiona; that's just a fact. Just like hers will include Josh. We have to accept that.

"We visited a few times after that," I continue. "I made friends on the restoration committee and started doing volunteer woodwork during the off-season. After a few years, when one of the old houses went on the market, I had enough credibility in the community to get approval.

It's almost impossible to buy unless you're a year-round resident, but they made an exception for me."

"So it's your vacation home."

"That's right. We spent time up there every summer and a lot of Christmases too. It was our favourite spot. Sam learned to ride a bike there. Jamie used to wake up early just to feed the horses down at the town stables."

She stares out the window, her jaw still a little tighter than usual. "If it's a special place for your family, maybe I shouldn't be going there."

"That's exactly *why* I want you there," I counter. "I want new memories in that house, memories that don't include Fiona. I want you there because what we're building matters to me, and I want that house to hold part of the story too."

She doesn't say anything for a while, but her hand finds mine over the console and squeezes gently.

The rest of the drive is uneventful, though clouds are gathering by the time we reach the ferry terminal. We'll leave the truck here, and I grab both our bags as we head towards the boat.

"There are really no cars on the island at all?" Maxine asks curiously. The more I told her about Mackinac on the drive, the more intrigued she became. I know she's going to love it.

"Emergency vehicles, but that's it. Most people get around by snowmobile."

She glances at the bags over my shoulder. "What do we do with our bags?"

"Do you think I don't have a plan?" I ask, letting my voice take on the firmer edge I know will get to her. It works. Her eyes roll, but she's grinning as the ferry pulls away from the mainland.

The trip is slow in the winter and we mostly stay inside where it's warm, but as we approach the island, we duck out onto the deck for the final approach. Maxine's cheeks are flushed with cold and wonder, her eyes wide as the island grows closer, rooftops and treetops dusted in white, and the steeple of the old church peeking through like something out of a snow globe.

Waiting for us at the dock is a horse-drawn carriage with sleigh bells and thick wool blankets. Maxine clutches my arm in excitement, letting out a delighted laugh.

"This is straight out of a Christmas movie."

"Does that make me the romantic lead?" I ask sarcastically.

She purses her lips, pretending to think about it. "You've definitely got the brooding part nailed."

"Watch it, sweetheart."

My warning only makes her smile more as our driver helps her up into the carriage.

The house is up the hill with sprawling views over the harbour, but it also makes a pretty impressive sight on its own with its wraparound porch, gables, and hand-restored trim. White siding, forest-green shutters, and a red front door greet us, already adorned with a pine wreath. Inside, the warmth hits us immediately along with the fresh smell of pine from the towering Christmas tree in the front room and garlands draped over the banister.

Maxine walks through slowly, taking it all in. Fresh logs sit stacked beside the fireplace, and I kneel to get a fire going. We're going to need it tonight.

"Who decorated all of this?" she asks.

"I pay someone from the town to get it ready for me. We're stocked up with food too, but for tonight, we'll order something in. It's been a long day already."

She kneels beside me as the fire crackles to life, her eyes dancing in the growing glow.

"I didn't expect it to be this... beautiful," she whispers. "It feels like a dream."

I turn towards her, but she's still watching the fire.

"I actually used to fantasize about this, you know," she says, soft and half-laughing. "A cozy cabin in the snow, a roaring fire, and sex on a bearskin rug. The usual clichés."

She has my full attention now. "Oh, really?"

Her cheeks flush a little but she nods, her eyes darting over to meet mine. "It always sounded so romantic."

I don't know about romance, but her naked on a rug in front of the fire is definitely an image I'd like to see in the flesh.

Leaning closer to her, I let my voice drift into its lowest register.

"Maybe it's time to show me just how much you missed me. Are you going to be good for me tonight, or do I need to remind you how I deal with brats?"

She pretends to think that over for a second before shooting me a mischievous grin. "Why don't you find out for yourself?"

And just like that, the fire blazing beside us takes a back seat to the one igniting between us.

Chapter Thirty-Nine

The fire crackles behind me, casting flickering shadows across the walls. The afternoon sun is disappearing fast and we haven't turned on all the lights inside yet, but the fire provides just the right amount of light. Its warmth seeps into my skin, mingling with the heat building under the surface.

Reid pushes to his feet and circles me slowly, rolling up the sleeves of his flannel shirt. My pulse is already racing, a quick, steady beat throbbing through my whole body. When he reaches down and removes the belt from his jeans with one hand, I have to bite my lip to keep from whimpering.

It might have only been a couple of days apart, but I missed him. I missed *this*.

"Take your sweater off," he orders to start. "Leave the bra on."

My lips twitch as I try not to smile. "That might be a problem."

"Why?" he demands.

"Because you said we had to take a break, so I couldn't message you last night asking which underwear to wear."

I leave it there, letting him put the pieces together for himself.

It doesn't take him long.

"Are you telling me you haven't been wearing underwear all day?"

His voice is so tight, it must physically hurt him to squeeze the words out.

"You punished me for wearing the wrong ones the other day," I remind him. "I didn't want to risk picking the wrong thing again."

I blink up at him as innocently as possible, remembering that he told me once that it drives him crazy.

"You…"

I know I've struck gold when his words choke off and he forces out a hard breath to bring himself back under control. I've got him right where I want him.

"Should I still take my sweater off, or…?"

I reach down and lift the bottom of it just enough to reveal a sliver of skin, enough to give him a taste of what's there, almost giddy in my boldness. Not only did I miss him, I missed who I am with him.

"Take it all off and lie down on your back. Now."

Victory tastes sweet, but it's also short-lived. As soon as I'm naked and on the throw blanket that Reid grabbed off the couch for me to lie on, he wraps his belt around my wrists and pulls them up over my head. The other end, he loops around one leg of the heavy coffee table between the fireplace and the sofa. When I give a testing tug on my arms, there's no give at all.

With calm, measured movements, he walks over to the bags we brought and pulls out a toy I haven't seen before. At first, I almost mistake it for a microphone, but reality quickly sets in when he starts fiddling with the settings and the large head of it begins to vibrate. *Oh, shit.*

"Knees up," Reid orders. "Legs spread."

Since I'm already in trouble, I do as he says. Maybe not wearing underwear today wasn't such a good idea after all.

The first touch of the vibrating head against my clit makes me gasp, but it's not rough. The intensity is low, the vibration gentle and constant. My muscles relax as Reid fixes the vibrator in position, stands back up and pulls out his phone.

"Wh-what are you doing?" I stammer.

Is he going to record this?

Is it wrong that the idea kind of turns me on?

That's not his answer, though. "Setting a timer. You get a minute at that speed, a minute at the medium speed, and a minute at the top speed. Every time you move, the timer resets and adds another thirty seconds. Got it?"

Quite honestly, no. The sensation against my skin is distracting me. The wide head of the wand covers not only my clit but down towards my pussy as well, the friction barely a tease. I need *more.*

"Why does it have to be so complicated?" I complain, and the buzzing against my clit suddenly ramps up. With another gasp, my thighs clench and Reid lets out a disappointed *tsk.*

"You moved. Now, it's 90 seconds at this speed."

"Wait. What? How did you..."

The vibration accelerates again, just for a second, and that's when I finally see the remote in his other hand. *That fucker.*

"Stay still."

"I didn't move, I..."

Buzz. Again, the speed changes, and again, my hips buck. Not even a lot, just an involuntary twitch.

"Two minutes now."

"This is..."

He gives me a look that stills my words in my throat. "Think long and hard about what you want to say next."

After thinking about it for a few seconds, I decide to stay silent and Reid nods in approval.

"Good call."

I make it through the two minutes at the lowest speed, and the vibrations intensify. I can't even tell if it feels better or worse. My body is throbbing, my legs aching from holding still. My hands grip the belt that's tying them together, desperate for something to anchor me.

When a minute passes and it goes to the next level, my hips shift. Instantly, the vibrator drops back to the slowest speed. "Two minutes at each speed now."

A dozen curse words fly to the tip of my tongue but I close my eyes and take a few deep breaths, focusing on the sensation between my legs and the heat of the fire on my bare skin, the scent of fresh pine from the Christmas tree and the softness of the blanket beneath me. When my eyes open again, Reid is watching me with something close to pride.

"There you go," he murmurs. "Stop fighting it."

This time, when the vibration increases, a small whimper is all I allow myself. Two minutes pass with Reid's eyes on me and the tension in my body coiling tighter. My jaw clenches as the rhythm increases again. I want it to stop and I want it to be even harder. Most of all, I want to come. *Fuck*, I want to come.

As the seconds tick by, the sound of a zipper fills the air. It must be Reid's pants, and although I want to lift my head for a better view, I don't dare. Instead, I listen to the rustle of the fabric as he pulls off his clothes, anticipation building even higher with each beat of my heart.

It must be getting close. *I'm* getting close. I just need…

The timer beeps on Reid's phone, and before I can react, he's kneeling between my legs. He presses the wand down onto my clit, twisting it 180 degrees, the handle now flat across my stomach, and without any warning, he drives his cock into me.

"Oh, fuck!"

Filled with him, the wand still on my clit between us, I fall apart. My orgasm crashes down hard, my arms thrashing against their restraint, my legs trembling around the solid man on top of me.

I always knew he would feel good inside me, but after our conversation on Sunday, knowing that he's emotionally invested in this as well as physically, it feels even better than I dreamed to finally have him buried there, his thick cock stretching me in the best way.

"Fuck, yes," Reid groans as my pussy clenches him tight. At last, he removes the wand, letting him settle down onto me fully, and he begins to fuck me like he's trying to drive me straight through the floor.

Each thrust is punishing, deep and possessive, and I cry out his name along with some other noises that might be words, but I honestly can't tell. My brain has stopped recognizing anything other than the pleasure of Reid inside me. One large, rough hand, finds my breast, palming and squeezing it while he continues to fuck me like his life depends on it

This isn't the romantic lovemaking I imagined in front of the fire, but it's so much better.

His hand leaves my breast and comes to my face. Two fingers press against my lips and my mouth parts for him, sucking as hard on them as if they were his cock.

"You wanted this," he growls above me. "And you're going to take every second of it."

I am. I'll take it all and beg you for more if you'll let me.

I can't say that because my tongue is wrapped around his fingers, but I nod up at him, and Reid groans. Pulling his wet fingers from my mouth, he slips his hand between us to find my still-sensitive clit.

"Show me how much you want this," he commands, and I arch up into him as a second orgasm hits. It's slower than the first one, but it lasts longer, hitting me in rolling waves, and I'm only vaguely aware of Reid's pace slowing, his breathing ragged as he comes deep inside me.

He stills, his weight pressing me into the floor, and for a moment, there's no noise but the fire and our breathing. When he finally lifts his head, his icy-blue eyes are uncharacteristically soft and satisfied.

"That's one new memory for the house. I can't wait to make some more."

Chapter Forty

~Reid~

After we're both spent and breathless, I help Maxine to her feet. On wobbly legs, she leans into me, trusting me to guide her.

I'll never take that trust for granted.

"C'mon," I murmur, pressing a kiss to her temple. "Let's get you cleaned up."

In the bathroom, she leans against the counter, flushed and relaxed, her body humming in the afterglow as I wipe her down gently with a warm cloth. She lets me fuss over her, the playful brat temporarily subdued. Once I'm satisfied, I wrap her in a thick blanket and carry her back to the sofa, settling her down with a pillow behind her head.

"You need rest," I tell her, brushing her hair back from her forehead. "Just a short nap while I unpack."

She murmurs something that sounds like agreement, her eyelids already fluttering closed.

I grab her discarded clothes and poke at the fire before leaving the room. In the kitchen, I grab my phone and call the number pinned to the fridge. The woman on the other end picks up with a bright voice, even as I hear wind howling faintly through her line.

"Sally's Kitchen, hello?"

"Still delivering up the hill?" I ask, glancing towards the large windows at the back of the house. Outside, snow swirls fast. While Maxine and I were busy in front of the fire, the wind picked up.

"For now," she replies cheerfully. "But it's lucky you called when you did. Looks like we might get a full blizzard tonight."

I place an order for supper, big enough for the two of us and some leftovers, and thank her, hanging up just as another gust rattles the panes. The old construction might sound creaky at times but I know it's solid. It'll keep the cold out and keep us warm and safe inside, no matter how bad it gets out there.

In the bedroom, I begin unpacking our things, sorting them into drawers and shelves. I brought a few things for Maxine along with the clothes she brought herself, so her belongings end up taking up a large portion of the dresser, but I don't mind. The sight of her belongings mixed with mine looks *right*.

When I'm finished, I pause in the hallway and glance into the smaller room beside it, the one that used to belong to the kids. The paint inside is still a little chipped from where Sam taped posters to the wall, and the bookshelf holds a few forgotten paperbacks, dog-eared and sun-bleached.

One hand on the doorframe, it almost feels like if I squint hard enough, I'll see Jamie tucked up in one of the twin beds, or Sam reading with a flashlight under the covers of the other one.

The house holds plenty of good memories and I don't want to erase that, but I know that I can't go back either. Having Maxine here doesn't replace anything that came before, it just adds another layer to what this house means to me.

The same is true of our relationship in general, and I hope Sam will be able to see that when she's had time to adjust to it.

A knock at the door startles me out of my musing.

As I reach the end of the hall, Maxine stirs on the couch, eyes blinking open. "What was that?"

"Food," I reply automatically, already heading towards the door. "I'll get it."

It isn't until I unlock the door, my hand already on the knob that I realize it's too soon for the food to be here already, especially in this weather. But who else would be here?

I open the door and everything seems to stop.

"Hey, Dad." Sam smiles up at me, cheeks pink from the cold, bundled in a thick coat and scarf. Josh stands beside her, holding two suitcases, his eyes focused on my knees. "We just made the last ferry, they're shutting everything down!"

The wind whips flakes of snow around them. At the end of the driveway, a snowmobile speeds away. That explains how they got here but doesn't begin to touch on *why* they're here.

"Dad?" Sam's smile turns a little bemused at my lack of response. "Can we come in? It's freezing out here."

In? They can't come in, but with the ferry shut down and no vacant hotels on the island at this time of year, I can't send them away either.

I throw a glance over my shoulder to the living room where Maxine is staring at me with wide, horrified eyes over the back of the couch. From this angle, it's not immediately apparent that she's only wearing a blanket, but I know she is. At least I grabbed her clothes earlier, but fuck, this is a disaster waiting to happen. She also can't get to the bedroom to get dressed without walking directly past the front door.

I'll have to give her as much help as I can, so I step forward, blocking the doorway with my body as much as possible. Sam takes a surprised step back as I motion behind my back for Maxine to move.

I just hope she understands what I'm trying to tell her without saying a word.

"You're supposed to be with your mother," I point out uselessly.

"We were, but she told us you were coming up here. Complained about it a lot, actually. And since they couldn't come here, she and Connor decided to go to a casino resort instead. Josh and I didn't want to do that, so I thought it would be a great opportunity for you two to get to know each other better. And now you won't have to spend Christmas alone either. It's perfect."

It's very much *not* perfect. How typical of Fiona to change her plans without any consideration for anyone else. And what does Sam really want? Last time we spoke, she was still stiff and awkward following her discovery that I was seeing someone. Now, she's acting like everything's normal. Is that for my benefit, or Josh's?

Either way, I still can't see any alternative. They're going to have to stay here, at least tonight.

Leaning back, I glance into the living room again. The couch is now empty, no sign of Maxine. She must have taken the hint, so I reluctantly step aside.

"Get in out of the cold."

"Finally," Sam laughs, stepping past me and stamping her boots on the rug at the door to shake off the snow.

Josh follows her in, giving me a nod. "Nice to see you, Mr Larson."

He might not be saying that in a minute.

When the door closes behind them, I break the first piece of news to them. "You need to know that I'm not alone here."

Sam freezes halfway through unzipping her winter coat, the smile falling from her face. "You mean..."

"The woman you met the other day," I confirm bluntly. "She's spending Christmas here with me."

My daughter throws a look back at the door, as if debating whether leaving is an option, but she quickly reaches the same conclusion I did: there's simply nowhere for them to go.

"Oh," is all she manages when she turns back around.

But I'm not done yet. "There's more."

"What else?" she asks warily.

I don't get a chance to answer. The floor creaks, and everyone's heads turn to see Maxine walk back into the room, dressed in her red Christmas sweater, looking flushed and defiant and gorgeous.

Josh's eyes nearly bug out of his head as he stammers, "M-Max?"

Chapter Forty-One

~**Maxine**~

The second I step into the living room, I know the storm outside has nothing on the one about to unleash inside this house.

Josh stutters my name and his face twists with disbelief as his eyes rake over me. Sam's head snaps in my direction, the colour draining from her face.

So much for a peaceful Christmas.

When I sprinted back to the bedroom while Reid covered for me, I debated crawling under the covers and hiding there until they left. This is *not* the Christmas getaway I signed up for. If there could be anything worse than spending the holiday with my ex-boyfriend and the girl he cheated on me with, I can't imagine it.

However, realization quickly sank in that hiding wouldn't solve anything. I've been trying that for weeks now, and it's only getting more complicated by the day.

The time had come to get it all out in the open, so I pulled my clothes on and strode back to the living room with all the confidence I could muster.

Now, I keep my chin up, refusing to shrink under the weight of either of their stares. I haven't done anything wrong and I won't act like I have. *They're* the ones who should be apologizing to *me*.

"Hi," I say evenly. "We weren't expecting company."

Josh takes a step forward, squinting at me like he's trying to figure out if I'm a hallucination. "What... what are you doing here?"

It's the first time I've seen him since our break-up, the first time in weeks that I've laid eyes on the man I used to think I was going to spend my life with, and I feel... *nothing.* Not a hint of attraction or a twinge of regret. Looking at him, I see a selfish man-child who took far more than he gave during our years together.

I see Reid's polar opposite.

As he crosses my mind, I glance over at Reid and find him watching me with a measured, steady look that conveys so much without him saying a word. He's giving me the space to answer how I want to, letting me take the lead, but the second I want backup, he'll be there.

For now, I stick to the basic facts.

"Reid invited me here for Christmas."

Josh's jaw tenses, but it's Sam who speaks up. "Max?" Her eyes dart back and forth between me and Josh with growing dread. "As in your ex-girlfriend Max?"

"That's me." I offer her a tight smile. "Nice to know I did come up in conversation."

I force myself not to look away, not from Sam's wide, betrayed eyes and not from the stunned confusion on Josh's face. Tension thickens in the room until I can almost feel it pressing down on me. Still, I hold my ground. We wouldn't be here if the two of them hadn't started this, so if they're looking for someone to blame for this awkwardness, they can start with a mirror.

Sam recovers first. "Dad, did you know?" she asks, her voice high and tight. "Did you know she and Josh used to be together?"

Reid's jaw tics, but he nods once. "I did. I knew the day we met, but Maxine didn't find out that you're my daughter until later."

The words hit like a slap. Sam blinks several times in quick succession, as if she expected him to deny it and doesn't know what to do with the alternative.

"Oh my God," she breathes, her voice cracking. She shakes her head, her cheeks flushing as the tension in her frame builds into something that can't be contained. "I... I need a few minutes."

She doesn't wait for anyone to answer before turning on her heel and stalking down the hallway. I'm not sure where she's going, but she knows this house better than I do. A door slams a second later.

Josh exhales slowly, as if waking from a dream. Or more likely a nightmare.

"I guess this is why you asked me for that reference," he says to Reid, shaking his head the same way Sam just did. "You knew she wouldn't give me one and you wanted me to embarrass myself."

Reference? His words make no sense to me but Reid seems to know what he's talking about. He stares Josh down as he bites out each word. "I didn't need to make you embarrass yourself. You seem to be capable of doing that just fine on your own. You cheated on Maxine, and I don't believe for a second you wouldn't do it again to Sam, so don't pretend you're some kind of victim here."

Josh flinches beneath Reid's controlled anger but doesn't back down when he really, really should.

Instead, he turns to me. "So, this is your way of getting revenge?"

"Are you seriously making this about *you*?" I scoff. "I met a charming, handsome, talented man who actually knows how to treat a woman, but I only decided to date him because it would annoy you? That's delusional."

Reid's hand covers his mouth and I could swear he's trying not to laugh.

"But you barely know him," Josh tries to argue. "You can't..."

"I wouldn't say another word if I were you," Reid interrupts, any trace of humour gone as he steps forward. "Maxine didn't do anything but move on with someone who actually sees her worth. She only did that because you chose someone else over her. And that someone else is currently upset, and instead of comforting her, you're standing her making an ass of yourself even further. Go and check on your girlfriend."

Josh's shoulders drop and, for a moment, he just looks... *tired.* Thankfully, he listens and stalks off down the hall in search of Sam.

Silence settles over the living room and I exhale slowly, tension draining out of me like air from a bicycle tire.

"You okay?" Reid asks.

I do my best to smile. "It could have been worse."

His hand finds the small of my back as he chuckles. "Give it time. We're just getting started."

I lean into his chest, inhaling his cedar and spice scent. Only when I'm resting against his solid bulk do I realize I've been trembling. "I'm sorry you're in the middle of this."

"I chose to be here," he reminds me. "And things *will* calm down. It's a shock to them right now, but we're going to be stuck here together for the next day at least, depending on the weather. We'll have a chance to talk again when they've gotten used to the idea."

I honestly don't see how this ends well, but I trust Reid.

Outside, the wind howls. The fire next to us crackles in the hearth. But the only sound I care about is the steady beating of his heart against my ear, promising me that no matter what comes next, he's not going anywhere.

Chapter Forty-Two

The knock on the door a few minutes later startles us both. Maxine and I have been sitting on the couch while I explained to her why Sam and Josh need to stay with us until the storm lifts, and although she doesn't love the idea, she understands.

Me? I'm torn between worrying about Sam, disliking Josh more with every second I spend in the guy's presence, and basking in the pride of hearing Maxine stand up for herself with him and tell him our relationship has nothing to do with him.

She's told me that before, but it hits differently when she says it so confidently to *him*.

"That'll be the food," I murmur, and Maxine lifts her head from where it's been resting against my shoulder and gives me a faint, rueful smile.

"Do you want me to get it?"

"No, I'll get it. Why don't you head into the kitchen and find the plates in the cupboard beside the fridge. Grab four."

Her eyebrows lift, but she nods without comment, a quiet agreement that we need to at least aim for civility.

It's a good thing I ordered extra food tonight.

I open the front door to find Sally's son on the porch, red-faced from the cold and layered in enough wool to insulate a house.

"You're our last one tonight," he says, handing over two bags. "If the power goes out, light some candles and stay close to the fire."

"We'll manage," I assure him, tipping generously. As the snow whips around me, I hope we won't have to test that theory.

Inside, Maxine is already setting the table in the dining room. Her movements are graceful but tight, a clear sign of the storm brewing under her skin.

"Where are the glasses?" she asks.

"In there." I gesture to the hutch behind her, an antique I found and fixed up. "We'll have wine. I'll go get the others."

The floorboards creak beneath my weight as I walk back down the hall to the bedrooms. The door to the room Sam and Jamie shared as kids sits closed, murmured voices going quiet as I get closer.

My knuckles rap softly on the door. "We just got supper delivered. There's enough for you."

"I'm not hungry," is Sam's muffled reply.

My jaw sets. "This is the only food available tonight. If you don't eat now, you're not eating."

A little harsh maybe, but hiding in her room isn't going to fix anything. She's an adult now; we all are, and we need to act that way.

By the time I get back, Maxine has the table ready. Roast chicken, mashed potatoes, spiced carrots and warm rolls make my mouth water as I open the containers and push them into the middle of the table. From the wine cabinet, I grab a bottle of Pinot Noir and pour out our two glasses to start with.

Maxine and I are just sitting down next to each other when Sam and Josh appear in the doorway. Sam enters first, her face neutral in the way people get when they've decided to be polite but aren't fooling anyone. Josh trails behind, hands stuffed in his pockets, looking like he'd rather be anywhere else. They take the two seats opposite us, leaving the head and foot of the table free.

The table is wide enough that it creates physical distance, but not emotional. That kind of space is harder to find right now.

Sam reaches for the chicken at the same moment that Maxine does, and both immediately pull their hands back. I break the stalemate by picking up the container and handing it to Maxine.

"Start with the potatoes," I instruct Sam.

We serve ourselves in silence until Maxine clears her throat. "This looks great. Are there a lot of restaurants on the island?"

"We always get food from Sally's Kitchen when we arrive," Sam answers before I can say anything. "It's a tradition."

She looks at Josh as she says it, like she's having a conversation with him instead of with Maxine, but I can read between the lines easily enough. She wants to send Maxine a message that we have history in this house, history that doesn't include her.

It's not the first time lately she's reminded me of her mother.

"There are quite a lot of restaurants," I tell Maxine since Sam didn't actually answer the question. "More in the summer, which is prime tourist season. This time of year, less than half of them are open."

Sam reaches for the bottle of wine I left on the table, pouring a glass for herself and one for Josh. She drains half of hers in one gulp.

"If this weather keeps up, they won't be open at all," I continue. "But we'll be fine here. We're stocked with groceries, and even if the power goes out, we have the fire."

"Is that likely? That the power's going to go out?" Josh asks, keeping his eyes fixed on his plate.

I'm not sure if he's talking to me or Sam, but I answer. "Hard to say. It does happen, but like I said, we'll be fine. These old houses are built tough."

When no one responds to that, the conversation withers. Everyone sticks to eating in silence that's far from comfortable. Every fork scrape is loud. Every glance is loaded. Maxine takes tiny bites, and I'd be surprised if she's even tasting the food at all.

Fuck, this isn't at all the getaway I wanted.

After a painful minute or two of awkward silence, I try again.

"Did you already open your presents at your mom's?" I ask my daughter.

"Some of them," she answers, her gaze darting to Maxine before returning to me. "I got Josh Bears tickets. He's never been to a game."

Maxine stiffens beside me, obviously taking that as some kind of slight. From the smirk that momentarily flashes across Sam's face, she meant it as one too.

But Maxine quickly fires back. "Reid actually just took me to my first game this past weekend. It was incredible."

Her hand comes to rest on my arm as she says it, a possessive little gesture that makes Sam's nostrils flare. My grip tightens on my fork.

Josh reaches for his wine glass. "You were sitting next to some blonde woman on TV, not... him."

The way he says the word 'him' like it's an insult does nothing to help calm things down. I step in before things get out of hand.

"That was Olivia Stamer. Noah invited us to his box at the game."

Josh's jaw drops. "The guy who owns Stamer Hotels?"

That's right, you little piece of shit, is what I'd like to say, but as the oldest person here, I need to set an example.

"Yeah. I've done some work with them in the past and might be doing more soon."

Sam blinks over at me with a feigned innocence that I immediately clock as being insincere. "Oh, is that for the new hotel in Denver? It's going to take a few months, right?"

Fuck.

Next to me, Maxine coughs like something got caught in her throat. I grab her wine glass and offer it to her but she waves it off. "You're going to Denver?" she asks when the coughing stops, and the hurt in her voice is unmistakable.

I haven't had a chance to talk to her about it yet, between our argument on Sunday and the unfinished business between her and Josh. The timing hasn't felt right. But it's something I absolutely want to discuss with her, and now, it sounds like I've been hiding it.

Sam appears to be trying not to gloat but failing. "Didn't he tell you?"

I fix her with a hard stare. As much as I love my daughter, I'm not liking this version of her at all. "Who told *you*?"

She shrugs. "I heard about it somewhere," she says to me before refocusing on Maxine. "I guess you don't know each other that well yet. How long has this been going on anyway?"

Her index finger flicks between the two of us dismissively, and Maxine sucks in a breath. When she speaks, her words come out jagged and sharp. "It started after Josh and I broke up, which is more than anyone can say for your relationship."

That shuts Sam up, and even though it's entirely deserved, I can't help feeling bad when her head drops.

To my surprise, Josh actually steps in on Sam's behalf. "Max, don't be mean to her because you're mad at me. She didn't..."

He trails off there but I'm not about to let that go. Sam told me Josh misrepresented the state of his relationship when they got together, and I want to hear from the horse's mouth if that's true. "She didn't what?"

"Don't bother," Sam mutters, pushing her chair back from the table. "This is useless."

With that declaration, she leaves her meal half-finished and heads back towards the bedroom. Josh casts a longing look down at his plate, but after a few beats, he does the right thing and follows her out of the room.

His footsteps have barely receded when Maxine also gets up. "I think I need a few minutes alone too."

I catch her by the wrist, my grip loose but unyielding. "We're going to talk about Denver. Nothing's settled yet. She was just trying to rile you up."

Although she nods, her face remains tight. "I know. I'll help you clean up. I just need a minute."

"Don't worry about that. Why don't you have a bath in the ensuite bathroom? Try to relax. There's no rush."

She blows out a breath before nodding. "That sounds perfect, actually."

"Of course it does. I always know what you need."

For the first time since Sam and Josh arrived, I catch a glimpse of a real smile, but it's gone again a second later as Maxine leaves the dining room and I'm left alone with three empty chairs, a supper quickly going cold, and no fucking idea what to do next.

Chapter Forty-Three

The bathwater has gone from scalding to merely warm, but I can't seem to move. My fingers trail slowly over the surface, chasing the tiny ripples my legs make beneath the water. My skin is pink from the heat, my heart heavy from everything else.

The conversation from the dinner table still echoes in my head, every sharp-edged comment Sam made scratched into my brain. After literally stealing my boyfriend, she has the nerve to act like *she's* the victim here? And even though Reid didn't take her side, he didn't fully take mine either.

Not that I want him to have to choose. I don't. I just wish he didn't have to be *her* father.

The door creaks behind me, and I sit up with a startled splash, my heart instantly hammering. *What the fuck?*

A second later, Reid steps inside, calm and unapologetic, a towel over one arm. "Don't panic. I have a master key for the house. No one else is coming in."

He flips the lock on the door again and I sink back down, my pulse still racing. "You nearly gave me a heart attack."

He grabs a chair from next to the wall and pulls it up to the side of the tub, his eyes scanning my face. "How are you feeling?"

"Fine," I try to bluff, but the stern look he gives me makes the lie wither in my throat. "Alright, not so fine."

He brushes a damp strand of hair behind my ear. "Talk to me."

Letting my head fall back against the edge of the tub, I blow out a cleansing breath. "I know you have my back, but she's your daughter, Reid. I'm a random woman you met not even a month ago. There's no comparison."

I'm not proud of it, but I keep waiting for the other shoe to drop, for Reid to decide that no matter how he feels about me, it's just not worth the fallout with his daughter.

He doesn't say anything for a beat, just runs a finger slowly down the side of my neck. His touch leaves a trail of heat behind it, and I shiver beneath the cooling water.

"No, there isn't any comparison," he finally says. "Sam will always be my daughter, but she's also an adult with a life of her own. I can offer her advice, give her my opinion, but I can't tell her what to do anymore, and she can't tell me what to do either. If she had a legitimate reason to dislike you, I'd consider her point of view. But you haven't done a damn thing wrong, Maxine."

Even though I already know that, it doesn't hurt to hear him say it.

"She's jealous that you have my interest, and she's worried that you'll replace her in my life. That's the only reason I can come up with for the way she behaved tonight. It doesn't make it any better, but she's not usually like that."

"I'm not trying to replace her."

"I know that," he assures me. "And you couldn't, because the place I want you to hold is completely separate from hers. She has a life of her own, but I want you to have one with me."

My heart kicks in my chest at the casual, confident way he states that, as if it's a completely normal thing to say to someone.

"I'll talk to her," he promises. "But first, lie back. Let me take your mind off all of it for a little while."

The shift in his tone is subtle but unmistakable, and his hand dips lower, trailing over my collarbone and beneath the water. I suck in a breath as Reid rolls up his sleeve.

How this man can make me go from listless to aching for him in a matter of seconds really should be studied. It can't be natural.

Firm fingers slip over my nipple as he cups my breast beneath the water. Rather than lingering, they drift lower, teasing over my stomach, and sliding between my legs. His touch is light but certain, the movement slow and coaxing.

I need no encouragement to spread my legs further, my hips instinctively lifting to seek him.

His chuckle warms me like sunshine on my skin. "Greedy."

"Only for you." A gasp cuts off my words as his fingers part me, circling my clit.

"And do you think anyone has the right to tell us that we can't do this?" he demands.

My breath quickens with each movement, the pressure of his hand almost unbearable. "N-no."

He hums in agreement, his fingers dipping even lower to tease at my entrance. "Who's the only person who gets to control your pleasure?"

"Me?" I guess, only half paying attention. His fingers are far too distracting.

A thick finger pushes into me, hard, impaling me on his hand. "Try again."

It takes a second for my brain to catch up and realize what answer he's looking for. "You."

"Damn right," he mutters, his finger swirling inside me until it presses down on my g-spot and I have to clamp a hand over my mouth to stop from crying out.

I have no idea how thick the walls are in this house, and we don't need an audience.

Reid works me over slowly, his fingers alternating between my clit and my pussy, teasing and tormenting me until I barely remember there's anyone else in this house. Or in this world, for that matter.

"Please," I whimper. "Please let me come."

For once, he goes easy on me, giving in to my request as his expert hand finds just the right combination of touch and tempo to send me crashing over the edge into my orgasm.

The now-cool water laps against my heated skin, my heart pounding as the room re-shapes around me.

Reid's hand leaves me, and he picks up the soap to wash his fingers before leaning in and kissing my temple.

"Feel better?"

"Much," I murmur happily.

"Good." He rises to his feet, pushing the chair back against the wall. "I'm going to go talk to Sam in the living room. If you want to speak to Josh alone, now's your chance."

A sigh escapes me as I pull myself upright. There's no good time to reopen an old wound, but maybe the only way to heal is to stop pretending it doesn't still sting. "Might as well get it over with."

His hand squeezes my shoulder. "It might not feel like it, but this is progress."

He's right: it doesn't feel like it.

But as he closes the door behind him and I start draining the tub, I'm more determined than ever to put Josh firmly in my past, where he belongs.

Chapter Forty-Four

~**Reid**~

The house is quieter now, the kind of quiet that settles over a place when no one's quite sure what to say next. The storm still howls outside, wind rushing over the roof and rattling old panes, but inside it's just the fire, crackling low and steady in the hearth, and the murmur of voices behind Sam's bedroom door.

I rap softly on the wood with my knuckles, not saying anything until the door creaks open and my daughter's somber face appears.

"C'mon," I say softly. "Let's go sit by the fire and talk."

Her blue eyes stare up at me, wary and uncertain, but eventually, she glances back over her shoulder to Josh. "I'll be back in a few minutes."

She follows me down the hallway without a word, arms crossed tightly over her chest and feet padding softly on the hardwood. In the fire's glow, we sit down on the couch, a good arm's length apart. I don't push her to move closer, nor do I start talking right away. Silence stretches between us until she's ready to speak.

Staring into the flames, she eventually does. "I always loved coming up here."

The words are neutral, and though she might be building to something, I don't try to anticipate it. I respond to her statement as it stands. "I remember. You and Jamie used to spend weeks planning for it and begging me to buy twice as many marshmallows as we needed."

If I squint hard enough, I can still see their heads, one blonde and one dark, as they sat side-by-side, roasting their marshmallows over the fire.

"He always burned mine," she complains, just as she did back then.

Those marshmallows summed up my kids in a nutshell: Sam wanting to do it the right way, taking her time to toast each side perfectly, while Jamie got impatient and stuck them straight in the flames until they caught on fire. He'd grab Sam's arm and pull hers down too so they'd both have the charred black version.

"I think he thought he was helping you. He didn't know you preferred your way."

She huffs a soft laugh, but it quickly evaporates, swallowed by the heavier thing sitting between us.

"I remember hanging stockings here," she says after a few more beats of silence. "Writing letters to Santa at the table. You'd drink cocoa with us and pretend not to see us trying to peek at the presents."

"You always confessed afterwards anyway," I remind her. "I could always count on you to tell me the truth."

Sam draws her knees up onto the couch, curling in tighter. "Until now, you mean."

It isn't anger that makes her voice tremble. It's fear, and a touch of vulnerability. A crack in the tough façade she's been wearing all day.

"Sam…"

She keeps going, not giving me a chance to interject. "I keep thinking about the conversation we had when I told you about Josh. I knew you were disappointed. I could see it in your face."

I nod slowly, not denying it.

Her eyes are glassy but fixed on me. "You'd never looked at me that way before, and I know how it ended between you and Mom. You walked away after she cheated and you didn't look back. You barely talk now, even when we're all in the same room."

"What happened between us doesn't…"

"I know," she interrupts me again. "But part of me keeps thinking: if you could cut her out so easily, what's stopping you from doing the same to me?"

My throat tightens, and for a moment, I don't trust myself to speak. I had no idea that thought had even crossed her mind, and as crazy as it sounds to me, it obviously feels like a real possibility to her.

After a deep breath, I make myself answer. "You're not your mother, and this isn't the same thing. Does it bother me that you got involved with a man who was already in a relationship? Yes. Does it mean I don't love you anymore? Of course not. We all make mistakes. And you *do* know it was a mistake, don't you?"

Her answer comes without hesitation. "Of course. I thought they were already over. That's what he told me, but I guess I should have asked more questions. Instead, I kept making excuses about why it was okay because I wanted him. I kept defending him, and myself, so I wouldn't have to face it."

I reach over and place my hand on her knee. She flinches, but doesn't pull away. "That right there? That's why you're nothing like your mother. She never regretted it, never apologized, never accepted that she might have been wrong. But you don't have to be that way. I don't expect you to change the past, just own your decisions and do better going forward."

A shaky breath shudders out of her, as if she really thought I might say otherwise. "Okay."

I give her knee a squeeze before pulling my hand back, and together, we watch the fire a few moments longer. The conversation isn't over, but I know from experience that it's best to let Sam lead so she doesn't feel put on the spot.

It works. Eventually, she clears her throat and speaks again. "I thought you called me out here to yell at me about dinner."

I raise an eyebrow. "Do you think you deserve it?"

A grimace stretches her face. "I don't know, I just... I felt defensive, I guess."

"Around Maxine?"

Sam nods miserably. "She hates me, and I understand that. I wasn't *trying* to hurt her, but I know that doesn't matter. I'm still guilty, and now, it feels like she's using you to get back at me."

There's a lot to unpack there, so I start with her last statement. "I promise you, she isn't with me because of you. As I told you at dinner, she didn't even know I was your dad at first."

The way her nose wrinkles suggests she doesn't fully believe me. "Then how did she even meet you? It's weird."

"It's unlikely," I have to agree. "She saw the person who keyed your car, so we started talking. Things grew from there."

That's not the full truth, of course, but she doesn't need to know *everything*. I'll take that secret to my grave.

"But what do you even have in common?" she asks.

'Getting cheated on' sits on the tip of my tongue, but I swallow it back down. Definitely not the right moment. "We just clicked. There's nothing unusual about it, except that it's always unusual when you meet someone special. And for the record, I don't think she hates you. Even if you didn't really help your case tonight."

Her bottom lip disappears beneath her teeth as she thinks that over. "I just don't see how we're supposed to be in the same room without everything that happened constantly hanging over us."

"It won't be easy," I admit. "And I'm not saying you'll be best friends, but you don't need to be enemies, either. Start with something simpler."

"Like what?"

"How about a truce?"

She nods slowly, eyes flicking back towards the fire. "I guess I can try that."

"Good." I sling my arm over the back of the couch, and Sam relaxes her grip on her knees. Her shoulders begin to lower. "We're all stuck here together for at least a little while longer, so it's a good chance to put it to the test."

We sit that way for a while, just watching the flames dance. The wind still rages outside, but in here, something has eased.

It might not be fixed yet, but it's a start.

265

Chapter Forty-Five

~Maxine~

The hallway creaks beneath my feet as I make my way to the guest room. Maybe I should feel nervous about facing Josh one-on-one, but mostly I just feel... done. Done with beating around the bush, done with bitterness, and very, very done with him.

When I knock on the door, it opens almost immediately. Josh doesn't look surprised to see me, and as I step past him, the scent of his body wash sets off a dozen different memories. He must have showered while I was in the bath. Looking closer, I can see the ends of his hair are still a little damp.

"You here to yell at me?" he asks dryly, watching as I move inside and take a seat on the bottom end of one of the twin beds. Staying standing feels confrontational, so I'd rather sit, even though I don't intend to stay for long.

"I don't think I ever yelled at you," I counter as mildly as possible, and it's true. When we fought, if I sharpened my tone just a little, he would retreat and sulk. We never made it as far as shouting.

He shrugs before flopping down onto the other bed across from me. "Maybe not, but I could always tell when you were unhappy with me. Which was a lot."

I'm starting to feel unhappy with him right now, but I force myself to take a deep breath and stay on topic.

"Look, I'm not here to argue. I just want to talk. Reid thinks it'll help to get some closure since we never really had it out when things ended."

"Reid?" His eyebrows lift as he repeats the name, as if he's never heard it before. "I can't wrap my head around the fact that you're actually dating him. Or even that you're on a first-name basis."

"Well, I am."

And I sure as hell don't call him Mr Larson when he fucks me.

That second part, I keep in my head.

Josh's lips tighten in an unhappy grimace. "Are you the reason he's been so hard on me about the app?"

I blink a couple of times, trying to figure out what he's talking about. Eventually, I have to give up and ask. "What?"

"The business proposal. He said he'd think about investing, but he's dragging his feet and nitpicking everything. I just figured..."

He trails off, eyeing me like I'm supposed to fill in the blanks.

I can only stare at him, genuinely stunned. "You think I'm dating Reid so I can scheme against your tech pitch?" The laugh that I let out isn't kind. "For fuck's sake, Josh. How do you manage to always be so self-centred?"

He frowns as if *I'm* the one who's delusional. "So I'm supposed to believe that this is entirely random? That you're completely over me and dating a guy old enough to be your father, a guy who just happens to be Sam's father, by complete coincidence?"

"Of course I'm over you," I snap. "You think I'm still hung up on a guy who made me handle every adult responsibility while he played video games? A guy who put all the bills in my name so it would be my responsibility? I love that Reid is older because he's *mature*. He takes care of things without me having to ask or remind him, and I love it."

"You always prided yourself on being independent," Josh scoffs. "You made a whole thing out of it."

My tone sharpens. "I *had* to be independent because you gave me no other choice. If I didn't book the appointments or budget the money or clean the apartment, it didn't get done. And I convinced myself I was okay with that until you threw everything away. With Reid, I finally know what I was missing."

That blow lands, and his chest caves inwards. For a split second, I almost feel bad, until I remind myself that we wouldn't be having this conversation if it weren't for the choices he made. So I force down the part of me that always wanted to comfort and support him and I let the words linger between us, waiting for him to make the next move.

"I'm sorry I hurt you," he finally says, eyes darting up to meet mine for only a second before they drop back to the floor. "I know it could have been handled better."

It's not much of an apology, but it's probably the best one I'm going to get, so I move on to getting answers for some of my lingering questions. "How long were you unhappy in our relationship?"

He shifts uncomfortably. "It wasn't unhappiness, exactly, but you were always nagging me. Always telling me what I was doing wrong. I never felt good enough for you."

Maybe if you'd acted like a grown man, I wouldn't have had to treat you like a child.

Again, I keep those words locked up inside, letting him continue.

"When I met Sam, she looked up to me. Believed in me. Made me feel special."

Even though I don't want Josh back, it still stings to be compared to her. Even more so when he adds one more sentence.

"Being with her felt like how it used to be with you, at the beginning."

I fight the reflex to argue with him and really *listen* to what he's saying instead. When I do, I notice something interesting.

"You're using the past tense. Have things changed?"

From the way his face twists, I can tell I'm onto something. "The last week hasn't been great, honestly. Her mom's awful, and Sam keeps pushing me to close this deal with her dad and make him like me, but I can tell he *doesn't* like me. Now, I know why. There's all this pressure and... well, being with you was a lot less stressful."

His lack of self-awareness truly stuns me. "It was less stressful because I did everything for you."

He has the audacity to try to argue that point as he pushes off the bed and comes to sit beside me. "No, I think it's because you're a nurturing person, Max. Maybe I didn't fully appreciate that when we were together, but I see it now. Maybe we just needed some time apart to see how good things were."

I must be hallucinating. There's no way he *actually* just said that.

"This time apart has definitely given me clarity, but that's not the conclusion I came to."

He smiles as if I were making a joke. "Seeing you here today was a shock, but the more I think about it, the more I think maybe it was fate. I mean, what are the odds?"

"Are you drunk?" I know he had some wine at dinner, but that doesn't explain this level of disconnect from reality.

"I know you're trying to say you're over it, but you wouldn't have been so nasty to Sam at dinner if you weren't jealous. You miss me."

"I absolutely do not..."

Before I can finish that sentence, he grabs my shoulder and pulls me towards him. His lips hit mine, too fast for my brain to register it. My breath catches in my throat, body stiff with shock as I sit there, not responding, not kissing back. Not anything.

"Josh?"

The disbelieving voice comes from the doorway and I take advantage of the interruption to shove Josh away as hard as I can.

When I turn to look, Sam is standing there, eyes wide and mouth parted in horror. A single beat passes; a long, impossible second that stretches forever. I'm waiting for Josh to do something, or say *something*, but he just sits there, useless as ever.

Gradually, Sam's expression hardens into one of pain and betrayal that I know all too well. My skin crawls at finding myself in the position of being the one to inflict that pain on someone else.

"This isn't..." I finally stutter out, but it's too late. She turns and bolts back to the living room before I can get out another word.

"Shit," Josh mutters behind me.

No kidding.

Chapter Forty-Six

~Reid~

As soon as I step out of the bathroom, the good mood brought on by my conversation with Sam immediately disappears.

"Sam?" I hear Josh call from the direction of the dining room.

"Her coat's gone," Maxine replies, genuine worry in every syllable.

I stride back towards the living room and they both turn towards me at once.

"What the hell's going on?" I ask, already dreading the answer.

Maxine rushes forward. "She's gone, Reid. I think Sam left."

It takes a second for her words to register, and even when they do, they don't make sense to me. "What?"

"We've searched every room. She's not here."

I don't even bother responding before I whip around and bolt for the front door. The moment I tug it open, a wall of ice-cold air slams into me. A sharp gust sends snow straight into the entryway, and when I glance down, I swear out loud.

Her boots are gone.

I grab my coat from the hook and shove my arms into the sleeves. "Sam!" I shout into the swirling dark, but the wind eats her name almost immediately.

Behind me, Maxine fumbles with her own coat. "I'm so sorry. I didn't hear her leave, but it must have only been a minute or two ago."

I figured as much since I was with her until then. She was heading for her room while I stopped in the bathroom before going to check in with Maxine.

"What the hell happened?" I demand.

Maxine winces while Josh looks anywhere but at me.

She's the one to answer. "Josh kissed me and Sam walked in on it. She must have thought... well, I don't know exactly what she thought but it couldn't have been good."

My eyes immediately dart over to where Josh seems to have shrunk a couple of inches, as if he could will himself to disappear into the floor. "You did *what?*"

Again, it's Maxine who answers, her eyes brimming with guilt and panic. "I didn't want this to happen. It wasn't mutual. I didn't even..."

"I believe you," I interrupt, no hesitation in my voice. We can deal with that bullshit later; right now, I need to find my daughter.

Josh continues to stand there, frozen and useless.

"Why aren't you putting on your coat?" I bark.

"I..."

I grab his coat off the peg and throw it at him hard enough he stumbles back. "You're going out too. If anything happens to her out there, you'll be leaving this island in multiple pieces. Is that clear?"

From the look on his face, he gets the picture. His coat is on by the time I pull on my boots.

We spill out into the storm. The wind howls across the island, sweeping the snow sideways in blinding waves. The trees resemble ghosts, barely outlined through the flurries, and the path that leads down to the harbour is completely covered, making it impossible to tell what's road and what's not.

"We split up," I shout, voice half-swallowed by the gale. "Maxine, head down into the town. Josh, go up the hill. I'll check the back and loop down towards the beach. If you find her, text me and bring her straight back here. Don't waste time, and don't put yourself in danger either."

That last part is mostly directed at Maxine, but they both nod before vanishing into the storm.

I head for the back. There's a pond behind the house that should be frozen by now, but the worst-case scenario I can think of is that she's somehow fallen through the ice. Best to rule that out first. The snow is already halfway up my calf and each step forward takes twice the effort. Wind claws at my face and my breath freezes in the air as I bellow her name again and again.

The only answer is the crunch of my boots and the roar of wind.

Trees sway dangerously along the edge of the woods. Snow blasts sideways in bursts that blind me, forcing me to crouch and shield my eyes. My cheeks are burning from the cold, my eyes watering, but I push forward.

The surface of the pond is undisturbed, no footprints and no breaks in the snow.

She's not here, thank fuck.

With that fear put to bed, I start to head down the back path to the beach. It's not easy to see, but I know it's there, and Sam would know it too. She's taken it enough times to remember the way.

As I trudge along, my lungs burning, I try to put myself in her shoes. It isn't hard. I know *exactly* how it feels to walk in on someone you trusted going behind your back, and I understand the urge to turn and run. I don't blame her for wanting some space. I just wish she didn't do it in the middle of a fucking blizzard.

Using my phone as a flashlight, I scan in every direction, hoping to catch a glimpse of her pink coat or blonde hair, anything that might be her. But all I see is white and gray; nothing else.

Up ahead, I see a shadow across the path and my heart leaps.

"Sam?"

I jog forward as fast as I can, only to find a broken tree pushed to the side by the howling wind. It's Sam's height, but there's still no sign of *her*.

The trail flattens out as I reach the beach. Up ahead, the windows of a house glow faintly through the storm, the coloured Christmas lights forming a kaleidoscope through the falling flakes. My face is numb, my hands frozen, but all I can think of is Sam freezing out here too.

If the others haven't found her by now...

My chest squeezes tight as I head towards the house. If I have to, I'll knock on every damn door on this island until I find her.

But just as I reach the bottom of the steps, my phone dings.

It's Maxine.

> I found her. She's okay. We're both okay. Heading back in a minute.

A deep, shuddering sigh of relief leaves me, and I close my eyes to whisper a thank you to the universe, and to Maxine.

Shoving the phone back in my pocket, I turn around and begin the trudge back up the hill.

Chapter Forty-Seven

~**Maxine**~

The wind cuts sideways as I make my way down the hill into town, ice slick beneath the new layer of snow. At one point, my boots slip, and I grab a fence post to steady myself, heart hammering. My breath fogs fast in the air and my nose already stings from the cold.

The streets are deserted. Not even snowmobile tracks disturb the snow, already covered by a fresh powder.

Where would Sam go to be alone? Did she have a plan or did she just start walking with no destination in mind? If I knew her better, I might be able to guess what she'd be thinking, but with no clues to guide me, I just keep walking.

At the curve in the road, just before the harbour, an old stone church sits quietly under a dusting of snow. Twinkle lights wrap around two spruce trees flanking the porch. It's the first real shelter I've seen and it beckons to me as another gust of wind hits. Maybe Sam felt the same? My teeth chatter as I quickly climb the steps.

As soon as I'm within the small, covered space, the wind stops and it immediately feels a hundred times warmer. Unfortunately, Sam's not here, but I pause a moment anyway, brushing the snow from my sleeves and trying to psych myself up to keep going.

This day has turned into a complete disaster. I'm disappointed that my time alone with Reid was interrupted, frustrated that things have to be so difficult with Sam, furious with Josh for kissing me and guilty that Sam saw it. Basically, I don't know *what* to feel other than cold. It's the thing I can't escape, and as I imagine Sam shivering somewhere out there on her own, I know I have to keep going.

Just as I'm about to head back out, though, a little voice in the back of my head tells me to try the door to the church. With my gloved hand, I push down on the door handle.

It opens.

Inside isn't much warmer than outside, but it *is* quieter. A few candles flicker near the altar, casting warm light and the faint scent of wax into the cold air. A figure sits in silhouette in the third pew from the front, hunched over with her arms wrapped tight around herself.

"Sam?"

She jumps at the sound of my voice, twisting around to face me. The light catches her blonde hair beneath her hood, her face hardening before she turns back around.

"Go away," she says, her voice a warning. "You're the last person I want to see right now."

"I understand," I say quietly, not moving. "But your dad's worried. I'm going to let him know you're safe."

When she doesn't argue, I send a quick text to Reid, then another to Josh. Both show as read almost immediately. I slide the phone into my pocket and lower myself into a pew a few rows behind her.

For a minute, I don't say anything. There's nothing I *can* say that she'll believe. Apologizing feels hollow, even if I did nothing wrong.

Instead, I decide to be honest with her in a different way, and start with a story.

"Josh and I met at a Super Bowl party. I brought bear-shaped snacks, so he asked if I was a Bears fan. Obviously, I am, so we started talking football."

Sam doesn't turn around, but I know she's listening, so I keep going.

"He told me his ex hated football and said how nice it was to talk to a girl who actually got it. I was flattered. We sat together and talked for hours. He made me feel special, and we started dating."

A bitter smile tugs at my mouth.

"Two years later, we were having some of his friends over to watch a game when I heard him telling a new coworker that I thought I knew the game better than anyone, so he should humour me. I was really hurt. I didn't say anything while everyone was there, but when they left, I confronted him about it. He said he just wanted to make the guy feel welcome and he didn't really mean it."

Still no movement from Sam, but since she hasn't walked out, I don't stop.

"Now, with the benefit of hindsight, I realize that's what he does. He compliments by putting other people down. I'm guessing he said some unflattering things about me when you guys got together, and tonight, he told me how stressful things have been with you and how it was easier when he was with me."

Her head dips lower, and although I could twist the knife here and remind her that she's reaping what she sowed for going after a guy in a relationship in the first place, I have a very odd urge to comfort her instead.

In the end, we're not so different.

"I fell for that trick at the beginning, obviously. For years. And I don't even think he knows he's doing it. I don't want to give him that much credit. It's just his instinct and it kind of sucks. That's not the kind of person I want to be with."

Reid's face flashes across my mind, his attention fixed solely on me. He doesn't need to belittle anyone else to lift me up. He knows exactly how to make me feel good about myself without any of that.

Finally, Sam speaks, her voice rough and raw, like she's been crying. "If that's true, why did you kiss him?"

I suck in a steadying breath. "I didn't. He kissed me and I froze. It was a shock, that's all. I didn't want it, I didn't enjoy it, and I pushed him away the second I realized what was happening."

Sam turns slightly, just enough for me to see her expression: jaw tight and eyes glassy with unshed tears.

"I don't want him," I add, just to be clear. "Not even a little. You're welcome to him if you still want him, but honestly? I wouldn't recommend it."

That draws a soft laugh, more air than sound. "I'm not sure I want him either."

"Well, you know your father better than I do, but I have a feeling Reid would have some ideas of how to get rid of the body if you wanted to be done with him permanently."

She turns to face me fully, staring at me in disbelief for several long, agonizing seconds, until finally, to my relief, she starts to laugh. It's a real one this time: dry and surprised and almost human.

"This is the weirdest conversation I've ever had."

I smile at her through the darkness between us. "Ditto."

A burst of wind hits the door, rattling it on its hinges. Sam and I both shudder, almost in unison, and she huffs out another small laugh.

"I guess we have to go back out in that."

"I don't think we have much choice," I agree, pushing to my feet. "I can walk in front of you to block the wind."

She stands too. "No, *I'll* go in front. I know the way better."

With a shrug, I let her lead the way as we walk uphill into the howling wind and blowing snow, back to Reid's house. Neither of us speaks; we couldn't even if we wanted to over the howling wind. Our boots crunch through the snow, our hoods drawn low.

But when she glances back to make sure I'm still behind her, I nod in encouragement. And when she nods back, I know we'll get where we're going, one step at a time.

Chapter Forty-Eight

~**Reid**~

The door creaks open and my head whips towards it. My coat and boots still sit in the entranceway, ready to be thrown back on at a moment's notice, and my hand clutches my phone, just in case either woman calls for help.

But Sam stands in the entryway, dusted in snow, cheeks a bright pink from the cold. Maxine is right behind her, looking winded but pleased, and the tightness in my chest finally eases.

I reach Sam in two strides and pull her into a hug before she can speak. She stiffens for just a second before sinking against me with a quiet exhale.

"You scared the hell out of me," I mutter into her hair, my eyes locking onto Maxine over the top of Sam's head. She gives me a smile that tells me she knows I'm not ignoring her; I just need to speak to my daughter first and she understands that.

"I know," Sam mumbles against my chest. "Sorry."

Leaning back, I hold her at arm's length so I can scan her face. "Are you okay?"

"Physically? Yes."

"Good." My tone sharpens just a little, enough to remind her that she's not entirely off the hook. "Don't ever do something that reckless again. You could've frozen out there."

"I know," she groans. "Can you lecture me about it tomorrow? I really just want to get warmed up."

That answer has more fire in it than I expected, and once again, my eyes flick to Maxine, wondering if she had something to do with it.

"Do you want to talk to Josh tonight?" I ask.

He arrived back at the house just after I did and I told him to get out of my sight. He didn't waste any time obeying and I haven't seen him since.

Sam's mouth pulls into a grimace. "Not really."

"Then you don't have to." I brush her hair back off her face, another strong wave of relief hitting me. "I'll take care of it. Go get warm and I'll see you tomorrow."

"Thanks." She leans in for one more quick hug before turning back to Maxine. "Good night."

Maxine looks almost as surprised as I am at the acknowledgement, but she quickly returns the greeting. "Good night."

She disappears down the corridor, and I turn to Maxine. She's still standing near the door, brushing flakes off her coat. Sam had been my primary worry because of her emotional state, but the relief I feel at seeing Maxine back safe too is sharper than I expected.

"Are *you* okay?" I ask.

She nods as she pulls off her coat, shivering as a trickle of melted snow sneaks beneath her sweater. "Yeah. Freezing, but otherwise fine."

Stepping closer, I cup her cheek. "Thank you for finding her."

She tries to brush it off. "I just got lucky that you sent me the right way."

"No. You put aside your own comfort to help someone who has been nothing but rude to you all day. I'm proud of you."

The cold from earlier fades into a distant memory as my body heats, relief mingling with arousal. The colour that creeps up her cheeks tells me she's feeling exactly the same, and her smile turns playful.

"Does that mean I get a reward?"

Lowering my voice, I tilt my head towards the bedroom. "Go strip off your wet clothes and get under the covers. Naked. Wait there for me."

Her breath catches, her eyes going wide in that fucking irresistible way of hers, and without another word, she slips away, footsteps quiet on the wooden floor.

That just leaves me with one person to deal with before I go and join her.

The house isn't so big that Josh can hide from me, so I find him the first place I look: in the dining room, hunched at the table, hands clasped like he's waiting for judgment.

Fitting, since I'm judging the hell out of him right now.

Arms crossed, I lean against the doorframe. "So. You kissed her."

His head jerks up, his face so pale, I wonder if he's going to pass out. "It wasn't like that."

"Wasn't it?"

"I... I don't know what I was doing," he stammers. "I didn't think... I mean, it wasn't planned. It just happened. This day has been crazy and she just showed up and we talked and it was... familiar. I got confused. Overwhelmed. And I just... I don't know. I wasn't trying to hurt anyone."

"You just have a habit of doing it anyway?"

In my experience, a kiss never 'just happens'. At some point, he made a conscious decision to kiss her, but he won't admit it, not even to himself.

He pushes up from the chair like he might try to run away like the coward he is, but I step into his path before he can move.

"You know what I see when I look at you? Not a fucking man, that's for sure. I see a boy who doesn't know who the hell he is and keeps dragging women down with him while he tries to figure it out."

Josh flinches but doesn't respond.

"You had a good woman and you didn't grow up enough to keep her. Somehow, you got another one, and you're so busy flailing you don't even see the damage you're doing. My daughter deserves a hell of a lot better."

He shakes his head like a petulant kid, looking exactly like the boy I just accused him of being. "I didn't mean for this to happen. Any of it."

My voice lowers to a gravelly warning. "Maybe not, but meaning well doesn't count for much when your actions say otherwise."

He opens his mouth, but I shut him down before he gets a word out. It's clear he doesn't plan on taking any accountability and I've had enough of his bullshit.

"If it weren't a blizzard outside, I'd have you out on your ass right now. I don't care if you freeze, but unfortunately, the police might disagree. Count yourself lucky that you're not worth going to jail over."

Josh somehow pales even further as I let that hang in the air for a moment.

"Sam doesn't want to see you tonight, so you're not going anywhere near her. Understood?"

At least he knows better than to argue, but he still sounds pathetic as he whines, "Where am I supposed to sleep?"

Fuck, this kid is useless. "I don't really care. There are usually blankets in the living room, although some of them are in the wash after I fucked Maxine on them this afternoon."

His jaw drops as I leave him standing there in the cold echo of his own failure, and head to my room and the beautiful woman waiting there for me.

Chapter Forty-Nine

~**Maxine**~

It takes a minute or two beneath Reid's heavy duvet until I stop shivering. As he instructed, I undressed and slipped beneath the sheets, my skin still prickling from the cold. From the way the house creaks, the storm obviously hasn't let up at all, but snuggled in the comfortable bed that smells of cedar, just like Reid, I don't mind the blowing snow anymore.

The confrontation with Josh is over and done with, Sam's safe, and Reid's declaration of pride in me made my whole body flush. I can't wait to see what he has in mind next.

The door opens with a soft click, and my head turns just in time to see Reid step inside, his silhouette backlit from the hallway. Without a word, he closes the door behind him and moves across the room, his eyes fixed on me with only the bedside lamp's dim light to guide him.

As I watch, he shrugs off his flannel shirt, unbuttons his jeans, and strips. Every movement is calm and deliberate. This is a man who will not be rushed, and his control is almost as sexy as his hard, muscled body. *Almost.* When he lifts the covers and slides in beside me, the heat of his body against mine is instant and overwhelming.

I shift towards him automatically, pressing into his warmth, and for a while, he simply holds me. One of his hands slides into my hair while the other finds my waist and curls there, grounding me.

"You okay?" he murmurs.

I nod against his chest. "Yeah. That was quite a day."

His hand strokes over my back, slow and gentle. "I'm proud of you."

I close my eyes, letting those words settle in places I hadn't realized were empty. "You already said that."

"I'll keep saying it."

When he tilts my chin up, I expect his mouth to go to my throat or my breast or somewhere lower, following his usual path. But this time, his gaze lingers on my mouth. A thumb trails across my bottom lip.

"I've been thinking about these lips since the night I first met you," he says, barely above a whisper. "You were electric that night: drunk and defiant and somehow still sexy as hell."

I call bullshit. "You were too busy lecturing me that night to think about my lips."

"I'm capable of multi-tasking."

His deadpan answer makes me giggle. It's so perfectly *Reid*.

"And I was lecturing you because it's what you needed at the time. I will always give you what you need."

The way he so casually tosses the word 'always' in there makes my heart stutter.

"But it doesn't change the fact that I *was* thinking about these lips, that night and most nights since then."His thumb traces my bottom lip again, his eyes following the movement like he's hypnotized, and I can barely breathe. I couldn't speak if I wanted to, but luckily, I don't have to.

Because Reid leans in, his breath warming my face, and kisses me.

Kissing has always been the first step towards intimacy in all my previous encounters, not the last. It's been a stepping stone, and something I've enjoyed, but it has never, ever felt like this.

This kiss is *reverent.*

His mouth moves over mine with a kind of slow certainty that makes everything else fall away. The drama with Sam and Josh, the doubts about whether we can overcome all the complications, and even the storm raging outside fade into the background. His hand slides up into my hair as he deepens the kiss, and I melt, falling into him completely.

His body shifts, covering mine, but he doesn't push. He just lets the kiss go on and on, exploring my mouth, my tongue, my lips, like they're something rare and precious.

When he finally lifts his head, I'm trembling beneath him, my body pulsing with need.

"Fuck, I needed that," he murmurs.

"Me too," I manage to whisper.

I know what it means to him, and I know what it means to me now too. The contract might have made this official, but that kiss just made it *real*.

His lips find mine again, his hips pressing his hard erection against my thigh, but still, there's no urgency. It feels like we have all the time in the world as his hands move, one moment wrapping loosely around my neck, the next kneading my ass, then pinching my nipple. I rock against him, needing more but never wanting this to end. And when he finally slides inside me, I whimper with the utter perfection of it.

Reid's forehead presses to mine as our breaths mingle. He moves slowly, our connection building with each roll of his hips, and I wrap around him, clinging to his solid form like he's the only thing in the world that makes sense.

And when my orgasm comes, it seems to overflow, every part of me opening to make room for him and the pleasure he knows exactly how to give me.

"That's it," Reid groans. "Now, give me another one, my little brat."

That name shouldn't make me shiver like it does.

A few minutes later, with his fingers on my clit, I give him what he wants, and another after that, before Reid finally gives in, coming inside me with a muttered, "Fuck, Maxine."

No one has *ever* said my name the way he does. If my whole body hadn't already turned to liquid, the sound of it might have made me come *again*.

And even though everything about this was sensual instead of rough, Reid doesn't skimp on taking care of me afterwards. Without even asking me, he gets to his feet and picks me up, cradling me to his chest. He carries me to the bathroom, leaving me alone so I can pee, but as soon as I turn the tap on to wash my hands, he's back, lifting me up to carry me back to the bed.

I could tell him it's overkill, but secretly? I kind of love it.

When we're back in bed, the lights off and his body once again curled around mine, I whisper the words that I've been wanting to say but haven't dared to, not sure if he'd believe me. Now that he's kissed me, the timing feels right.

"I'm falling in love with you, Reid."

Just for a second, I could swear the dominant, self-assured man beside me doesn't know what to say.

His voice is rougher than usual when he answers. "I wouldn't have kissed you if I didn't feel the same."

After a beat of silence, and with a throat-clearing cough, he takes back control with his usual firm instructions.

"Get some rest now. I've got you."

Warm in his embrace, I drift off to sleep.

Chapter Fifty

The smell of coffee hits me before we even reach the living room, confirming that Maxine and I aren't the first ones to wake up. Considering how we lingered in bed, enjoying the warmth and each other, I'm not surprised.

Now, she walks beside me, her hand brushing against mine as we move down the hall. Outside, the storm has finally passed, leaving behind a pristine white world that glows through the windows like something out of a Christmas card.

Everything is still and quiet and peaceful in a way that feels almost surreal after the chaos of yesterday. The living room is empty, but in the kitchen, we find Sam, hands wrapped around a mug, her hair pulled back into a low bun. She's dressed in one of her college sweatshirts, and although she looks tired, the tension she carried for most of the day yesterday seems to have eased, at least a little.

"Good morning," Maxine says carefully to test the waters.

Thankfully, Sam doesn't seem to be in a fighting mood. Her lips tighten into something that could almost be called a smile as she nods at us both. "Morning."

The coffee pot beckons, and I pour out two mugs, handing one to Maxine. She takes a sip before glancing around. "Where's Josh?"

Wordlessly, Sam reaches across the counter and slides over a folded piece of paper. Lips pursing into a frown, Maxine opens it, scans the words, and silently passes it to me.

I think it's better for everyone if I leave. We'll talk when you get back.

"Coward," I mutter, crumpling the note in my hand and tossing it back on the counter. "He won't have gotten very far. The first ferry won't leave for at least an hour so he's probably just sitting down at the terminal. I could go drag him back up here if you want me to."

My daughter shakes her head. "Don't bother. I don't think I want to talk to him right now anyway."

The coffee in her cup ripples as she blows on it, and she takes another sip before looking out the snow-dusted window to the bright blue sky above the blanket of white.

"I'll wait until we have confirmation that the first boat has gone, and then I'll get on the next one. I left my car in the lot on the other side."

If she drove, I'm not sure how Josh is planning to get back to the city, but I also don't give a fuck.

"You don't have to leave," I tell her.

"I don't want to intrude..."

"You wouldn't be," Maxine cuts in quickly, setting her coffee down. "You're not going to spend Christmas Eve travelling alone just because Josh is a jackass. Stay. Please."

Pretty much those exact words were on the tip of my tongue, but I'm grateful she beat me to it. It means a lot more coming from her.

Sam's eyes dart between us, her uncertainty clear. "I don't know..."

"There's pie," I add, preying on what I know is my daughter's weakness. "From the bakery downtown."

Her resistance starts to crack, and Maxine senses it too. "We can watch *Little Women*."

"Why *Little Women?*" I have to ask.

"It's a Christmas movie." When I arch an eyebrow at her, she wrinkles her nose back at me. "It is. Prove to me that it isn't."

That's not an argument I think I'll win, so I stick to a different question. "Do I get a say in what we watch?"

"No," both women reply in unison, and finally, Sam smiles fully.

"Alright, I guess I'll stay if you're sure that it won't be weird."

"Oh, it'll be weird," Maxine says, moving towards the fridge to see what there is to eat. "But at this point, we might as well just embrace it."

Amen to that.

We make a late breakfast, or perhaps a brunch, all three of us working together to fry the bacon, scramble the eggs and toast the bread. By the time we sit down at the dining table, the atmosphere is completely different to how it felt over dinner last night.

When the conversation falls into a natural lull as everyone starts eating, Maxine is the one to break it. "Tell me about this job in Denver."

She sounds more curious than cautious, which is a positive step, but there's still one thing I would like to know. "I will, but first: Sam, how did you hear about it? The truth this time."

Sam winces. "Mom told me."

Of course she did.

The ceramic coffee mug is warm in my hand as my grip tightens, but I force myself to hold my tongue. Years ago, I made a promise to myself not to badmouth Fiona in front of the kids, no matter how hard it is. And fuck, she makes it hard sometimes.

"You know how she is," Sam adds when I don't say anything. "She probably got it from one of her real estate friends, or overheard it at the party."

"Right." And she decided to tell Sam, hoping that it would cause trouble, which it almost did.

Maxine's hand finds my thigh under the table, a light, soothing touch that helps to ease the tension, and I exhale through my nose to release any lingering stress before answering her question.

"Stamer Hotels wants to expand their resort in the Rockies, just outside Denver. They're planning to add a series of luxury log cabins:

timber-frame builds with a rustic look, high-end interiors, really classy. Noah asked me to lead the build."

"That's exciting." Maxine's eyes light up with genuine delight, and I adore her even more for being so pleased on my behalf. "It sounds incredible."

"It is. It'll be months of work, could even stretch as long as a year. I'll be based out there starting mid-January."

Her smile falters slightly before she pushes it even wider, trying not to look as disappointed as she feels. Unfortunately for her, I know her well enough by now to see right through it.

Since I don't want that unhappiness to linger a second longer than necessary, I reach over and take her hand, brushing the back of it with my thumb. "How much notice do you have to give at your job?"

Thrown by the change of subject, she blinks up at me. "What?"

My gaze stays steady on hers. "Not the job you're doing for me, but your day job. How much notice do you need to give? Two weeks?"

"Um... yeah. Two weeks. Why?"

"Because you're coming to Denver with me."

Maxine simply stares at me, her brow furrowing as she tries to decide if I'm joking or not.

I'm not.

"You didn't think I'd leave without you, did you?"

"But what about..."

I don't even wait to hear what worries she might have; those are secondary to the more important question. "Do you *want* to come?"

Her mouth opens and closes again, her eyes darting across the table to Sam, who's wisely eating her breakfast and staying out of it.

"Well, yes, but..."

"But nothing. You want to come and I want you to come, so we'll figure the rest out."

Her lips purse. "It's not that simple. What about my apartment? What would I even do out there?"

"You can keep your apartment if you want or give it up and move your things into storage if you prefer. Either way, I'll look after it. As for work, you'll work for Bear Construction. You can be my assistant if you want to, or we'll find another way to use your talents."

Maxine studies me, the sunlight from the window reflecting in her eyes as she faces me. "Are you serious?"

"Dead serious."

Once again, she glances at Sam, as if she needs confirmation that someone else is hearing this too.

This time, Sam responds with a shrug. "Dad doesn't do anything halfway. You get used to it."

Maxine rubs a hand over her temple, like she can massage her brain into making sense of all of this. "You can't just..." she starts, but again, I don't need to hear the rest of that sentence.

"Yes, I can. I'm in charge and I meant what I said: I'll give you what you need."

My voice dips at the end of the sentence, probably a little *too* suggestively, and Sam pushes her chair back from her table. "I'm going to go... not be here anymore."

With a pained smile, she walks out of the dining room, taking her plate with her.

With no audience anymore, I lean over and kiss Maxine again. Now that I've crossed that line, I'm not sure I'm going to be able to stop kissing her every time we're alone together.

Luckily for me, she doesn't seem to mind at all.

Chapter Fifty-One

~**Maxine**~

Christmas morning in Reid's island house is ridiculously picturesque.

Outside, snow blankets the world in white, glowing against the soft blue of the sky. Inside, the fire crackles in the stone hearth and the scents of fresh coffee and pine needles surround me. Christmas music plays softly in the background as Reid walks out of the kitchen in his flannel shirt and jeans, and hands me a fresh mug before taking a seat next to me.

"You ladies ready for presents?"

Across from us, Sam's curled up in the armchair, already sipping from her cup. She placed a few gifts beneath the tree last night, the ones she brought from her mom's house to open here, and I added mine for Reid this morning. It could be awkward since I don't have a gift for her and she doesn't have one for me, but we seem to have collectively decided that things are only awkward if we make them that way. For now, I just want to enjoy the day, and I think Sam does too.

"I'll grab them," she offers, placing down her mug to retrieve the wrapped packages from beneath the tree. It's not a big haul, and none of the presents are very large, so she takes them all back to her chair with her.

From the pile, she pulls out a small, flat, rectangular parcel wrapped in flannel-patterned wrapping paper that matches Reid's shirt almost exactly. "Dad, this one's yours, from me."

Reid raises an eyebrow as he takes it, turning it over in his hands as if he could figure out what it is just from the feel and shape of it. When he can't seem to figure it out, he tears off the paper.

Inside is a pocket-sized leather notebook, monogrammed with his initials, and a pen that I can tell at a glance is a high-quality fountain pen.

Reid blinks at it, swallowing with more force than usual. Is he actually getting emotional over a *notebook?*

I look to Sam for an explanation and she gives me a hesitant smile. "Mom used to buy him these notebooks and a pen to keep field notes in, when he's on site. They were always in his truck or on the kitchen counter when I was growing up." Turning to Reid, she nods down at the items in his hand. "I realized a few weeks ago that I hadn't seen you with one in a long time, but I figured you still need them even if she doesn't buy them anymore."

"I do. Thank you. It's perfect." His voice sounds flatter than usual, but I'm not fooled and I don't think Sam is either. He's keeping it tight on purpose so it doesn't crack.

It *is* perfect, the sort of gift someone who's known him for years would get him, and mine seems inadequate in comparison. Not that it was really great to begin with.

With each passing second, I'm more nervous about him opening it.

"Open yours from me," he instructs Sam. "The one on the bottom."

From the stack of presents she brought with her, she pulls out the largest of the gifts. Unlike her father, Sam digs straight in, ripping off the paper, and a second later, she lets out a delighted squeal. "Ooh, yay! Thank you!"

"What is it?" I ask, craning my neck to try to make out something on the unfamiliar-looking box.

She turns it to show me, though that doesn't help much. Both the item and brand are unfamiliar. "It's a new piece of software I'm dying to learn how to use. It'll really help with simplifying a lot of the coding I do."

Reid shrugs when I glance over at him. "I have no idea what it does, just that she wanted it."

It sounds like the kind of thing Josh would have been thrilled about too, which makes me think that they might have actually been a good match if he wasn't such an idiot.

And as soon as Josh crosses my mind, Sam picks up another present from her dwindling pile, her lips pursing as she reads the tag.

"This one's from Josh. He wanted me to wait until Christmas to open it."

Reid says nothing but I notice the way his jaw tenses at the sound of Josh's name.

"You don't have to open it if you don't want to," I offer as I shift on the couch, my thigh pressing against Reid's. "Though, if it helps, I can probably guess what it is."

Sam's eyebrows draw together. "What do you mean?"

"Well, based on the size and shape of the box, I'd guess it's earrings. Small studs. Possibly hearts."

The furrow in her brow deepens. "That's oddly specific."

"Not really. Josh's go-to has always been jewellery that's safe and vaguely romantic."

Not to mention generic, with no personal thought behind it, but I leave that part out.

Still frowning, Sam tears the wrapping away. Sure enough, a pair of gold heart studs blink up at her from the velvet box.

"Nailed it," Reid mutters.

Her jaw tight, Sam closes the lid without comment and sets the box down. The disappointment written in the lines of her face is both unmistakable and familiar, but she does her best to put it behind her as she looks down at the remaining gifts in her lap.

"Only two left. Dad, looks like this one is for you."

She passes my gift to Reid and my heart beats a little faster as he turns it over, examining it while it's still wrapped, just like he did to Sam's.

Unable to take the suspense, I start rambling. "This is just a little something for fun. Fun for me, I mean, but hopefully you'll think it's fun too. I don't expect you to actually use it, or even put it up anywhere. I just thought..."

Reid's eyebrow lifts a little higher with each sentence until he finally cuts me off. "Let me see what it is first."

One hard swipe pulls the paper free, leaving him with the small canvas displaying the Bear Construction logo I created. It's based on the bear carving I saw on their website right after we met, the carving that I'm now certain he did himself, nestled within the frame of a house. The lines are strong and sturdy, like Reid himself, but the bear adds an artistic flair, just a hint of the passionate man underneath the stern exterior.

For a long moment, he doesn't speak. His eyes roam the canvas, studying it as though there's going to be a test on it later. My heart pounds harder, the wait for his verdict growing more unbearable with each silent second.

Finally, he looks up at me, his striking blue eyes almost taking my breath away in their intensity. "You made this?"

I nod a little more forcefully than necessary, the motion helping to expel some of my nervous energy. "You remember that I studied graphic design in college?"

"I remember."

His tone makes it sound like he remembers every word I've ever said.

"Well, I got inspired by all the beautiful things you create, and I thought the company logo could reflect that a little better. Not that there's anything wrong with it, but..."

I'm about to start rambling again, and Reid stops me before I can get too carried away. "I love it. After Christmas, I want you to bring your portfolio in and show Rebecca. We usually hire an external firm for our design needs and she's the one who manages it."

Heat floods my face, my cheeks warming with his approval.

"Jamie saw you drawing something in the office the other day and I meant to ask you about it. I must have gotten distracted." He shakes his head in a reprimand to himself. "You were asking me what you would do for work in Denver? Maybe this is it. You should be using this talent if it's what you'd like to do."

"Let me see," Sam says, holding out her hand for the canvas. Reid passes it over like it's something precious, and when Sam sees it full-on, her eyes widen. "Wow. This is really good, Max. I like it way better than the current logo."

"Thanks." I lean into Reid's side, suddenly embarrassed by so much appreciation, and he wraps his arm around me while holding out his other hand to Sam. At first, I think he's asking for the sketch back, but instead, he asks for the final present.

"That one's for Maxine, from me."

I immediately straighten. "What? You already gave me the jersey and took me to the game. I wasn't expecting anything else."

He's unimpressed with my reasoning. "I'll buy you whatever I want, whenever I want. Don't argue with me on this. You won't win."

The narrow box is placed in my hands, one that has a lid that can simply be opened rather than unwrapped, and I hesitate as I look down at it. "Is it safe to open in front of your daughter?"

Sam groans audibly. "Please tell me it's not inappropriate."

"It's perfectly appropriate," Reid says dryly. "Though some of my other ideas weren't."

I shoot him a warning glare before carefully lifting the lid. Inside sits a thick, silver chain, and hanging from it, a single *R* pendant made entirely of tiny, glimmering diamonds.

"Oh," I whisper on an exhaled breath. It's stunning, and unlike the heart studs Josh bought, this one was obviously personally chosen.

The *R* makes me pause, though.

"It's beautiful, but shouldn't it be an *M* for Maxine?"

Reid's lips twitch. "Do you need a reminder of your own name?"

My eyes roll as Sam chuckles. "No, but apparently, you think I need to remember yours."

"It's not a reminder for you," he says simply. "It's a statement to everyone else who sees it, to let them know that you belong to me."

Just like his name on the back of the jersey he got me, I suppose.

It's ridiculous.

It's arrogant and possessive and over-the-top.

And it makes my stomach flip in the most traitorous, infuriating way, because we both know it's completely true.

Chapter Fifty-Two

~**Reid**~

Only a few days after we get back from the island, I already find myself reminiscing on our short time there with nostalgia. The snow-covered afternoons, the fire crackling while Maxine curled into my side, and Sam humming Christmas songs off-key in the kitchen, pretending not to be sneaking an extra piece of pie.

I didn't expect it to feel so... *easy*. After the mess with Fiona and all the subsequent years of keeping people at arm's length, I thought it would be awkward to fit someone new into my life. I expected it to take time. But Maxine just slotted into the house, and my life, like she was always supposed to be there.

Now, it's the morning of New Year's Eve and I'm alone in the Bear Construction office. Everyone else has the day off, but I don't mind the solitude. It gives me time to breathe and time to think as I contemplate the end of the year and get ready for the new one.

I'm reviewing vendor bids when the door creaks open and Jamie walks in, a duffel bag slung over his shoulder. "Figured I'd find you here."

"Lucky guess," I deadpan, and he grins back at me, dropping into the chair across from me. "When did you get back?"

"Late last night."

"And you had a good time?"

"It was hot and perfect." The twinkle in his eye tells me he doesn't just mean the weather, but I don't pry. His personal life is his own business. "I'm hitting the gym but thought I'd come and see what I missed."

That's a loaded question, so like he did, I also stick to work. "We got the Colorado project."

Jamie's eyes light up. "Yes! That's fantastic. When are you leaving?"

"In a week or two. Just getting some details settled."

Like whether or not Maxine is coming with me, for one. She hasn't officially given me her answer yet, though every time it comes up, she speaks about it with a little more certainty.

"And I'll be in charge here while you're gone?" he asks a little *too* eagerly.

"What exactly do you plan to do that you can't do while I'm here?" I have to ask.

"Nothing," he assures me, and when I level a disbelieving look at him, he holds up his hands in surrender. "I mean it. It's just different when there's no one they can go to over my head. A lot of the guys still see me as the little kid who used to hang around the construction sites. When I have the final say, they'll have to give me a little more credit."

"Well, I'm trusting you to manage, but you can always reach me if you need to. And I'll want you to make at least one trip out there to see the project in person."

"Of course. Will anyone else be going to visit you too?"

There's no question who he's referring to, and I don't play dumb. "I've invited Maxine to go with me for the entire time."

Jamie lets out a low whistle. "That's pretty intense. Does mom know?"

"It doesn't concern her, but Sam knows. And speaking of Sam, there's something you should be aware of."

Briefly, I fill him in on the situation between Sam, Josh and Maxine, and how Sam and Josh ended up at the island house before Christmas.

"Damn it. I missed all the drama," he complains when I'm finished. "Are you going to invest in the app after all?"

I shake my head. "No. I'm pulling out."

Jamie's eyebrows lift. "Sam won't love that."

"It's time I let her figure things out without me always softening the consequences." She's my daughter and I don't want her to fail, but the past few weeks have shown me that she still has some growing up to do too. "However, if *you're* interested, I believe they're still looking for an investor."

He laughs under his breath, but I don't miss the spark of curiosity in his eyes. "I wouldn't mind hearing more. Think I could request a replacement for Josh as the team lead, though?"

"I'd be disappointed if you didn't."

As he stands to leave, my phone buzzes with a message from Maxine.

Getting ready for tonight. Here's a sneak peek.

Attached is a photo of her in a towel, just barely on the safe side of pornographic. She knows I'm at work and she's pushing her luck, but I can't tear my eyes away.

"Something tells me that's not work-related," Jamie declares, his eyes dancing as he heads towards the door. "Happy New Year, Dad."

If I have my way, it most certainly will be.

Chapter Fifty-Three

~**Maxine**~

Ellie's apartment is already humming with energy by the time I arrive. The insurance office closed at noon and most of my friends didn't have to work at all today, so we're spending the afternoon together for a New Year's Eve pre-party before we split up for our various commitments this evening.

Brad answers the door and his smile is polite but tight. "Hey, Max."

"Hey," I reply, toeing off my boots. "Happy New Year."

"Yeah." He steps aside to let me in and Ellie appears at my side to loop her arm through mine.

"Drinks are in the kitchen, and we saved you a spot on the couch."

Brad disappears with a mumbled excuse and I raise an eyebrow at Ellie. "Everything okay with him?"

She waves a dismissive hand. "He's busy cleaning up Josh's messes. I'll explain later."

After grabbing a glass of prosecco, we settle onto the couch where Tamara, Janine, and Willow are already huddled. A bowl of fancy popcorn sits on the coffee table next to a plate of Christmas cookies, but I don't even get a chance to grab one before Janine dives in.

"Alright, start from the top. Those pictures you sent? Where the hell were you, the North Pole?"

Reid and I explored Mackinac Island the day after Christmas, once Sam left, and I sent my friends some ridiculously picturesque photos to tease them. Looks like it worked to stoke their curiosity.

"It was magical... most of the time. Except for when Sam and Josh showed up."

"What?" Willow shrieks, making Tamara wince. "What do you mean they showed up? Showed up where?"

"At Reid's house."

My friends exchange astonished looks, but it's Tamara who gets the question out first.

"Why would they be at your boyfriend's house?"

Time to finally drop the bomb. "Because Sam is Reid's daughter."

As I expect, this news leads to complete and utter chaos. My friends shout over each other, leaving me unable to make out a word until Brad reappears in the doorway asking us to please keep it down for the sake of their neighbours.

That helps calm the room, but the energy doesn't lessen. It just focuses back on me again.

"Did you have to spend Christmas with them?" Janine asks, aghast.

"I mean they showed up, and yeah, Sam stayed for Christmas. Josh left early, which I assume Ellie already knew."

All eyes go to Ellie and she holds up her hands. "I knew Sam kicked him out. The rest of it is news to me too."

With their urging, I tell them the whole story. All about Reid's beautiful home, Sam and Josh's unexpected arrival, the awkward dinner, Josh's audacity in kissing me, and the search for Sam through the snow.

"I can't believe he kissed you!" Willow rages.

"I can't believe Reid didn't throw him out into the snow," Janine counters.

"That could be considered attempted murder during a blizzard," Tamara points out.

By the time I get to Reid inviting me to go to Colorado with him, they're on the edge of their seats.

"Are you going to go?" Ellie prompts.

It's all I've been thinking about since he made the offer. I haven't told him for sure yet, but to my friends, I confide the truth. "Yeah, I'm going to go."

The words feel more real now that I've said them out loud, and gasps and squeals fill the room.

"We should go and visit!" Willow exclaims. "Skiing in Colorado with a free place to stay? Sign me up!"

"I would love that," I tell them, even though I have no idea where we'll be staying or how much extra room there will be, or if Reid will mind me inviting them. I only know I'm going to miss them.

Tamara, however, has a different question. "Do you think all of this is a little fast, Max?"

I was waiting for that question since I've asked myself the same thing thanks to the cautious voice in the back of my head, put there by my parents.

"Maybe, but it still feels right. I know I don't know everything about him, but I understand him. I know who he is and I know how he makes me feel."

With Josh, I always felt like I was trying too hard. With Reid, it feels like breathing. He sees me, even the parts I'm still figuring out.

Ellie nudges me. "And who is he?"

"The perfect man," Janine declares.

Everyone laughs, and although I don't disagree, I add a small qualifier. "Maybe he's not perfect, but he's perfect for me."

Glasses clink, laughter bubbles up again, and the future has never felt brighter.

Chapter Fifty-Four

~**Maxine**~

By the time we pull into the underground parking for the club, I'm already squirming in my seat. A little from nerves, but mostly from anticipation. Reid hasn't said much about what he has planned for tonight, and the suspense is driving me crazy. He showed up at my apartment after I got home from Ellie's, kissed me like he hadn't seen me in a month, and made no mention of the photo I sent earlier. We ate dinner and talked about our days, like normal people.

As if he wasn't planning to ruin me in the best way possible later.

But I know better. I'm learning how to read the way his jaw sets and what each arch of his eyebrow means. He hasn't forgotten about my text; he's just waiting for the right moment to make me pay for it.

How he plans to do it, I have no idea. He won't do anything I truly don't want him to, that much is clear, but that leaves a lot of options still on the table.

The club's entryway feels less intimidating this time around. The soft lighting and the low thrum of music are still slightly hypnotic, but now it's also somewhat familiar. Last time, we were here to explore, but this time, Reid clearly has something specific in mind.

He checks us in and leads me with quiet authority through the lounge and down the wide staircase into the club's private wing. His hand at the base of my neck instructs without being too rough. At the end of the corridor, he stops in front of a door marked only with a silver 3, and a keycard swipe and a soft click later, the door opens.

Unlike the room we visited last time, this one is smaller and more intimate. No one else is here, and when Reid locks the door behind us, it's clear no one else is coming in. Three mirrored walls surround a padded mat in the centre of the black floor, a large cupboard lines one side of the room, and overhead lights cast a muted glow over everything.

In the mirrors, my reflection stares back at me, eyes wide and cheeks already turning pink. Behind me, Reid steps closer, each thud of his shoes on the soft padding rolling through me like thunder.

"Strip."

It isn't a request, and I don't hesitate.

Under his watchful eyes, I peel off the skirt I'm wearing, slow enough that we can both enjoy the anticipation. My shirt comes next, leaving me in the black lingerie he picked out for me the night before. I *did* briefly consider wearing something else, or maybe even going without altogether, but tonight already feels electric and I'm not brave enough to tempt fate twice.

By the time I'm naked, I'm already warm all over, but somehow, goosebumps still spread across my skin as Reid's gaze rakes over me.

"Hands over your head," he orders when he's satisfied with his inspection. My arms lift, and in the mirror, I watch Reid walk away from me, heading for the wall with the cabinet. Next to it, hooked to the wall, is a chain I hadn't noticed before. As he unhooks it, my eyes follow it up to a mounted roller on the ceiling, and back down to where Reid is loosening the thick, padded cuffs dangling from the other end.

Oh, shit.

The chain clanks as he pulls the roller over to me, and the cuffs close around my wrists one at a time with Reid's smooth, practiced precision. When he pulls the chain taut above me, raising my arms overhead, my weight shifts forward slightly so my back arches and my ass juts out.

It doesn't hurt, but it *is* deeply exposing, especially with the mirrors multiplying every angle.

Before I can feel any kind of self-consciousness, Reid takes a moment to step back and look at me, his eyes drinking me in like I'm an oasis in the desert, and any self-doubt vanishes.

"I was working this afternoon," he says as he begins to roll up his sleeves. "And I was meeting with someone."

My eyes stay trained on his reflection, my pulse hammering in my ears.

"Then my phone buzzed." Walking away from me again, he opens the cabinet and pulls out a long, black crop. I recognize it from the internet searches I've been doing since our last visit to the club. "What do I find when I check it? A photo of you designed to make me hard."

Although I try not to smile, my lips twitch, and he catches the movement in the mirror.

"Is that what you wanted, sweetheart?"

His voice is deceptively calm and my thighs press together involuntarily. "I just wanted to give you something to smile about."

The first swat is more noise than pain, a warning across the curve of my backside.

"Try again."

"I was thinking of you and I wanted you to be thinking about me."

He drags the crop across my skin before he strikes again, firm and fast. This time, it truly stings, and I gasp in surprise. The crop concentrates the pain much more than when he uses his hand.

A hand fists gently in my hair, lifting my face towards the mirror again. I hadn't even realized it had fallen forward, but Reid's lips brush my ear, his breath hot against my skin, as I meet his gaze through the glass.

"That's not a good excuse. I'm *always* thinking about you."

That sentence strikes somewhere deep, and I shudder from how *exposed* he makes me feel, right down to my soul.

Another blow lands and I moan, my body arching desperately towards him even when it shouldn't.

"This," he murmurs, dragging his fingers across the reddened skin of my ass, "is what happens when you act like a brat."

Another strike. Another moan. Our own kind of music filling the air.

"And this," he continues, tracing lower, slipping two fingers between my thighs and letting out a strangled groan when he finds me soaked, "is why you keep doing it."

"Yes," I whisper, not even sure what I'm agreeing to anymore. I don't care. Just *yes*.

One more smack of the crop leaves me trembling, and he steps back, placing the implement in a large bin next to the cabinet. He pulls out a flogger next, the tails of it feeling like feathers as he draws it gently across my back.

"So, the next time I'm at work and you feel like teasing me, what are you going to do?"

I can't resist pushing just a *little* more. "Put a 'not safe for work' warning on the photo?"

In the mirror, I see his lips twitch just before the flogger lands on my upper back. He thought that was funny, I know he did, even if he won't admit it.

Unlike the sharp sting of the crop, the flogger hits with a thud. The impact splits across the tails and spreads like ripples across the water's surface, stealing my breath.

"Try again," he commands.

I suck in air, steeling myself against the pain. My pussy throbs with need, so I give him the words I know he actually wants to hear. "I won't text until you've left the office."

The flogger trails lightly over my shoulder. "And how will you know when I've left?"

There's a sarcastic response ready to slip off my tongue, but I catch it just in time. "I'll wait until you tell me."

"Good," he breathes. "Now, apologize for distracting me."

The tails of the flogger dip lower over my shoulder, dragging over my sensitive nipples, and I could almost cry from the overstimulation.

At this point, I'll say whatever he wants as long as he makes me come. "I'm sorry, Reid."

A sharp smack on my ass makes me jump. He used his palm that time. "Like you mean it, Maxine."

In the mirror, I see us: me, bared and bound, and him, unrelenting and completely in control, and I whimper in need.

"I'm sorry for teasing you. I've learned my lesson."

"Hmmm," is all he says in response, the sound inconclusive. "Maybe we need a little positive reinforcement to really cement it."

My arms immediately drop when he releases the cuffs around my wrist. Instantly, my muscles protest, aching more than I realized with the distraction of the crop and flogger. I'm going to be sore as hell tomorrow.

Patient as always, Reid pulls the chain out of the way and returns to the cupboard by the wall. He pulls out a small, padded... stool, maybe, and something else that he screws into it. I'm watching through the mirror, so it's hard to tell exactly what he's doing, but I can't seem to turn around either. My body feels rooted to the spot.

When at last he returns, my eyes widen at the object in his hands. It's not a stool, exactly, but it's roughly rectangular in shape, black and padded. But it's the *other* item, the thing he screwed into it, that draws my attention.

A large, anatomically accurate dildo, sticking straight out of it.

Reid places the contraption on the floor at my feet. "Climb on."

A string of words, completely incoherent, spills out of my mouth. "I... you... how... what?"

His gaze hardens. "On your knees, and mount it. Don't play innocent."

It's not playing, exactly. Yes, I have a dildo at home, but not like this. I've never done *this* before.

Curiosity urges me on, though, especially when it's coupled with the trust I have in Reid. More than anything, my pussy wants to be filled, so I do as he says, getting down onto my knees with the mounted dildo between my legs, and slowly lower myself onto it. A moan slips out of my mouth almost without me noticing. It feels so good, but I need movement. I need friction. I need *more*.

Reid steps back and unbuckles his belt with slow, deliberate movements, his eyes never leaving mine and his voice a low promise. "Now, for your reward."

Finally. Happy New Year to me.

Chapter Fifty-Five

~**Reid**~

Maxine's eyes are fixed to my cock as soon as it's free, her tongue swiping over her lips subconsciously in a way that sends a rush of adrenaline through my body. I'm already rock-hard from the way she took her punishment, teasing and pushing just enough to keep me on my toes before submitting. She's such a fucking natural at this that when she asked me what to do with the saddle, I almost forget that she's never used one before.

Which makes what's about to happen even more fun.

Fisting the base of my cock, I run the head across Maxine's lips. They open for me eagerly, but before I slide into her warm, welcoming mouth, my other hand reaches down and presses a button on the remote I pocketed earlier.

The saddle beneath Maxine begins to rock gently and she yelps in surprise.

"You didn't tell me it moves!"

"It does more than that," I promise, unable to hold back my smirk as her eyes widen. *Now* she's getting it. "No other man is ever putting his dick inside you while I'm around, but that doesn't mean I don't have other ways of making use of *all* of you."

Her eyes go even wider, her thighs clenching together out of instinct, and I press the second button to start the vibration on the dildo.

"Oh, God," she gasps, and while her mouth is still open, I push my cock past her lips.

Her wet tongue sliding along my shaft makes it hard to think straight, even without the accompanying visual. Seeing her lips wrapped around me while her hips roll beneath her is damn near perfection.

She moans around me, the vibration from her throat traveling up the length of my cock like a jolt of electricity. My hand curls into a fist in her hair, not enough to hurt but just enough to remind her who she belongs to.

"Keep your eyes on me," I order.

She lifts her gaze, obedient and blazing with heat, and *fuck*, I could come just from the sight of her like this: on her knees, impaled, writhing slowly as the saddle moves beneath her, her mouth full of me.

I guide her rhythm with one hand, not thrusting, just holding her where I want her and letting her take me deeper at her own pace. She's almost *too* good at this, willing and enthusiastic, and that hungry little hum she makes every time the movement below her intensifies is testing every last shred of my control.

"Greedy girl," I murmur, brushing her cheekbone with my thumb. "You like being used like this?"

Her eyes flutter shut as she nods, my cock still resting on her tongue, and that honest surrender sets something off inside me I don't know how to name. All I know is that there's nothing I wouldn't do for her when she puts her trust in me this way.

When her breathing hitches and her thighs tremble harder around the saddle, I know she's close.

"Don't come yet." I pull back, letting her take a breath. "We're doing this one together. I'll tell you when."

A frustrated whimper escapes her, and I can't help the chuckle that rumbles out of me. I love pushing her right to that edge and watching her fight to obey, even when her whole body is begging to break.

I love it because she loves it too, even when she complains.

And just to raise the stakes a little more, I give the button on the remote one more press, and the saddle doesn't just rock beneath her, it begins to thrust.

"Fuck," she stutters. "Reid, I want..."

My cock fills her mouth again before she has to say it. Holding tight to her hair, I thrust in rhythm with the mechanical cock beneath her. Maxine grabs my thighs to steady herself, holding on for dear life as she's fucked from both ends. Her body begins to shudder and her big brown eyes plead with me for mercy.

"Now," I command, the word almost catching in my throat as my own orgasm passes the point of no return. A moment later, I'm filling her mouth as Maxine's body convulses in pleasure. The feeling's so intense that I almost miss the back of her hand gently tapping twice against my leg.

Almost, but not quite.

My pleasure is forgotten in an instant as I withdraw from her mouth and pull her off the saddle, not even bothering to turn it off first. I drop onto the padded floor, pulling her into my lap.

"What's wrong? Are you okay?"

My thumb strokes her cheek, trying to calm her as she coughs, gasping for air.

Fuck.

She might be the one struggling, but my heart is pounding.

"Talk to me, Maxine. Are you alright?"

Finally, the coughing stops and an airy laugh takes its place. "Sorry. Some of that went down the wrong way."

Thank fuck. Not that she inhaled my cum, obviously, but for a second, I thought I'd pushed her too far. That doesn't seem to be the case, though, not when she snuggles into me and sighs contentedly. In a matter of seconds, she's practically boneless in my arms, blinking slowly as her cheek rests against my shoulder.

"You're fine now," I whisper. "I've got you."

She hums something unintelligible but she doesn't move, her weight a welcome pressure in my arms. Her breath is coming in shudders, a natural aftermath of so much pleasure. My own heartbeat finally slows as I stroke her back, the silence between us charged with affection rather than tension, and we stay that way for several long, languid minutes.

We both needed that tonight, but now, she needs something else just as much.

In the small private shower off the playroom, I help her clean up, taking slow, careful passes with a warm cloth across her thighs, her ass, her back, and her wrists. When she's clean, I rub on some lotion to help ease any lingering sting. She doesn't say much, just watches me with those big eyes that are somehow more trusting than ever.

It's this part of the scene that she never fights. No sharp comebacks or teasing, just quiet, open surrender, and it undoes me every time.

I redress her and carry her back to the car. No one even bats an eye as I walk out of the club with a near comatose woman in my arms. By the time we reach my place, she's half-asleep in the passenger seat, legs tucked up beneath her and lips parted like she's dreaming of something sweet.

In the bedroom, I help her undress again, get her under the covers, and climb in behind her, pulling her close.

"You okay?" I ask, pressing a kiss to her shoulder.

She nods, her voice soft and far-away-sounding. "Wonderful."

I pull the duvet higher around us, my palm smoothing over her hip. There in my arms, she's warm and pliant and relaxed. The tension she's been carrying without even realizing it for the past few weeks, over Sam and Josh and this new relationship, has finally started to melt away. I can feel it in the way she curls against me.

In the mess of tangled limbs, her hand finds mine under the covers and laces our fingers together like it's the most natural thing in the world.

Maybe it is.

When I wake the next morning, the pale, clean light through the window makes it *feel* like the first day of the new year, when everything is fresh and new. Maxine is lying on her stomach, her face buried in my pillow, one leg kicked out and hair tangled like a halo around her.

I'm not sure I've ever seen anything more beautiful.

I slide out from under the covers to make some coffee and bring it back to bed. She stirs when I set the mug down, blinking slowly as she turns to face me.

A sleepy smile curves across her lips. "Happy New Year."

"Happy New Year, sweetheart."

She stretches, catlike, then pulls the covers higher before sitting up and accepting the mug. "So... I did something yesterday."

"Oh?" I raise an eyebrow, leaning back against the headboard. "I thought we did quite a few things yesterday."

She wrinkles her nose at me in protest of my sarcasm.

"I mean: I handed in my notice at work."

That gets my full attention. "Really?"

She takes a long sip of coffee before answering, her eyes brightening with excitement the more she wakes up. "I talked to my boss before I left work. She tried to offer me a raise to talk me out of it, but I told her I don't have a choice. I have to go."

"You *do* have a choice," I remind her.

"I know, but I've been playing it safe for too long. It's time I jumped. And if that means Colorado with you, then I'm in."

A slow grin pulls at my mouth, one I don't even bother to fight.

"You're sure?" I ask, even though I already know the answer.

"Positive." She leans over and sets the coffee on the nightstand before crawling into my lap, straddling my thighs. "I want to start this year right. All in with you."

My hands run down her back, pulling her closer until our foreheads touch. "You have no idea how good that sounds."

She laughs softly, pressing a kiss to the corner of my mouth. "I think I do."

For years, I kept my walls up, convinced there was no one on the other side worth opening them for, until she appeared, key in hand, and carved out a place in my life right alongside those scratches on Sam's car.

It's not all going to be smooth sailing; I know that better than anyone. The build in Denver will be challenging, and so will being in a new place with a new relationship that's still under construction. But none of that feels particularly daunting right now, not with her here with me.

Building is literally what I do, and we're just getting started.

Chapter Fifty-Six

~**Maxine**~

The office is quiet when I arrive at Bear Construction on the evening of January 2nd. The holiday lights are still strung along the edges of the lobby, their faint glow already seeming a little out of place. Outside, the Chicago streets are damp and gray, but inside, the building is warm and familiar.

Reid isn't here tonight, and neither is Rebecca. She's not due back for a couple more days, and without her steady presence, the place feels both larger and emptier. Still, I'm buzzing with nervous energy after the whirlwind of Christmas and New Year's. Everything between Reid and me feels so new, so sharp-edged and thrilling, like the first inhale after breaking through the surface of cold water. I still catch myself smiling for no reason at all.

At my desk, I boot up the computer and check my inbox. Most of the emails are routine: updates from different departments as they kick off the new year, and a few project notes I'm supposed to file. As a temp, I don't get much that's personal.

Which is why the message sitting near the top makes me pause.

There's no sender name, which is strange enough, and the subject line is simply my name.

Frowning, I hover the cursor over it. It came in earlier today, around noon, and is probably spam considering there's no sender. Still, curiosity outweighs hesitation, and I click.

The message is short, just one line with no greeting and no signature.

If you go to Colorado, you'll regret it.

Instantly, my blood runs cold. For a moment, I can only stare at the words, and a chill crawls across my skin despite the warmth of the room.

Suddenly hyper-aware of the people sitting at nearby desks, I glance furtively around the office, looking for anyone who might be gauging my reaction. Everyone looks absorbed in their screens, fingers tapping quietly on keyboards, their brows furrowed at spreadsheets or blueprints.

Nobody's looking at me, but I can't shake the feeling of being watched.

With a trembling hand, I minimize the email, as if hiding it could make me forget about it, but the words are already seared in the back of my mind.

If you go to Colorado, you'll regret it.

Who would send that? Why? What does it mean? Regret it how? Is it a warning? A threat? A prank?

All I have are more and more questions as the monitor's glow flickers across my face, and after one more moment's hesitation, I reach for my phone and dial Reid's number.

Thank You For Reading

I hope you enjoyed Reid and Maxine's story! If you'd like more of them, their second book *Valentine Dom* will follow their relationship as they head to Colorado. Preorder now for the 2026 release!

In the meantime, if you'd like more spicy and sweet Christmas romance, the *Christmas in the City* series follows the Stamer family and their close friends as they discover love, kink, and holiday spirit in different cities around the world. Start with *Mistletoe Mistake*, or skip straight to *Tinsel Temptation* for Noah and Olivia's story.

Thank you to my readers on Ream for being the first audience for this book and for all of your comments and suggestions. Shout out to Ahja, Amber, Amy, Angela, Ashley, Brandi, Cyndy, Debra, Grelyn, Jody, Kathy, Ljiljana, Lois, MiniMouse, Ngawang Chodron, Robyn, Saily, Shelby, Tabby, Tanja, Valerie and Wendy!

Melanie Yu at Made Me Blush Books, thank you for your very helpful beta read feedback.

Arya Jacobs and Scott Rose, thank you for bringing Maxine and Reid to life for the audiobook, and thanks to Epilogue Audio for putting it all together.

And thank you to my fellow author and partner-in-crime, Emma Lee-Johnson, for always being there to talk through plot points and to give me a confidence boost when needed!

More from the Author

<u>**Contemporary Romance – 18+**</u>

Callahan Series
A Matter of Time
A Piece of Land
A Change of Heart
A Work of Art

Christmas in the City Series
Mistletoe Mistake
Candy Cane Challenge
Tinsel Temptation
Gingerbread Gamble
Stocking Standoff
Eggnog Experiment

Standalones

Brat Christmas

X-Rated

Loyalty Test

In Too Deep

Leading Lady

A Set of Three

Charity Case

Hired Lover

<u>Contemporary Romance – New Adult/Closed Door</u>
It Figures duet
It Figures
Figuring It Out

<u>Historical Romance – 18</u>+
Lady in Waiting Series
Lady in Waiting
King in Training
Princess in Hiding

<u>Paranormal Romance – 18</u>+

Rocky Mountain Wolves Series
Fated to the Enemy
Honour Among Rogues
Hidden in Plain Sight
Wishes in the Moonlight
Death Knows Our Name

Cold Lake Pack Series
The Curse and the Prophecy
The Spell and the Legacy
The Dream and the Destiny

Mismatched Mates Series
Mismatched Mates
Misguided Motives
Mistaken Meanings

Serena's Story
The Alpha's Second Chance
The Returned Mate
The Vampire's Consort

Sacrifice Series
Blood Donor
Life Giver

Out of My Depth (standalone)

Paranormal Romance – New Adult/Closed Door
The Alpha's Prey

Keep in Touch

For more about my other books and to keep up-to-date with new releases, find all the links here:
https://linktr.ee/melodytyden

www.ingramcontent.com/pod-product-compliance
Lightning Source LLC
Chambersburg PA
CBHW070829190726
48292CB00006B/2155